Heart
Bones

Also by Colleen Hoover

SLAMMED SERIES
Slammed
Point of Retreat
This Girl

HOPELESS SERIES
Hopeless
Losing Hope
Finding Cinderella
Finding Perfect

MAYBE SOMEDAY SERIES
Maybe Someday
Maybe Not
Maybe Now

IT ENDS WITH US SERIES
It Ends with Us
It Starts with Us

STAND-ALONES
Ugly Love
Confess
November 9
Without Merit
All Your Perfects
Too Late
Regretting You
Heart Bones
Layla
Verity
Reminders of Him

Also by Colleen Hoover and Tarryn Fisher

Never Never:
The Complete Series

Heart Bones

A Novel

Colleen Hoover

ATRIA PAPERBACK

NEW YORK LONDON TORONTO SYDNEY NEW DELHI

ATRIA
PAPERBACK

An Imprint of Simon & Schuster, Inc.
1230 Avenue of the Americas
New York, NY 10020

This Atria Paperback edition January 2023

ATRIA PAPERBACK and colophon are
trademarks of Simon & Schuster, Inc.

For information about special discounts for bulk purchases, please contact Simon & Schuster Special Sales at 1-866-506-1949 or business@simonandschuster.com.

The Simon & Schuster Speakers Bureau can bring authors to your live event. For more information or to book an event, contact the Simon & Schuster Speakers Bureau at 1-866-248-3049 or visit our website at www.simonspeakers.com.

Manufactured in the United States of America

5 7 9 10 8 6

Library of Congress Control Number: 2022945359

ISBN 978-1-6680-2191-0
ISBN 978-1-6680-2192-7 (ebook)

*Kelly Garcia, this book is for you,
your husband, and your happily ever after.*

Heart
Bones

One

Summer 2015

There's a picture of Mother Teresa that hangs on our living room wall where a television would go if we could afford the kind of television that hangs on the wall, or even a home with the kind of walls that could hold a television.

The walls of a trailer house aren't made of the same stuff walls in a normal house are made of. In a trailer house, the walls crumble beneath your fingernails like chalk if you so much as scratch at them.

I once asked my mother, Janean, why she keeps a picture of Mother Teresa on our living room wall.

"The bitch was a fraud," she said.

Her words. Not mine.

I think when you're the worst of people, finding the worst in others becomes a survival tactic of sorts. You focus heavily on the darkness in people in the hopes of masking the true shade of your own darkness. That's how my mother has spent her entire life. Always seeking the worst in people. Even her own daughter.

Even Mother Teresa.

Janean is lying on the couch in the same position she was in when I left for my shift at McDonald's eight hours ago. She's staring at the picture of Mother Teresa, but she's not actually *looking* at it. It's as if her eyeballs have stopped working.

Stopped absorbing.

Janean is an addict. I realized this around the age of nine, but back then, her addictions were limited to men, alcohol, and gambling.

Over the years, her addictions became more noticeable and a lot deadlier. I think it was five years ago, right around when I turned fourteen, when I caught her shooting up meth for the first time. Once a person starts using meth regularly, their life span shortens drastically. I googled it in the school library once: *How long can a person live with meth addiction?*

Six to seven years is what the internet said.

I've found her unresponsive several times over the years, but this feels different. This feels final.

"Janean?" There's a calmness to my voice that certainly shouldn't be present right now. I feel like my voice should be shaky or unavailable. I feel somewhat ashamed of my lack of reaction in this moment.

I drop my purse at my feet as I stare intensely at her face from across the living room. It's raining outside and I haven't even closed the front door yet, so I'm still getting soaked. But shutting the door and sheltering my back from the rain is the least of my concerns right now as I stare at Janean as she stares at Mother Teresa.

One of Janean's arms is draped over her stomach and the other is dangling off the couch, her fingers resting gently against worn carpet. She's a little swollen and it makes her look younger. Not younger than her age—she's only thirty-nine—but younger than what her addictions have made her appear to be. Her cheeks are slightly less concave and the wrinkles that have formed around her mouth over the last few years look as if they've been smoothed out by Botox.

"Janean?"

Nothing.

Her mouth is hanging slightly open, revealing yellow slivers of chipped and rotted teeth. It's like she was in the middle of a sentence when the life slipped out of her.

I've imagined this moment for a while now. Sometimes when you hate someone enough, you can't help but lie awake in bed at night, wondering what life would be like if that person were dead.

I imagined it differently. I imagined it would be much more dramatic.

I stare at Janean for another moment, waiting to see if she's just in some kind of trance. I take a few steps toward her and then pause when I see her arm. There's a needle dangling from the skin just underneath the inside of her elbow.

As soon as I see it, the reality of the moment slips over me like a slimy film and it makes me nauseated. I spin around and run out of the house. It feels like I'm about to be sick, so I lean over the rotten railing, careful not to put too much pressure on it so it doesn't buckle beneath my grip.

I'm relieved as soon as I get sick because I was beginning to worry about my lack of reaction to this life-altering moment. I may not be as hysterical as a daughter should be in this moment, but at least I feel *something*.

I wipe my mouth on the sleeve of my McDonald's work shirt. I sit down on the steps, despite the rain still pummeling down on me from the heartless night sky.

My hair and my clothes are soaking wet. So is my face, but none of the liquid streaming down my cheeks is tears.

It's all raindrops.

Wet eyes and a dry heart.

I close my eyes and press my face into my hands, trying to decide if my detachment is because of my upbringing or if I was born broken.

I wonder what kind of upbringing is worse for a human. The kind where you're sheltered and loved to the point that you aren't aware of how cruel the world can be until it's too late to acquire the necessary coping skills, or the kind of household I grew up in. The ugliest version of a family, where coping is the only thing you learn.

Before I was old enough to work for the food I buy, there were many nights I'd lie awake, unable to sleep because my stomach would be cramping from hunger. Janean told me once that the growl coming from my stomach was a ravenous cat that lived inside me, and the cat would growl if I didn't feed it enough food. Every time I got hungry after that, I'd imagine that cat in my belly searching for food that wasn't there. I feared it would eat away at my insides if I didn't feed it, so sometimes I'd eat things that weren't food just to satisfy the hungry cat.

She once left me alone for so long, I ate old banana peels and eggshells from the garbage. I even tried eating a few bites of stuffing from inside the couch cushion, but it was too hard to swallow. I spent most of my childhood scared to death that I was slowly being eaten from the inside by that starving cat.

I don't know that she was ever actually gone for more than one day at a time, but when you're a child, time feels stretched out when you're alone.

I remember she'd come stumbling through the front door and fall onto the couch and stay there for hours. I'd fall asleep curled up at the other end of the couch, too scared to leave her alone.

But then in the mornings following her drunken return, I'd wake up to find her cooking breakfast in the kitchen. It wasn't always traditional breakfast. Sometimes it would be peas, sometimes eggs, sometimes a can of chicken noodle soup.

Around the age of six, I started to pay attention to how she worked the stove on those mornings, because I knew I'd need to know how to work it for the next time she disappeared.

I wonder how many six-year-olds have to teach themselves how to work a stove because they believe if they don't, they'll be eaten alive by their internal ravenous cat.

It's the luck of the draw, I guess. Most kids get the kind of parents who'll be missed after they die. The rest of us get the kind of parents who make better parents after they're dead.

The nicest thing my mother has ever done for me is die.

Buzz told me to sit in his police car so I'd be out of the rain and out of the house while they retrieved her body. I watched numbly as they carried her out on a gurney, covered with a white sheet. They put her in the back of a coroner van. Didn't even bother taking her in an ambulance. There was no point. Almost everyone under the age of fifty who dies in this town dies from addiction.

Doesn't even matter what kind—they're all deadly in the end.

I press my cheek against the car window and try to look up at the sky. There are no stars tonight. I can't even see the moon. Every now and then, lightning strikes, revealing clumps of black clouds.

Fitting.

Buzz opens the back door and bends down. The rain has slowed to a mist now, so his face is wet, but it just makes him look like he's dripping sweat.

"Do you need a ride anywhere?" he asks.

I shake my head.

"Need to call anyone? You can use my cell."

I shake my head again. "I'll be fine. Can I go back inside now?"

I don't know that I really want to go back inside the trailer where my mother took her last breath, but I don't have a more appealing alternative at the moment.

Buzz steps aside and opens an umbrella, even though the rain has slowed and I'm already soaking wet. He stays a step behind me, holding the umbrella over my head as I walk toward the house.

I don't know Buzz very well. I know his son, Dakota. I know Dakota in so many ways—all ways I wish I didn't.

I wonder if Buzz knows what kind of son he's raised. Buzz seems like a decent guy. He's never given me or my mother too much shit. Sometimes he stops his car on his patrol through the trailer park. He always asks how I'm doing, and I get the feeling when he asks this, he half expects me to beg him to get me out of here. But I don't. People like me are extremely skilled at pretending we're just fine. I always smile and tell him I'm great, and then he sighs like he's relieved I didn't give him a reason to call Child Protective Services.

Once I'm back inside the living room, I can't help but stare at the couch. It looks different now. *Like somebody died on it.*

"You good for the night?" Buzz asks.

I turn around and he's standing right outside the door with the umbrella over his head. He's looking at me like he's trying to be sympathetic, but his mind is probably working out all the paperwork this has just caused him.

"I'm good."

"You can go down to the funeral home tomorrow to plan the arrangements. They said anytime after ten is good."

I nod, but he doesn't leave. He just lingers for a moment, shuffling from one unsure foot to the other. He closes the umbrella just outside the door like he's superstitious, then takes a step into the house. "You know," he says, creasing his face so hard his bald head spills wrinkles over his forehead, "if you don't show up at the funeral home, they can declare it an indigent burial. You won't be able to have any type of service for her, but at least they can't stick you with a bill." He looks ashamed to have even suggested that. His eyes dart up to the Mother Teresa picture and then he looks down at his feet like she just scolded him.

"Thanks." I doubt anyone would show up if I held a service, anyway.

It's sad, but it's true. My mother was lonely, if anything. Sure, she hung with her usual crowd at the bar she frequented for almost twenty years, but those people weren't her friends. They're all just other lonely people, seeking one another out so they can be lonely together.

Even that crowd has dwindled thanks to the addiction that's ravaged this town. And the type of people she did hang out with aren't the type to show up for a funeral. Most of them probably have outstanding warrants, and they avoid any kind of organized events on the off chance it's a ploy by the police to do a warrant roundup.

"Do you need to call your father?" he asks.

I stare at him a moment, knowing that's what I'll end up doing but wondering how long I can put it off.

"Beyah," he says, pronouncing my name with a long *e*.

"It's pronounced *Bay*-uh." I don't know why I correct him. He's said it wrong since I've known him, and I've never cared enough to correct him before this moment.

"*Beyah*," he corrects. "I know this isn't my place, but . . . you need out of this town. You know what happens to people like—" He stops talking, as if what he was about to say would insult me.

I finish the sentence for him. "To people like me?"

He looks even more ashamed now, even though I know he just means *people like me* in a broad sense. People with mothers like mine. Poor people with no way out of this town. People who end up working fast food until they're numb inside, and the fry cook offers them a hit of something that makes the rest of the shift feel like they're at a disco, and before they know it, they can't survive a single second of their miserable day without hit after hit, chasing

g faster than they chase the safety of their own
l they're shooting it straight into their veins and
Mother Teresa while they accidentally die, when
all they ever really wanted was an escape from the ugliness.

Buzz looks uncomfortable standing inside this house. I
wish he'd just leave. I feel sorrier for him than I do myself,
and I'm the one who just found my mother dead on the
couch.

"I don't know your father at all, but I know he's been
paying the rent on this trailer since you were born. That
right there tells me he's a better option than staying in this
town. If you have an out, you need to take it. This life you've
been living here—it's not good enough for you."

That might be the nicest thing anyone has ever said to
me. And it's coming from Dakota's dad, of all people.

He stares at me a moment, like he wants to say something else. Or maybe he wants me to respond. Either way,
the room stays silent until he nods and then leaves. Finally.

After he shuts the front door, I turn and stare at the
couch. I stare so long, I feel like I'm in a daze. It's weird how
your whole life can completely change in the hours between
waking up and going to bed.

As much as I hate to admit it, Buzz is right. I can't stay
here. I never planned to, but I at least thought I had the
summer left to prepare for my exit.

I've been working my ass off to get out of this town, and
as soon as August hits, I'll be on a bus to Pennsylvania.

I received a volleyball scholarship to Penn State. In

August, I'll be out of this life, and it won't be because of anything my mother did for me or because my father bailed me out of here. It'll be because of *me*.

I want that victory.

I want to be the reason I turn out the way I'm going to turn out.

I refuse to allow Janean to receive any credit for any good things that might happen in my future. I never told her about the volleyball scholarship I received. I didn't tell anyone. I swore my coach to secrecy and wouldn't even allow a write-up in the paper or a photo op for the yearbook.

I never told my father about the scholarship, either. I'm not even sure he knows I play volleyball. My coaches made sure I had everything I needed as far as supplies, equipment, and a uniform. I was good enough that they weren't going to allow my financial situation to prevent me from being part of the team.

I haven't had to ask my parents for a single thing related to volleyball.

It feels strange even referring to them as parents. They gave me life, but that's about the only thing I've ever received from them.

I am the product of a one-night stand. My father lived in Washington and was in Kentucky on business when he met Janean. I was three months old before he even knew he'd gotten Janean pregnant. He found out he was a dad when she served him with child support papers.

He came to see me once a year until I was four; then he started flying me to Washington to visit him instead.

He knows nothing about my life in Kentucky. He knows nothing about my mother's addictions. He knows nothing about me, other than what I present to him, and that's very little.

I'm extremely secretive about every aspect of my life.

Secrets are my only form of currency.

I haven't told my father about my scholarship for the same reason I never told my mother. I don't want him to take pride in having a daughter who accomplished something. He doesn't deserve to feel prideful of a child he puts a fraction of his effort into. He thinks a monthly check and intermittent phone calls to my work are enough to cover up the fact that he barely knows me.

He's a two-weeks-out-of-the-year dad.

Because we're so far apart on the map, it's convenient for him to excuse his absence in my life. I've stayed with him fourteen days out of every summer since I was four, but in the last three years, I haven't seen him at all.

Once I turned sixteen and joined the varsity team, volleyball became an even bigger part of my daily routine, so I stopped flying out to see him. I've been making excuses for three years now as to why I can't make our visits.

He pretends to be bummed.

I pretend to be apologetic and busy.

Sorry, *Brian*, but a monthly child-support check makes you responsible; it doesn't make you a father.

There's a sudden pounding on the door that startles me enough that I let out a yelp. I spin around and see the landlord through the living-room window. Normally, I wouldn't open up for Gary Shelby, but I'm not really in a position to ignore him. He knows I'm awake. I had to use his phone to call the police. Plus, I kind of need to figure out what to do about this couch. I don't want it inside the house anymore.

When I open the door, Gary hands me an envelope as he pushes his way inside to get out of the rain.

"What's this?" I ask him.

"Eviction notice."

If this were anyone but Gary Shelby, I'd be surprised.

"She literally just died. You couldn't wait a week?"

"She's three months late on rent, and I don't rent to teenagers. I'll either need a new lease with someone over the age of twenty-one, or you're gonna have to move out."

"My father pays her for the rent. How are we three months behind?"

"Your mother said he stopped sending her checks a few months ago. Renaldo's been looking for a bigger place, so I'm thinking I might let them switch to—"

"You're an asshole, Gary."

Gary shrugs. "It's business. I've already sent her two notices. I'm sure you have somewhere else to go. You can't just stay here by yourself, you're only sixteen."

"I turned nineteen last week."

"Either way, you gotta be twenty-one. Terms of the lease. That and actually paying the rent."

I'm sure there's some sort of eviction process that has to go through the courts before he could actually force me out the door, but it's pointless to fight when I don't even want to live here anymore.

"How long do I have?"

"I'll give you the week."

The week? I have twenty-seven dollars to my name and absolutely nowhere to go.

"Can I have two months? I leave for college in August."

"Maybe if you weren't already three months behind. But that's three months on top of two months and I can't afford to give *any*body almost half a year of free rent."

"You're such an asshole," I mutter under my breath.

"We covered that already."

I go through a mental list of potential friends I could possibly stay with for the next two months, but Natalie left for college the day after we graduated to get a head start on summer classes. The rest of my friends either dropped out and are on their path to becoming the next Janean, or they have families I already know wouldn't allow it.

There's Becca, but she's got that sleazy stepfather. I'd rather live with Gary than be near that man.

I'm down to my last resort.

"I need to use your phone."

"It's getting late," he says. "You can use it tomorrow."

I push past him and walk down the steps. "You should have waited until tomorrow to tell me I'm homeless, then, Gary!"

I walk in the rain, straight to his house. Gary is the only one left in this trailer park who still has a landline, and since most of us here are too poor to have cell phones, everybody uses Gary's phone. At least they do if they're caught up on their rent and aren't trying to avoid him.

It's been almost a year since the last time I called my father, but I have his number memorized. It's the same cell number he's had for eight years now. He calls me at work about once a month, but most of the time I avoid his call. There's not much conversation that can be had with a man I barely know, so I'd rather not speak to him than spew lies like, *Mom's good. School's good. Work's good. Life's good.*

I swallow my thick, compacted pride and dial his number. I expect it to go to voicemail, but my father answers on the second ring.

"This is Brian Grim." His voice is scratchy. I woke him up.

I clear my throat. "Um. Hey, Dad."

"Beyah?" He sounds way more awake and worried now that he knows it's me. "What's wrong? Is everything okay?"

Janean died is on the tip of my tongue, but I can't seem to get it out. He barely knew my mother. It's been so long since he's been to Kentucky, the last time he laid eyes on her, she was still kind of pretty and didn't look like a shallow, stumbling skeleton.

"Yeah. I'm fine," I say.

It's too weird telling him she died over the phone. I'll wait and tell him in person.

"Why are you calling so late? What's wrong?"

"I work late shift and it's hard for me to get to a phone."

"That's why I mailed you the cell phone."

He mailed me a cell phone? I don't even bother inquiring about that. I'm sure my mother sold it for some of the stuff that's sitting frozen in her veins right now.

"Listen," I say. "I know it's been a while, but I was wondering if I could come visit before I start college classes."

"Of course," he says without hesitation. "Name the day and I'll buy a plane ticket."

I look over at Gary. He's just a few feet away, staring at my breasts, so I turn away from him. "I was hoping I could come tomorrow."

There's a pause, and I hear movement on the other end, like he's crawling out of bed. "Tomorrow? Are you sure you're all right, Beyah?"

I let my head fall back and I close my eyes while I lie to him again. "Yeah. Janean just . . . I need a break. And I miss you."

I don't miss him. I barely know him. But whatever will get me a flight out of here the fastest.

I can hear typing coming from my father's end, like he's on a computer. He starts muttering times and names of airlines. "I can get you on a United flight to Houston tomorrow morning. You'd need to be at the airport in five hours. How many days do you want to stay?"

"Houston? Why Houston?"

"I live in Texas now. Have for a year and a half."

That's probably something a daughter should know about her father. At least he still has the same cell phone number.

"Oh. Yeah, I forgot." I grip the back of my neck. "Can you just buy a one-way ticket for now? I'm not sure how long I want to stay. Maybe a few weeks."

"Yeah, I'll buy it now. Just find a United agent at the airport in the morning and they'll print your boarding pass. I'll meet you at baggage claim when you land."

"Thanks." I end the call before he can say anything else. When I turn around, Gary throws a thumb in the direction of the front door.

"I can give you a ride to the airport," he says. "It'll cost ya, though." He grins, and the way his lips curl up makes my stomach churn. When Gary Shelby offers to do a favor for a woman, it isn't in exchange for money.

And if I'm going to be exchanging favors with someone for a ride to the airport, I'd rather it be Dakota than Gary Shelby.

I'm used to Dakota. As much as I despise him, he's been dependable.

I pick up the phone again and dial Dakota's number. My father said I need to be at the airport in five hours, but if I wait until Dakota is asleep, he may not answer the phone. I want to get there while I still have the opportunity.

I'm relieved when Dakota answers the call. He sounds half asleep when he says, "Yeah?"

"Hey. I need a favor."

There's a moment of silence before Dakota says, "Really, Beyah? It's the middle of the night."

He doesn't even ask what I need or if everything is okay. He's immediately annoyed with me. I should have put an end to whatever this is between us as soon as it started.

I clear my throat. "I need a ride to the airport."

I can hear Dakota sigh like I'm a nuisance to him. I know I'm not. I may not be more than a transaction to him, but I'm a transaction he can't seem to get enough of.

I hear the creak of his bed like he's sitting up. "I don't have any money."

"I'm not— I'm not calling you for that. I need a ride to the airport. Please."

Dakota groans, and then says, "Give me half an hour." He hangs up. So do I.

I walk past Gary and make sure to slam his screen door as I leave his house.

Over the years, I've learned not to trust men. Most of the ones I've interacted with are like Gary Shelby. Buzz is okay, but I can't ignore that he created Dakota. And Dakota is just a better-looking, younger Gary Shelby.

I hear people talk about good men, but I'm starting to think that's a myth. I thought Dakota was one of the good ones. Most of them just appear to be Dakotas on the outside, but beneath all those layers of epidermis and subcutaneous tissue, there's a sickness running through their veins.

When I'm back inside my own house, I look around my bedroom, wondering if there's anything I even want to take with me. I don't have much that's worth packing, so I grab a few changes of clothes, my hairbrush, and my toothbrush. I stuff my clothes in plastic sacks before putting them in my backpack so they don't get wet in case I get stuck in the rain.

Before I head out the front door to wait on Dakota, I take the picture of Mother Teresa off the wall. I try to shove it in my backpack, but it won't fit. I grab another plastic sack and put the picture in it, then carry it with me out of the house.

Two

One dead mother, one layover in Orlando, and several hours of weather delays later, I'm here.

In *Texas*.

As soon as I step off the plane and onto the jet bridge, I can feel the late-afternoon heat melting and sizzling my skin like I'm made of butter.

I walk, lifeless, hopeless, following signs for baggage claim to meet the father I'm half made of, yet somehow wholly unaccustomed to.

I have no negative experiences of him in my memories. In fact, the times I did spend with my father in the summer are some of my only good childhood memories.

My negative feelings toward him come from all the experiences I *didn't* have with him. The older I get, the clearer it becomes to me what little effort he's made to be a part of my life. I sometimes wonder how different I would be had I spent more time with him than Janean.

Would I have still turned out to be the same untrusting, skeptical human I've become had I experienced more good times than bad?

Maybe so. Or maybe not. Sometimes I believe personalities are shaped more by damage than by kindness.

Kindness doesn't sink as deep into your skin as damage does. Damage stains your soul so bad, you can't scrub it off. It stays there forever, and I feel like people can see all my damage just by looking at me.

Things might have been different for me if damage and kindness had held equal weight in my past, but sadly, they don't. I could count the kindness shown to me on both hands. I couldn't count the damage done to me even if I used the hands of every person in this airport.

It's taken me a while to become immune to the damage. To build up that wall that protects me and my heart from people like my mother. From guys like Dakota.

I am made of steel now. *Come at me, world. You can't damage the impenetrable.*

When I turn the corner and see my father through the glass that separates the secured side of the airport from the unsecured, I pause. I look at his legs.

Both of them.

I graduated from high school just two weeks ago, and while I certainly didn't expect him to show up to my graduation, I kind of held out a small sliver of hope that he would. But a week before I graduated, he left me a message at work and told me he broke his leg and couldn't make the flight out to Kentucky.

Neither of his legs look broken from here.

I'm immediately grateful that I am impenetrable because this lie is probably something that would have otherwise damaged me.

He's next to baggage claim with no crutches in sight. He's pacing back and forth without a limp or even a hitch in his step. I'm no doctor, but I would think a broken leg takes more than a few weeks to heal. And even if it did heal in that short amount of time, surely there would be residual physical limitations.

I already regret coming here and he hasn't even laid eyes on me yet.

Everything has happened so fast in the last twenty-four hours, I haven't had a chance for it all to catch up to me. My mother is dead, I'll never step foot in Kentucky again, and I have to spend the next several weeks with a man I've spent less than two hundred days with since I was born.

But I'll cope.

It's what I do.

I walk through the exit and into the baggage claim area just as my father looks up. He stops pacing, but his hands are shoved inside the pockets of his jeans and they stay there for a moment. There's a nervousness to him and I kind of like that. I want him to be intimidated by his lack of involvement in my life.

I want the upper hand this summer. I can't imagine living with a man who thinks he'll be able to make up for lost time by over-parenting me. I'd actually prefer it if we just coexisted in his home and didn't speak until it was time for me to leave for college in August.

We walk toward each other. He took the first step, so I make sure to take the last. We don't hug because I'm holding my backpack, my purse, and the plastic sack that contains Mother Teresa. I'm not a hugger. All that touching and squeezing and smiling is not on my reunion agenda.

We awkwardly nod at each other and it's obvious we're strangers who share nothing but a dismal last name and some DNA.

"Wow," he says, shaking his head as he takes me in. "You're grown-up. And beautiful. And so tall . . . and . . ."

I force a smile. "You look . . . older."

His black hair is sprinkled with salty strands, and his face is fuller. He's always been handsome, but most little girls think their fathers are handsome. Now that I'm an adult, I can see that he is actually a handsome man.

Even deadbeat dads can be good-looking, I guess.

There is something else different about him in a way that has nothing to do with aging. I don't know what it is. I don't know that I like it.

He gestures toward the baggage carousel. "How many bags do you have?"

"Three."

The lie comes out of my mouth immediately. Sometimes I impress myself with how easily fabrications come to me. Another coping mechanism I learned living with Janean. "Three big red suitcases. I thought I might stay a few weeks, so I brought everything."

The buzzer sounds and the carousel begins to turn. My father walks over to where the luggage begins spilling out of the conveyor belt. I pull the strap of my backpack up onto my shoulder—the backpack that contains everything I brought with me.

I don't even own a suitcase, much less three red ones. But maybe if he thinks the airport lost my luggage, he'll offer to replace my nonexistent belongings.

I know that pretending to lose nonexistent luggage is deceitful. But his leg isn't broken, so that makes us even.

A lie for a lie.

We wait for several minutes in complete awkwardness for luggage I know isn't coming.

I tell him I need to freshen up and spend at least ten minutes in the bathroom. I changed out of my work uniform before I got on the plane and put on one of the sundresses that had been wrinkled up in my backpack. Sitting around all day in airports and in a cramped airplane seat has made it even more wrinkled.

I stare at my reflection in the mirror. I don't look much like my father at all. I have my mother's dull, lifeless brown hair and my father's green eyes. I also have my father's mouth. My mother had thin, almost invisible lips, so at least my dad gave me something other than his last name.

Even though pieces of me resemble pieces of them, I've never felt like I've belonged to either one of them. It's as if I adopted myself when I was a kid and have been on my own since then. This visit with my father feels like just that: a visit. I don't feel like I'm coming home. I don't even feel like I just left home.

Home still feels like a mythical place I've been searching for my whole life.

By the time I make it out of the bathroom, all the other passengers have gone and my father is at a counter filling out a form for my missing luggage.

"It shows there were no bags checked with this ticket," the agent says to my father. "Do you have the receipt? Sometimes they stick them on the back of the ticket."

He looks at me. I shrug innocently. "I was running late, so Mom checked them for me after they handed me my ticket."

I walk away from the counter, pretending to be interested in a sign posted on the wall. The agent tells my father they'll be in touch if they find the bags.

My father walks over to me and points at the door. "Car is this way."

The airport is ten miles behind us. His GPS says his home is sixty-three miles ahead of us. His car smells like aftershave and salt.

"After you're settled in, Sara can run you to the store to get whatever you need."

"Who's Sara?"

My father looks over at me like he isn't sure if I'm joking or not.

"Sara. Alana's daughter."

"Alana?"

He glances back at the road and I see a tiny shift in his jaw as it tightens. "My wife? I sent you an invitation to the wedding last summer. You said you couldn't take off work."

Oh. *That* Alana. I know nothing about her other than what was printed on the invitation.

"I didn't realize she had a daughter."

"Yeah, well. We haven't really spoken much this year." He says this like he's harboring some resentment of his own.

I hope I'm misinterpreting his tone, because I'm not sure how he could be resentful of me in any way, shape, or form. He's the parent. I'm just a product of his poor choices and lack of contraception.

"There's a lot to catch you up on," he adds.

Oh, he has no idea.

"Does Sara have siblings?" I ask. I pray she doesn't. The thought of spending the summer with more than just my father is already a shock to my system. I can't handle more voltage.

"She's an only child. A little older than you, a freshman in college, home for the summer. You'll love her."

We'll see. I know all about Cinderella.

He reaches toward the vent. "Is it hot in here? Too cold?"

"It's fine."

I wish he'd play some music. I don't know how to have a comfortable conversation with him yet.

"How's your mother?"

I stiffen when he asks that question. "She's . . ." I pause. I don't even know how to say it. I feel like I've waited so long to bring it up that now it would seem strange or worrisome that I didn't tell him on the phone last night. Or when I first saw him in the airport. And then there's the lie I told the ticket agent—that my mother was the one who dropped me off at the airport.

"She's better than she's been in a long time." I reach down to the side of my seat to find the lever to lean it back. Instead of a lever, I find a bunch of buttons. I push them until my seat finally starts to recline. "Wake me when we get there?" I see him nod, and I feel kind of bad, but it's going to be a long drive and I really just want to close my eyes and try to sleep and avoid questions I don't know that I can answer.

Three

My head is knocked around by a violent shake. My eyes flick open and my whole body jerks awake.

"It's a ferry," my father says. "Sorry, it's always bumpy on the ramp."

I glance over at my father, a little discombobulated. But then everything comes back to me.

My mother died last night.

My father still has no idea.

I have a stepsister and a stepmother.

I look out my window, but there are rows of cars blocking my view in every direction. "Why are we on a ferry?"

"GPS said there was a two-hour traffic backup on Highway 87. Probably a wreck. I figured the ferry to Bolivar Peninsula would be faster this time of day."

"Ferry to *where*?"

"It's where Alana's summerhouse is. You'll love it."

"*Summer*house?" I cock an eyebrow. "You married someone who has seasonal homes?"

My father chuckles lightly, but it wasn't a joke.

When I last stayed with him, he lived in a cheap one-bedroom apartment in Washington and I slept on the couch. Now he has a wife with more than one home?

I stare at him a moment, realizing why he seems different. It isn't the age. *It's the money.*

He's never been a rich man. Not even close. He made enough to pay his child support and afford a one-bedroom apartment, but he was the type of man who used to save money by cutting his own hair and reusing plastic cups.

But looking at him now, it's apparent that the small changes in him are because he has money. A haircut he paid for. Name-brand clothes. A car that has buttons rather than levers.

I look at his steering wheel and see a shiny silver leaping cat in the center of it.

My father drives a Jaguar.

I can feel my face contorting into a grimace, so I look out the window before he can see the repugnance radiating from me. "Are you rich now?"

He chuckles again. I hate it. I hate hearing people chuckle; it's the most condescending of all laughs. "I did get a promotion a couple of years ago, but not the kind of promotion that would afford me seasonal houses. Alana's divorce left her with a few assets, but she's also a dentist, so she does okay for herself."

A dentist.

This is so bad.

I grew up in a trailer house with a drug addict for a mother, and now I'm about to spend the summer in a beach house with a stepmother who holds a doctorate, which means her offspring is more than likely a spoiled rich girl I'll have nothing in common with.

I should have stayed in Kentucky.

I don't people well as it is, but I'm even worse at peopling with people who have money.

I need out of this car. I need a moment to myself.

I lift in my seat, trying to get a better look out the window to see if other people are out of their cars. I've never been to the ocean before, nor have I been on a ferry. My father lived in Spokane most of my life and it isn't near the water, so Kentucky and Washington are the only two states I've been to until now.

"Am I allowed to get out of the car?"

"Yep," he says. "There's an observation deck upstairs. We have about fifteen minutes."

"Are you getting out?"

He shakes his head and grabs his cell phone. "I've got some calls to make."

I get out of his car and look toward the back of the ferry, where there are families tossing pieces of bread at hovering seagulls. There's also a crowd at the front of the ferry, as well as at the observation deck above me, so I walk until I'm out of my father's sight. There's no one on the other side of the boat, so I make my way between the cars.

When I reach the railing, I grip it and lean forward, staring out over the ocean for the first time in my life.

If clear had a smell, this would be it.

I'm convinced I've never inhaled purer breaths than the ones I'm inhaling now. I close my eyes and breathe in as much of it as I can. There's something about the saltiness of the air that feels forgiving as it mixes with the stale Kentucky air still clinging to the walls of my lungs.

The breeze whips my hair around, so I grab it in my hands and twist it, then secure it with the rubber band I've had on my wrist all day.

I look to the west. The sun is about to set and the whole sky is swirls of pink and orange and red. I've seen the sunset countless times, but I've never seen the sun when it's separated from me by nothing more than ocean and a small sliver of land. It looks like it's dangling above the earth like a floating flame.

It's the first sunset I've ever felt this deep in my chest. I feel my eyes begin to tear up at the sheer beauty of it.

What does that say about me? I've yet to shed a tear for my mother, but I can somehow spare one for a repetitive act of nature?

I can't help but be a little moved by this, though. The sky is swirled with so many colors, it's as if the earth has written a poem using clouds, communicating her appreciation to those of us who take care of her.

I inhale another deep breath, wanting to remember this feeling and this smell and the sound of the seagulls forever. I'm scared the power of it all will fade the more I experience it. I've always been curious about that—if people who live on the beach appreciate it less than people whose only view is the back porch of their shitty landlord's house.

I look around, wondering if the people on this ferry are taking this view for granted. Some of them are looking at the sunset. A lot of them remain in their cars.

If I'm about to spend the summer with views like this, will *I* start to take it for granted?

Someone from the front of the ferry yells that there are dolphins, and while I would love to see a dolphin, I like the idea of going in the opposite direction of the crowd even more. The people at the back of the ferry are like June bugs to a porch light as they flock to the front.

I take the opportunity to move to the back of the ferry. It's empty and more secluded from the cars now.

I notice a half-empty loaf of Sunbeam bread lying on the deck of the ferry near my feet. It's what the kids have been using to feed the seagulls. Someone must have dropped it in their rush to go look at the dolphins.

My stomach rumbles as soon as I see the bread, reminding me that I've hardly eaten in the last twenty-four hours. Besides a bag of pretzels on the plane, I haven't had anything to eat since my lunch break at work yesterday, and even then, all I ate was a small order of fries.

I look around to make sure there are no people lingering, then I pick up the loaf of bread. I reach my hand inside and pull out a slice, then put the loaf back where it was discarded.

I lean against the railing and tear the bread off in pieces, slowly wadding them up and putting them in my mouth.

I've always eaten bread this way. Slowly.

It's a misconception, at least in my case, that people who live in poverty scarf down food when they do get it. I've always savored it because I never knew when it would come again. Growing up, when I'd get to the heel of a loaf of bread, I'd make that slice last all day long.

That's something I'll have to get used to this summer, especially if my father's new wife cooks. They probably have family dinners together.

This is going to be so strange.

It's sad that it's strange that I'll have regular access to food.

I pop another piece of bread into my mouth and then turn around to get a look at the ferry. *Robert H. Dedman* is written on the side of the upper deck in big white letters.

A ferry named Dedman? *That's not comforting at all.*

Several people have returned to the back of the upper deck now. The dolphins must have disappeared.

My eyes are pulled to a guy on the upper deck who is

holding a camera like it means nothing to him. The strap isn't even wrapped around his wrist. It's just dangling, like he has replacement cameras at home if he were to drop his.

The camera is pointed right at me. At least it seems that way.

I glance behind me, but there's nothing there, so I'm not sure what else he'd be taking a picture of.

When I look back at him, he's still staring at me. Even with him being a level higher than me on this ferry, my defense mechanisms kick in immediately. They always do when I find someone attractive.

In a way, he reminds me of the guys back in Kentucky who came back to school after being out on the farm all summer in the assailing sun. Their skin was kissed with a tan, their hair full of light blond streaks from the sun's rays.

I wonder what color his eyes are.

No. I don't wonder. I don't care. Attraction leads to trust leads to love, and those are things I want no part of. I've trained myself to turn off faster than I can be turned on. Like a switch, I find him unappealing as instantly as I found him appealing.

I can't decipher what the look on his face means from down here. I don't know how to read people my age very well because I've honestly never had many friends, but I definitely don't know how to read the expressions of *rich* people my age.

I look down at my clothes. My wrinkled, faded sundress.

My flip-flops that I've managed to keep intact for two years. The half slice of bread remaining in my hand.

I look back up at the guy with the camera that's still pointed in my direction and suddenly feel embarrassed.

How long has he been taking pictures of me?

Did he take a picture of me stealing the slice of discarded bread? Did he photograph me eating it?

Is he planning on posting the pictures online in hopes they go viral like those heartless *People of Walmart* posts?

Trust and love and attraction and disappointment are just many of the things I've learned to protect myself from, but embarrassment is still one I'm working on, apparently. It envelops me in a wave of heat from head to toe.

I glance nervously around me, recognizing the mixture of people on this ferry. The vacationers in their Jeeps, wearing flip-flops and sunscreen. The businesspeople still sitting in their cars in their business suits.

And then there's me. The girl who can't afford a car *or* a vacation.

I don't belong on this ferry, transporting these fancy cars full of fancy people who hold cameras like they're as cheap as a MoonPie.

I look back up at the guy with the camera and he's still staring at me, probably wondering what I'm doing on this ferry with all his people while I wear my faded clothes and sport my split ends and dirty fingernails and nasty secrets.

I look in front of me and see a door that leads to an enclosed area of the ferry. I dart for the door and duck inside. There's a bathroom to my immediate right, so I retreat into it and lock the door behind me.

I stare at myself in the mirror. My face is flushed and I don't know if it's from embarrassment or from this intense Texas heat.

I pull the rubber band out of my hair and try to comb through the messy strands with my fingers.

I can't believe I look like this and I'm about to meet my father's new family for the first time. They're probably the type of women who go to salons to get their hair and nails done, and to doctors to smooth out their imperfections. They're probably well-spoken and smell like gardenia.

I'm pasty and sweaty and smell like a mixture of mildew and grease from a McDonald's deep fryer.

I toss the rest of my bread in the bathroom trash can.

I stare back at the mirror, but all I see is the saddest version of myself. Maybe losing my mother last night is affecting me more than I want to admit. Maybe my decision to call my father was made in haste, because I don't want to be here.

But I don't want to be there, either.

Right now, it's just hard to *be*.

Period.

I pull my hair back up, sigh, and push open the door to the bathroom. It's a heavy door made of thick steel, so it slams when it shuts behind me. I'm not even two steps from the bathroom when I pause because someone pushes off the wall of the tiny corridor and blocks my way to the exit.

I find myself looking into the impenetrable eyes of the guy with the camera. He's looking back at me like he knew I was in the bathroom and he's here with a purpose.

Now that I'm much closer to him, I think I was wrong about him being my age. He may be a few years older than me. Or maybe being rich just makes you seem older. There's an air of confidence that surrounds him, and I swear it smells like money.

I don't even know this guy, but I already know I dislike him.

I dislike him as much as I dislike the rest of them. This guy thinks it's okay to take pictures of a poor girl during a slightly vulnerable and embarrassing moment, all the while holding his camera like a careless douchebag.

I try to take a step around him to get to the exit door, but he steps to the side in order to remain in front of me.

His eyes (they're light blue and striking, sadly) scroll over my face and I hate that he's this close to me. He glances over his shoulder as if to ensure our privacy, then discreetly slips something into the palm of my hand. I look down and see a folded-up twenty-dollar bill.

I look from the money back up to him, realizing what he's offering. We're near a bathroom. He knows I'm poor.

He assumes I'm desperate enough to hopefully drag him into the bathroom and earn the twenty bucks he just slipped into my hand.

What is it about me that makes guys think this? What vibe am I putting off?

It infuriates me so much, I wad up the money and throw it toward him. I was aiming for his face, but he's graceful and leans out of the way.

I grab his camera out of his hand. I flip it over until I find the slot for the memory card. I open it and pull out the card, then toss the camera back at him. He doesn't catch it. It falls to the floor with a crash and a piece of it breaks off and flies at my feet.

"What the hell?" he says, bending to pick it up.

I turn around, prepared to rush away from him, but I bump into someone else. As if being trapped in a tiny corridor with a guy who just offered me twenty bucks for a blow job wasn't bad enough, now I'm trapped by *two* guys. This new guy isn't quite as tall as the guy with the camera, but they smell the same. Like golf. *Is golf a smell?* It should be. I could bottle it up and sell it to pricks like these.

This second guy is wearing a black shirt with the word *HisPanic* on it, but *his* and *panic* are in two separate fonts. I take a moment to respect the shirt because it really is clever, but then I attempt to step out of the way.

"Sorry, Marcos," the guy with the camera says as he tries to piece it back together.

"What happened?" the guy named Marcos asks.

For a fleeting moment, I thought maybe this Marcos guy might have seen our interaction and came to my rescue, but he looks more concerned about the camera than me. I feel a little bad about tossing the camera now that I know it didn't belong to the guy who was using it.

I press my back against the wall, hoping to squeeze past them unnoticed.

The guy holding the camera waves a flippant hand in my direction. "I accidentally bumped into her and dropped it."

Marcos looks at me and then back at Douchebag Blue Eyes. There's something in the way they look at each other—something unspoken. It's as if they're communicating in a silent language I don't understand.

Marcos squeezes past us and opens the bathroom door. "I'll meet you in the car, we're about to dock."

I find myself alone with Camera Guy again, but all I want to do is escape and go back to my father's car. The guy is focusing on Marcos's camera, attempting to piece it back together, when he says, "I wasn't propositioning you. I saw you take the bread and thought you could use the help."

I tilt my head when he makes eye contact with me, studying his expression as I search for the telling lie. I don't know what's worse—him propositioning me, or him feeling sorry for me.

I want to respond with something clever—or anything at all, really—but I just stand frozen as we stare at each other. Something about this guy is digging into me, like his aura has claws.

There's a heaviness behind his reflective eyes that I assumed only people like me were familiar with. What could possibly be so terrible about this guy's life that would lead me to believe he's damaged?

But I can tell he is. Damaged people recognize other damaged people. It's like a club you don't want a membership to.

"Can I have my memory card back?" he asks, holding out his hand.

I'm not returning every picture he just took of me without my permission. I bend down and retrieve the twenty from the floor. I put it in his hand. "Here's twenty bucks. Buy yourself a new one."

With that, I spin and escape out the door. I grip the memory card in my hand while I make my way back through the rows of cars, toward my father's.

I climb into the passenger seat and close the door quietly because my father is on the phone. It sounds like a business call. I reach into the back seat and slip the memory card into my backpack. When I face forward again, the two guys are exiting the indoor section of the ferry.

Marcos is on his phone and the other guy is staring down at the camera, still trying to put it back together as they make their way over to a car near ours. I sink into my seat, hoping they don't see me.

They climb into a BMW two rows over, on my father's side of the car.

My father ends his phone call just as the ferry begins to dock. Only half of the sun remains dangling in the sky. The other half is swallowed by earth and sea, and I kind of wish the sea could do the same to me right about now.

"Sara is so excited to meet you," my father says, starting the car. "Other than her boyfriend, there aren't a lot of regulars on the peninsula. It's mostly vacation homes. Airbnb, Vrbo, things like that. It's a lot of new people coming and going every few days, so it's good she'll have a friend."

The cars begin exiting the ferry by row. I don't know why, but I glance past my father at the BMW as it crawls past us. Camera Guy is looking out his window now.

I stiffen when he spots me in the passenger seat.

We lock eyes, and his stare is unwavering as they pass. I don't like that my body is responding to that stare, so I look away and glance out my window. "What is Sara's boyfriend's name?"

Everything in me is hoping it isn't Marcos or his douchebag friend with the pretty eyes.

"Marcos."

Of course it is.

Four

The house isn't quite as extravagant as I had feared, but it's still the nicest house I've ever been in. It's beachfront and two-story, built high up on stilts like every other house in this neighborhood. You have to climb two sets of stairs before you even reach the first floor.

I pause when we reach the top of the second set of steps before following my father into his house to meet his new family.

I take in the view for a moment. It's like a wall of ocean and beach in front of us as far as I can see. The water looks like it's alive. Heaving. Breathing. It's both magnificent and terrifying.

I wonder if my mother ever saw the ocean before she died. She was born and raised in Kentucky, in the same town she died in last night. I don't ever remember hearing stories of any trips she took or seeing pictures of childhood vacations. That makes me sad for her. I didn't realize what seeing the ocean would mean to me, but now that I've seen it, I want every human on earth to experience it.

Seeing the ocean in person feels almost as important as having food and shelter. It doesn't seem far-fetched to believe a charity should exist for the sole purpose of allowing people to afford a trip to the beach. It should be a basic human right. A necessity. It's like years of therapy, rolled up into a view.

"Beyah?"

I look away from the beach and toward a woman standing in the living room. She's exactly how I pictured her. Bright, like a Popsicle, with white teeth and pink manicured nails and blond hair that looks expensively maintained.

I groan, but it isn't meant to be heard by anyone. I think maybe it came out louder than I expected it to because she tilts her head. She smiles anyway.

I came prepared to ward off hugs, so I'm holding my Mother Teresa picture and my backpack against my chest as a barrier.

"Hi." I step into the house. It smells like fresh linen and . . . *bacon*. What a strange pairing, but even a linen/bacon combination is a nice change from the mildew and cigarette smoke our trailer always smelled like.

Alana seems confused as to how to greet me since she can't really hug me. My father tosses his keys on a mantel above a fireplace and says, "Where's Sara?"

"Coming!" A high-pitched, manufactured voice is

accompanied by the sound of bouncing feet on the stairs. A younger version of Alana appears, beaming a smile with teeth somehow whiter than her mother's. She does this thing where she hops and claps and releases a squeal, and it's honestly terrifying.

She rushes across the room and says, "Oh my God, you're so pretty." She grabs my hand and says, "Come on, I'll show you your bedroom."

She doesn't even give me time to object. I follow behind her and her swishy ponytail. She's wearing jean shorts and a black bikini top, but no shirt. She smells like coconut oil.

"Dinner is in half an hour!" Alana yells from downstairs.

Sara releases my hand and pushes open a door when we reach the top floor.

I look around my new bedroom. The walls are painted a calming blue, almost the exact same color as the eyes of the guy from the ferry. The bedspread is white, with a giant blue octopus on it.

The bed is perfectly made, with an offensive amount of pillows.

It all smells and looks too clean to touch, but Sara plops down on the bed and watches me while I take in the room. It's three times the size of the bedroom I grew up in.

"My room is across the hall," Sara says, pointing at the door we just came through. Then she tosses a hand toward two doors that open up to a balcony with an unobstructed view of the beach. "This room has the nicest view in the whole house."

There must be something wrong with it if it has the nicest view, yet no one chooses to stay in this room. Maybe the beach is too loud and active in the mornings and this room feels the brunt of it.

Sara hops off the bed and opens a door, then flips on a light to a bathroom. "No tub, but the shower is nice." She opens another door. "Walk-in closet. Some of my shit is in there, but I'll move it out this week." She closes the door.

She walks to the dresser and opens the bottom drawer. It's full of stuff. "Junk drawer, but the other three drawers are free." She closes it and sits back down on the bed. "So? You like it?"

I nod.

"Good. I don't know what kind of house you live in now, but I was hoping you didn't have to downgrade." She reaches to the nightstand beside the bed and grabs a remote control. "All the rooms have everything. Netflix, Hulu, Prime. You can just use our accounts, they're all ready to go."

She has no idea she's saying this to a girl who has never even had a television. I haven't moved or spoken since we walked into the room. She's doing enough for the both of us, but I manage to mutter, "Thanks."

"How long are you here for?" she asks.

"Not sure. The summer, maybe."

"Oh, wow. Awesome."

I press my lips together and nod. "Yep. Awesome."

Sara doesn't catch the sarcasm. She smiles, or maybe she's still smiling. I'm not sure she ever stopped. "You can move, you know. Put your things down."

I walk over to the dresser and set the plastic sack on top of it. I toss my backpack on the floor.

"Where's the rest of your stuff?" she asks.

"The airport lost my luggage."

"Oh, *God*," she says, overly empathetic. "Let me get you some clothes until we can get to a store." She hops off the bed and walks out of the room.

I can't tell if the smile on her face is genuine. It has me even more on edge than before I met her. I'd trust her more if she were standoffish, or even a bitch.

It feels a little like the girls at my high school. I call them locker-room girls. They're nice on the court, in front of the coach. But in the locker room, it's a different story.

I can't tell if we're on the court or in the locker room right now.

"What size are you?" she yells from across the hall.

I move to my doorway and can see her digging through a dresser in the other bedroom. "A two, I think? Maybe a four?"

I see her pause for a moment. She looks across the hall at me and nods tightly, like my answer disturbed her in some way.

Being as skinny as I am isn't something I strive for. It's been a constant battle trying to consume enough calories to maintain the energy I need for volleyball, while also not having as much access to food as most people. I'm hoping before the end of summer, I can put on some much-needed weight.

"Well, I'm *not* a four," Sara says, walking back into my room. "Triple that, actually. But here are some shirts and two sundresses." She hands me the stack of clothes. "I'm sure they'll be baggy on you, but they'll work until you get your stuff from the airline."

"Thanks."

"Do you diet?" she asks, looking me up and down. "Or have you always been this skinny?"

I can't tell if that's a backhanded remark. Maybe it's because she has no idea *why* I'm as thin as I am, so it feels like an insult. I shake my head a little, needing this conversation to end. I want to shower and change and just be alone for a while. She hasn't stopped talking since I met her.

She doesn't leave. She walks over to the bed and sits down again, this time falling onto her side and resting her head on her hand. "Do you have a boyfriend?"

"No." I walk the clothes to the closet.

"Oh, good. There's a guy I think you'll like. Samson. He lives next door."

I want to tell her not to bother, that men are scum, but she probably hasn't had the same types of interactions with guys that I have. Dakota wouldn't offer a girl like Sara money. He'd just hit on her for free.

Sara hops off the bed again and walks across the room

to the other wall of curtains. She pulls one open. "That's Samson's house right there," she says, pointing out the window. "He's super rich. His dad is in the oil business or something." She presses her forehead to the glass. "Oh my God, come here."

I walk over to where she's standing and look out the window. Samson's house is even bigger than the one we're in. There's one light on in his house, in the kitchen, which Sara is pointing toward. "Look. He's got a girl in there."

There's a guy standing between the legs of some girl who is seated on his kitchen island. They're kissing. When they break apart, I suck in a quiet gasp.

Samson is Douchebag Blue Eyes. Samson is the same guy who just tried to pay me twenty bucks to join him in a ferry bathroom.

Gross.

But slightly impressive. He works fast. He was on the same ferry I was on, which means he just got home ten minutes ago. *I wonder if he offered that girl twenty bucks.*

"That's the guy you want to set me up with?" I ask as we watch his tongue explore another girl's neck.

"Yeah," Sara says, matter-of-fact.

"Looks like he's taken."

Sara laughs. "No, he's not. She'll be gone soon. Samson only makes out with the girls who are here for a weekend."

"He sounds terrible."

"He's your typical spoiled rich kid."

I look at her, confused. "But you want to set me up with him?"

"He's cute," Sara says with a shrug. "And he's friends with my boyfriend. It would be cool if we all coupled up. Did stuff together. Sometimes Samson feels like a third wheel."

I shake my head and walk away from the window. "Not interested."

"Yeah, he said the same thing when I told him you might be here for the summer. But you could change your mind after you meet him."

I have met him. And I'm still not interested. "The last thing I need right now is a boyfriend."

"Oh, God. No," Sara says. "I wasn't saying you should date him like *that*. I just mean . . . you know. Summer fling, but whatever. I get it." She sighs, like that saddens her.

I'm just waiting for her to leave so I can have some privacy. She stares at me a moment, and I can see her mind trying to come up with another question or anything else to say. "My mom and your dad won't be very strict since we're out of high school. They just want to know where we are at all times, which is basically in the front yard, at the beach. We make a fire every night and hang out."

It just occurred to me that this girl knows my father's parenting style better than I do. I hadn't thought about that before this moment. I know his name is Brian, his leg isn't broken, and he's a financial planner. That's about it.

"Where do you want to go shopping for new stuff tomorrow? We'll have to go to Houston, all they really have here is a Walmart."

"Walmart is fine."

Sara laughs, but when she sees I'm not laughing, she bites her lip to stop her smile. "Oh. You were serious." Sara clears her throat, looking hella uncomfortable now, and this might be the moment she realizes we're nothing alike.

I don't know how I'm going to last an entire summer with a girl who thinks Walmart is laughable. I've shopped at thrift stores and garage sales my whole life. Walmart is a step up for me.

I feel like I'm about to cry and I don't know why.

I can sense the tears coming. I suddenly miss my old house and my addict mom and my empty fridge. I even miss the smell of her cigarettes, and I never thought that would happen. At least that smell was authentic.

This room smells rich and sophisticated and comfortable. It smells fraudulent.

I point toward the bathroom. "I think I'm gonna shower now."

Sara looks at the bathroom and then at me. She realizes that's her cue to leave. "Try to hurry because Mom likes to have dinner as a *family* on the weekends." She rolls her eyes when she says *family*, then closes my bedroom door.

I stand in the center of this unfamiliar room, feeling more than a little overwhelmed.

I'm not sure I've ever felt more alone than I do right

now. At least when I was in the house with my mother, it felt like I fit there. We belonged there together, no matter how mismatched we were. We learned to navigate and weave our lives around each other, and in this house, I'm not sure I can invisibly weave around any of these people. They're like brick walls I'm going to crash into at every turn.

It feels claustrophobic.

I walk over to the balcony doors and I open one of them and step outside. As soon as the breeze hits my face, I start crying. It's not even a discreet cry. It's an almost-twenty-four-hour-delayed sob.

I press my elbows onto the railing and cover my face with my hands, trying to suppress it before Sara decides to pop back into my room. Or worse, my father.

Nothing works. I just keep crying. Five whole minutes probably pass while I stand and look out at the water through blurry, tear-filled vision as I sob.

I need to tell my father what happened last night.

I inhale several breaths and wipe my eyes, mustering up every ounce of resolve in me in order to regain control of my emotions. I eventually wipe enough tears out of my eyes so that I can actually appreciate the view of the ocean under the moonlight.

The girl Samson was kissing in his kitchen earlier has just crossed over the sand dune between the two houses. She joins a crowd of people gathered around a fire. They're all young, probably in their late teens and early twenties. They're likely all rich and carefree and confident. This is probably what Sara does every night, and those are probably her friends.

More people I have nothing in common with.

I don't want anyone to see me up here crying, so I spin to go back into my room.

I freeze.

Samson is standing alone on the balcony next door. He's staring at me with an unreadable expression.

I stare back at him for two seconds, and then I walk into the bedroom and close the door.

First, he sees me eating bread off the deck of a ferry. Then he offers me money, and I'm still not sure of his motives behind that offer. Then I find out he's my new neighbor for the summer.

And now he's witnessed the first breakdown I've had in years.

Great.

Fuck this summer.

Fuck these people.

Fuck the whole current state of my life.

Five

I had my first kiss when I was twelve.

It was a Saturday morning. I was standing at the stove about to cook scrambled eggs. I didn't hear my mother return the night before, so I assumed I was in the house alone. I had just cracked two eggs into a pan when I heard my mother's bedroom door open.

I looked over to see an unfamiliar man walking out of her bedroom holding a pair of work boots. He paused when he saw me at the stove.

I'd never seen him before. My mother was always in a new relationship or a new breakup. I did my best to stay out of her way, whether she was falling in love or getting her heart broken. Both were equally dramatic.

I'll never forget the way the man looked at me. It was a slow gaze, from head to toe, like he was hungry and I was a meal. It was the first time a man had ever looked at me like that. I instantly felt the hair on my arms rise and I immediately turned my attention back to the stove.

"You not gonna say hello?" the man asked.

I ignored him. I was hoping if he thought I was rude, he'd leave. But instead, he walked into the kitchen and leaned against the counter next to the stove. I was focused on stirring the eggs. "You make enough for me?"

I shook my head. "We only had two eggs."

"Sounds like just enough. I'm starvin'."

He walked over to the table and started putting on his work boots. I had finished scrambling the eggs by the time he had his boots on. I didn't know what to do. I was hungry and they were our only two eggs, but he was sitting at the table like he expected me to feed him. I didn't even know who the hell he was.

I transferred the eggs to a plate, grabbed a fork, and tried to rush out of the kitchen toward my bedroom. He reached me in the hallway, grabbing my wrist and pushing me against the wall.

"Is this how you treat guests?"

He grabbed me by the jaw and kissed me.

I was struggling to get away from him. His mouth was painful. Stubble dug into my face and he smelled of rotten food. I kept my teeth clenched tight, but he just kept squeezing my jaw harder, trying to pry my mouth open. I finally hit him upside his head as hard as I could with the plate of eggs.

He pulled back and slapped me.

Then he left.

I never saw him again. I never even knew his name. My mother woke up a few hours later and saw the broken plate and the uneaten eggs sitting at the top of the trash can. She yelled at me for wasting the last two eggs.

I haven't eaten eggs since that day.

But I've slapped plenty of my mother's boyfriends since then.

I say all this because when I stepped out of the shower a few minutes ago, all I could smell were eggs. The smell is still lingering.

It's making me sick to my stomach.

There's a knock at my door as soon as I finish dressing. Sara peeks her head in and says, "Baptismal dinner in five minutes."

I have no idea what that means. Are they super religious or something?

"What's a baptismal dinner?"

"Marcos and Samson have dinner with us every Sunday night. It's our way of celebrating the end of the influx of renters. We eat together and wash away the weekenders." She opens the door more and says, "That dress looks good on you. Want me to do your makeup?"

"For dinner?"

"Yeah. You're about to meet *Samson*." She grins, and it makes me realize how much I hate being set up, even though this is my first experience with it. I start to tell her I already met Samson, but I keep that to myself and hoard it along with all the other secrets I've kept in my life.

"I don't really want makeup. I'll be down in a few minutes."

Sara looks disappointed, but she leaves. At least she takes hints well.

A few seconds later, I hear voices downstairs that don't belong to any of the people who live in this house.

I stare at the wrinkled sundress I've been wearing all day. It's wadded up on the floor by the bed. I pick it up and change back into it. I'm not about to go downstairs and try to impress anyone. If anything, I'd like to achieve the opposite.

My father is the first to notice me when I reach the bottom of the stairs and make my way into the kitchen.

"You look refreshed," he says. "Is the room okay?"

I nod, tight-lipped.

Sara spins around and I can see the surprise in her eyes that I've changed back into my old sundress. She hides her shock well, though. Marcos is standing next to her, pouring himself a glass of iced tea. When he makes eye contact with me, he does a double take. It's obvious he didn't expect to see the girl from the ferry at dinner tonight.

Samson must not have told him about seeing me sob on the balcony earlier.

Speaking of Samson, he's the only one who doesn't look

at me. He's digging through the refrigerator as Sara lifts a hand and waves it toward me. "Marcos, this is my stepsister, Beyah. Beyah, this is my boyfriend, Marcos." She throws a thumb over her shoulder. "That's Samson, third wheel and next-door neighbor."

Samson turns around and eyes me for a moment. He lifts his chin in a nod as he pops open a can of soda. All I can think about as he presses the can to his lips to take a sip is how I just saw his mouth on some other girl's neck.

"Welcome to Texas, Beyah," Marcos says, pretending he didn't meet me on the ferry earlier.

I appreciate that the two of them aren't making a thing of it.

"Thanks," I mutter. I walk into the kitchen, not sure what to do. I don't feel comfortable enough to ask for a drink or to make my own plate of food. I just stand still and watch everyone else move about comfortably.

As hungry as I am right now, I'm dreading this dinner. For whatever reason, people feel the need to alleviate awkwardness with questions no one really cares to know the answers to. I have a feeling that's how this entire dinner is going to go. They're probably all going to be batting questions at me the entire meal, and I really just want to make a plate of food, take it to my room, eat it in silence, and then go to sleep.

For two straight months.

"I hope you like breakfast, Beyah," Alana says, walking

a plate of biscuits to the table. "We sometimes like to switch things up and have it for dinner."

My father sets down a pan of scrambled eggs. There are bacon and pancakes already on the table. Everyone starts taking their seats, so I do the same. Sara grabs the seat between Marcos and her mother, which means I'm left with the seat next to my father. Samson is the last to sit, and he pauses when he realizes he's seated next to me. He sits reluctantly. Maybe it's just me, but it seems he's trying to subtly shift his attention away from me.

Everyone begins passing food around. I skip the eggs, naturally, but the smell is overpowering all the other foods. My father starts in on the questions as soon as I take my first bite of a pancake.

"What have you been up to since graduation?"

I swallow, then say, "Work, sleep, repeat."

"What do you do?" Sara asks. She asks that in a rich way. Not "Where do you work?" but "What do you do?," like my job is some kind of skill.

"I'm a cashier at McDonald's."

I can tell she's taken aback. "Oh," she says. "Fun."

"I think it's great that you chose to work while still in high school," Alana says.

"It wasn't a choice. I had to eat."

Alana clears her throat and I realize my honest response makes her uncomfortable. If that bothers her, I wonder how she's going to take the news that my mother died of an overdose?

My father tries to skip over the moment and says, "I guess you changed your mind about summer courses. You starting in the fall now?"

That question confuses me. "I'm not enrolled in summer courses."

"Oh. Your mom said you needed summer tuition when I sent her money to cover the fall."

My mother asked him for tuition?

I earned a full ride to Penn State. I don't even have to pay tuition.

How much did he give my mother that I never even knew about? There was obviously a cell phone shipped to me at some point that I never received. And now I find out she asked him for tuition to an education she never even cared enough to ask me about.

"Yeah," I say, trying to come up with an excuse as to why I'm here in Texas and not in the summer classes he paid for. "I signed up too late. The classes were full."

I suddenly have no appetite at all. I can barely finish the second bite of pancake I took.

My mother never asked me about college at all. Yet she asked my father for tuition money that probably ended up in a slot machine at a casino or running through the vein in her arm. And he paid it without question. If he would have just asked me, I would have told him I could have gone to community college for free. But I didn't want to stay in that town. I needed as far away from my mother as I could get.

I guess that wish came true.

I put down my fork. I feel like I'm about to be sick.

Sara sets her fork down, too. She takes a sip of her tea, watching me.

"Do you know what you're going to major in?" Alana asks.

I shake my head and pick up my fork, just so I can pretend to be interested in eating. I notice Sara picks up her fork as soon as I do. "I'm not sure yet," I say.

I poke at pieces of pancake but don't actually put a piece in my mouth. Sara does the same.

I put down my fork. So does Sara.

More conversation passes around the table, but I ignore most of it when I can. I can't stop focusing on the fact that Sara is following my every move while trying to be discreet about it.

I'm going to have to be cognizant of this all summer. I think the girl might need to be informed that she should eat when she feels like eating and not base her food intake around how much *I* eat.

I make sure to eat a few bites, even though I'm nauseated and nervous and every bite is a struggle.

Luckily, it's a quick meal. Twenty minutes at most. Samson said nothing the entire time he ate. No one acted like this was abnormal. Hopefully he's always this quiet. It'll be easier to pay less attention to him.

"Beyah needs some stuff from Walmart," Sara says. "Can we go tonight?"

I don't want to go tonight. I want to sleep.

My father pulls several one-hundred-dollar bills out of his wallet and hands them to me.

I changed my mind. I want to go to Walmart.

"You should wait until tomorrow and take her somewhere better in Houston," Alana suggests.

"Walmart is fine," I say. "I don't need much."

"Get one of those prepaid phones while you're there," my father says, handing me even more money.

My eyes are wide. I've never held this much money in my life. There's probably six hundred dollars in my hands right now.

"You driving?" Sara says to Marcos.

"Sure."

I suddenly don't want to go again if that means Marcos and Samson are coming.

"I'm not going," Samson says as he picks up his plate and walks it to the sink. "I'm tired."

Well. Now that Samson isn't going, I want to go.

"Don't be rude," Sara says. "You're coming."

"Yeah, you're coming," Marcos adds.

I can see Samson glance at me out of the corner of his eye. At least he seems as disinterested in me as I am in him. Sara starts walking toward the door.

"Let me grab some shoes," I mutter, and head back upstairs.

Apparently, there isn't a Walmart on Bolivar Peninsula, which means you have to take the ferry to Galveston Island. It makes no sense to me. You have to take a ferry from the mainland to an island to do any shopping. This place is confusing.

The ferry takes approximately twenty minutes to get from here to there. As soon as Marcos parked the car, everyone got out. Sara noticed I hadn't opened my door, so she opened it for me. "Come on, let's go to the top deck," she said.

It wasn't really an invite so much as a command.

We've been standing up here for less than five minutes and Sara and Marcos have already snuck off, leaving me alone with Samson. It's getting late, probably around nine thirty, which makes for a mostly empty ferry. We're both staring out over the water, pretending this isn't awkward at all. But it is, because I don't know what to say. I have nothing in common with this guy. He has nothing in common with me. We've already had two less-than-stellar interactions since I arrived a few hours ago. That's two more than I'd like.

"I get the feeling they're trying to set us up," Samson says.

I glance over at him, but he's staring out at the water. "It's not a feeling. It's a fact."

He nods but says nothing. I don't know why he brought it up. Maybe to clear the air. Or maybe he's entertaining the idea.

"Just so you know, I'm not interested," I say. "And not

the kind of not interested where I hope you still pursue me because I like games. I'm *legit* not interested. Not just in you, but in people in general, really."

He smirks but still doesn't look over at me. It's like he's too good for eye contact. "I don't remember expressing my interest," he says coolly.

"You didn't *not* express interest, so I'm putting it out there. Just so we're clear."

His eyes find mine with a slow turn of his head. "Thanks for clearing up something that wasn't even confusing in the first place."

My God, he is good-looking. Even when he's being an asshole.

I can feel my cheeks burning. I quickly glance away, not sure how to come back from this. Every encounter I've had with him has been humiliating and I'm not sure if that's his fault or mine.

I think it might be mine for allowing myself to *get* embarrassed by him. You can't really be embarrassed in the presence of someone whose opinion you don't give two shits about. That has to mean that somewhere inside me, I give a shit what he thinks.

Samson pushes off the railing and stands up straight. I'm tall for a girl. Five-ten. But even at my height, he towers over me. He has to be at least six-three. "Friends it is, then," he says, shoving his hands in his pockets.

I unintentionally let out a dry laugh. "People like you aren't friends with people like me."

He tilts his head a little. "That's a bit presumptuous."

"Says the guy who assumed I was homeless."

"You ate bread off the ground."

"I was hungry. You're rich, you wouldn't understand."

His eyes narrow a bit, then he looks out at the ocean again. He stares so hard at it, it's like it's speaking to him. Giving him silent answers to all his silent questions.

Samson eventually looks away from both me and the water. "I'm going back to the car."

I watch him disappear down the stairs.

I don't know why I'm so defensive around him. After all, if he really did think I was homeless, he didn't ignore that. He offered me money. There must be a soul in there somewhere.

Maybe *I'm* the soulless one in this situation.

Six

To say I was relieved when Marcos and Samson split apart from us when we arrived at the store is an understatement. I've only been in Texas for a few hours and too much of that time has been spent in Samson's presence.

"What else do you need besides clothes?" Sara asks me as we walk through the health and beauty section.

"Pretty much everything," I say. "Shampoo, conditioner, deodorant, toothbrush, toothpaste. All the things I used to steal off maid carts every Saturday."

Sara pauses and stares at me. "Is that a joke? I don't know your humor yet."

I shake my head. "We couldn't afford necessities." I don't know why I'm being so blunt with her. "Sometimes, when you're poor, you have to get creative." I turn down the next aisle and Sara takes a moment to catch up to me.

"But didn't Brian pay child support?"

"My mother was an addict. I never saw a penny of that money."

Sara is walking next to me now. I'm trying not to look at her because I feel like my truth is stripping away her innocence. But maybe she needs a dose of reality.

"Did you ever tell your father that?"

"No. He hasn't seen my mother since I was four. She wasn't an addict back then."

"You should have told him. He would have done something about it."

I drop a can of deodorant in the cart. "I never felt it was my duty to let him know what my living conditions were. A father should be more aware of what's going on in his child's life."

I can tell that comment bothers Sara. She obviously has a different perspective of my father than I do, so maybe planting that one little seed is enough to get her to see outside her protective little beach-house bubble.

"Let's go look at the clothes," I say, changing the subject. She's quiet as we make our way through the clothing section. I grab several things, but I'm honestly not sure what will fit me. We make our way to the dressing rooms.

"You'll need a bathing suit, too," Sara says. "A couple, actually. We spend almost every day on the beach."

The swimsuit section is near the dressing rooms, so I grab a couple and head into a stall with the rest of my clothes.

"Come out after you change, I want to see how everything fits," Sara says.

Is that what girls do when they shop? Pose for each other?

I put on the bikini first. The top is a little big, but I hear the boobs are the first place you gain weight, and I'm sure I'll be gaining weight this summer. I walk out of the stall and stand in front of the mirror. Sara is sitting on a bench looking at her phone. She glances up at me and her eyes widen. "Wow. You could probably even go down a size."

I shake my head. "No, I plan on gaining weight this summer."

"Why? I'd kill to have a body like yours."

I hate that comment.

She's staring at me in a pouty way. It makes me think she's internally comparing our bodies, pointing out things about herself she deems as flaws.

"Your thighs don't even touch," she whispers almost wistfully. "I've always wanted a thigh gap."

I shake my head and walk back into the stall. I put on the second bathing suit and pull a pair of jean shorts over it to make sure they fit. When I walk out, Sara groans.

"My God, you could pull off anything." She stands up and positions herself next to me. She stares at our reflections in the mirror. She's only about two inches shorter than I am, fairly tall herself. Sara turns to the side and rests her hand on her shirt, right over her stomach. "How much do you weigh?"

"I don't know." I do know, but telling her my weight would only give her a goal she doesn't need to chase after. She sighs, sounding frustrated. She plops back down onto the bench. "I'm still twenty pounds shy of my summer goal. I just need to try harder," she says. "What's your secret?"

My secret?

I laugh while I stare at myself in the mirror again, running a hand over my slightly concave stomach. "I've spent most of my life hungry. Not everyone has food in their houses all the time." I look directly at Sara and she's staring up at me with an unreadable expression.

Her eyes flitter away before landing on her phone screen. She clears her throat. "Is that true?"

"Yeah."

She chews on her cheek for a moment and says, "Then why did you barely eat tonight?"

"Because I've had the worst twenty-four hours of my life and I was sitting at a dinner table with five people I don't know, in a house I've never been in, in a state I've never been to. Even hungry people lose their appetites sometimes."

Sara doesn't look at me. I don't know if I make her uncomfortable with how blunt I am or if she's grappling with the fact that our lives are so different. I want to bring up what I noticed at dinner earlier—how she only ate when I ate. But I don't. I feel like I've already wounded her enough tonight and we just met.

"Are you hungry?" I ask her. "Because I'm starving."

She nods with a small smile, and for the first time, I feel like there's some connection between us. "I am so fucking hungry right now it's unreal."

I laugh when she says that. "That makes two of us."

I walk into the dressing room and change back into my clothes. When I walk out, I grab Sara's hand and pull her up. "Come on." I throw the clothes into the cart and turn toward the grocery section.

"Where are we going?"

"To the food section."

We work our way to the bread aisle. I stop the cart in front of the boxed pastries. "Which is your favorite?"

Sara points to a white bag of mini-chocolate donuts. "Those."

I grab a bag off the shelf and open it. I take a donut and stick it in my mouth and hand her the bag. "We're gonna need milk, too," I say with a mouthful.

Sara looks at me like I'm insane, but she follows me to the dairy section regardless. I retrieve two individual chocolate milks and then point to a spot over by the eggs. I move the cart and then I sit down and lean against the long floor cooler that holds all the eggs.

"Sit down," I say to her.

She looks around us a moment, then she slowly lowers herself to the floor next to me. I hand her one of the chocolate milks.

I open mine and take a big drink of it and then grab another donut.

"You're crazy," Sara says quietly, finally taking a donut for herself.

I shrug. "There's a fine line between hungry and crazy."

She takes a drink of her chocolate milk and then leans her head against the cooler. "My God. This is heaven." She stretches her legs out in front of her, and we sit together in silence for a while, eating donuts and watching shoppers give us strange looks.

"I'm sorry if anything I said about your weight offended you," Sara finally says.

"It didn't. I just don't like seeing you compare yourself to me."

"It's hard not to. It doesn't help that I'm spending the summer on the beach. I compare myself to every girl in a bikini."

"You shouldn't," I say. "But I get it. It's weird, though, isn't it? Why do people judge other people based on how tightly their skin clings to their bones?" I shove another donut in my mouth to shut myself up.

Sara mutters, "*Amen,*" right before she takes another swig of her chocolate milk.

A store employee walks by and pauses when he sees us sitting on the floor eating food. "We're gonna pay for it," I say, waving a flippant hand at him. He shakes his head and walks away.

Another stretch of silence passes between us, and then Sara says, "I was really nervous to meet you. I was scared you hated me."

I laugh. "I didn't even know you existed until today."

My comment looks like it hurts Sara's feelings. "Your father never talked about me?"

I shake my head. "Not because he was trying to hide the fact that you existed. We just . . . We don't have a relationship. At all. We've barely spoken since he got married. I actually forgot he was even married."

Sara looks like she's about to say something, but she's interrupted.

"You two good?" Marcos asks.

We both look up to find Samson and Marcos looking back and forth between us.

Sara holds up her chocolate milk. "Beyah told me to stop obsessing about my weight and made me eat junk food."

Marcos laughs and reaches down into the bag for a donut. "Beyah is right. You're perfect."

Samson is staring at me. He never smiles like Marcos. Marcos always seems to be smiling.

Sara pushes herself off the floor and helps me up. "Let's go."

Seven

We loaded everything into the trunk except the prepaid phone. I've been trying to figure out how to set it up, but it's dark in the car and the instructions are hard to read. I don't even know how to power on the phone.

I'm struggling with it when Samson says, "Want me to help?"

I glance over at him and he's holding out his hand. I give him the package and he uses his own phone to light up the directions.

He's still working on it when Marcos parks the car on the ferry. "Coming?" Sara asks, opening her door.

I point to the phone in Samson's hands. "In a sec. He's setting up my phone."

Sara grins before she closes the door, like Samson setting up my phone is somehow going to lead to a summer fling. I hate that it's a goal of hers. I really have no interest in someone who has such little interest in me.

Samson has to dial a number to finalize the setup, which tells him there will be a two-minute hold time while the phone is activated.

Two minutes doesn't seem that long, but it feels like I'm entering into eternity. I glance out my window, trying to ignore the quiet tension that's filling the space between us.

It's so incredibly uncomfortable, I find myself hoping he'll say something after only ten seconds.

After twenty seconds, I start to feel nervous, so I blurt out the only thing I can think to say: "Why were you taking pictures of me on the ferry today?"

I glance at him and he's leaning an elbow into the area where the car door and the window meet. He's lightly dragging his fingers over his bottom lip, but he pulls them away when he sees me staring at him. He makes a fist and taps it against the window. "Because of how you were looking at the ocean."

His answer wraps like a ribbon around my spine. "How was I looking at it?"

"Like it was the first time you'd ever seen it."

I adjust myself in the seat, suddenly uncomfortable by how his words drape over me like silk.

"Have you looked at them yet?" he asks.

"Looked at what?"

"The pictures."

I shake my head.

"Well. When you do, feel free to delete what you don't want, but I'd really like the memory card back. There are pictures on there I'd like to have."

I nod. "What else do you take pictures of? Besides girls on ferries?"

He smiles at that. "Nature, mostly. The ocean. Sunrises. Sunsets."

I think about the sunset from earlier and how he might have gotten a picture of me with it. I'll see if Sara has a computer I can borrow so I can look at everything on the memory card. I'm curious now. "The sunset was really pretty tonight."

"Wait until you see the sunrise from your balcony."

"Yeah, I'm not waking up that early," I say with a laugh.

Samson looks down at my phone after the call notifies us setup is complete. "You want me to enter everyone's numbers?" He's opening up the contacts on his phone to Sara's name.

"Sure."

He enters Sara's number. Then Marcos's. Then his own. He does a few more things to the phone, then eventually hands it over to me. "You need a tutorial?"

I shake my head. "A friend from back home had one like this. I can figure it out."

"Where's back home?"

It's a simple question, but it sets my skin on fire. It's a question you ask someone you want to get to know better.

I clear my throat. "Kentucky," I say. "What about you?"

His eyes linger on me for a quiet moment. Then he looks away and grabs the door handle, as if starting a conversation with me is something he immediately regrets. "I'm gonna get some fresh air," he says, opening the door. He closes it and walks away from the car.

I should probably be offended by his strange reaction, but I'm not. I'm relieved. I want him to be just as disinterested in me as I am in him.

Or at least as disinterested as I'm *trying* to be in him.

I look down at my phone and add in Natalie's number. She was one of the few friends I had back home and I've been wanting to talk to her since last night. I'm sure she heard through her mother that my mother passed away, and if so, she's probably worried sick not knowing where I am. It's been hard for us to keep in touch since she left for college because I don't have a phone. That's a contributing factor as to why I don't have a lot of friends. It's hard to keep in touch with anyone when you're technologically out of the loop.

I get out of the car and walk to an empty spot on the ferry to make the call. I face the water and dial her number, waiting as it rings.

"Hello?"

I breathe a sigh of relief when I hear her voice. Finally, something familiar. "Hey."

"Beyah? Holy shit, I've been worried sick. I heard what happened, I'm so sorry." Her voice is so loud. I try to figure out how to take the phone off speaker, but the screen is just numbers. I look around, but no one is near us, so I just muffle the phone with my hand to keep the call from disturbing anyone in the vicinity.

"Beyah? Hello?"

"I'm here, sorry."

"Where are you?"

"Texas."

"Why the hell are you in Texas?"

"My dad moved here. I figured I'd stay with him for the summer. How's New York?"

"Different," she says. "In a good way." There's a pause before she says, "God, I still can't believe Janean is dead. You sure you're okay?"

"Yeah. I had one good cry, but like . . . I don't know. Maybe I'm broken."

"Whatever. She was the worst mother I've ever met."

And that's why I like Natalie. She says what she means. Not many people are as forthcoming as her.

"What about your dad? Hasn't it been a while since you've seen him? Is it awkward?"

"Yeah. It might even be worse now that I'm an adult. But he lives in a beach house, so that's a huge plus. He's married, though. Has a new stepdaughter."

"Yay for the beach house, but oh no. A stepsister? Is she your age?"

"About a year older. Her name is Sara."

"She sounds blond and pretty."

"She is."

"Do you like her?"

I think about that for a moment. "I'm still not sure what to think of her yet. I feel like she might be a locker-room girl."

"Ugh. Those are the worst. Any cute guys, at least?"

Right when Natalie asks that question, something catches my attention out of the corner of my eye. I turn my head and Samson is walking toward me. He's staring, like he might have caught the end of my conversation. I clench my jaw. "No. No cute guys. But hey, I gotta go. Save my number."

"Okay, got you."

I end the call and grip my phone in my hand. I swear to God, he shows up at all the worst times.

He takes a couple of steps closer until he's next to me at the railing. He narrows his eyes in my direction, looking at me curiously. "What's a locker-room girl?"

I hate that he heard that. I really do like Sara. I don't know why I said that to Natalie.

I sigh and then turn, resting my back against the railing. "It's what I called the mean girls at my school."

Samson nods, like he's processing my answer. "You know . . . when Sara found out you were coming, she moved

to the guest room. She wanted you to have the better room."
With that, he pushes off the railing, walks around me, and
heads back toward the car.

I turn and press my hands against my face and groan.

I have never made an ass out of myself in front of one
person so much in my life, and I've only known him for half
a day.

Eight

It's late by the time we get back and I get all my new stuff put away. These last twenty-four hours have been grueling, to say the least. I'm exhausted. Grief might even be catching up to me. And even though Sara and I shared an entire bag of chocolate donuts, I'm still hungry.

I go to the kitchen and find my father sitting at the table, a laptop in front of him and several books spread out over the table. He glances up when he hears me.

"Hey," he says, straightening up in his chair.

"Hi." I point to the pantry. "Just grabbing a snack." I open the pantry door and grab a bag of chips. When I close it, I fully intend to sneak back up to my room, but my father has other plans.

"Beyah," he says as soon as I reach the bottom step. "You got a sec?"

I nod reluctantly. I walk over to the table and take the seat across from him. I pull my knee up and try to seem casual. He leans back in his chair and rubs a hand across his jaw like whatever he's about to say is going to be a little uncomfortable.

Did he hear about my mother? I don't know that there are any people who connect them other than me, so I don't know how he'd have found out.

"I'm sorry I didn't go to your graduation."

Oh. It's about him. I stare at him for a moment, then open my bag of chips. I shrug. "It's fine. Long drive for someone with a broken leg."

He presses his lips together and leans forward, resting his elbows on the table. "About that," he says.

"I don't care, Dad. Really. We all tell lies to get out of things we don't want to do."

"It's not that I didn't want to be there," he says. "I just . . . I didn't think you *wanted* me there."

"Why wouldn't I have wanted you there?"

"I just got the impression that you've been avoiding me for the past couple of years. And I don't blame you. I don't feel like I've been a very good father to you."

I look down into my bag of chips and shake them around. "You haven't been." I casually eat another chip like I didn't just deliver the worst insult a child could hand to a parent.

My father's expression falls into a frown, and he opens his mouth to respond, but Sara spills out of the stairwell and into the kitchen with way too much energy for this time of night.

"Beyah, go put on your bathing suit, we're going to the beach."

My father looks relieved by the interruption. He gives his attention to his computer. I stand up and pop another chip in my mouth. "What's at the beach?"

Sara laughs. "The *beach* is at the beach. That's all you need." She's back in her bikini top and shorts again.

"I'm really tired," I say.

She rolls her eyes. "Just for an hour and then you can go to bed."

When we make it past the dunes, I deflate. I was hoping more people would be out here so I could be invisible, but it seems the crowd that was here earlier dissipated and the only two people remaining are Samson and Marcos. Plus a couple of people out in the water swimming.

Marcos is sitting by the fire, but Samson is sitting alone in the sand several feet away, staring out at the dark ocean. I know he hears us approaching, but he doesn't turn around to look at us. He's either lost in thought or making a concerted effort to ignore me.

I'm going to have to figure out a way to be at ease in his presence if this is how the summer is going to go—him always being around.

There are six seats set up around the fire, but two of them have towels draped over them and beers on the armrests, so they appear to be taken. Sara sits next to Marcos, so I take one of the last two empty chairs.

Sara looks out at the water, at the two people swimming. "Is that Cadence out there with Beau?"

"Yep," Marcos says flatly. "I think she's leaving tomorrow."

Sara rolls her eyes. "Can't wait. I wish she'd take Beau with her."

I don't know who Beau and Cadence are, but it doesn't sound like Sara and Marcos are big fans.

I try not to stare at Samson, but it's hard. He's about ten feet away, sitting with his arms wrapped around his knees, watching the waves claw at the sand. I hate that I'm wondering what he's thinking about, but he has to be thinking about something. That's what staring at the ocean produces. Thoughts. Lots of them.

"Let's go swimming," Sara says as she stands up and shimmies out of her shorts. She looks at me. "Wanna come?"

I shake my head. "I already showered tonight."

Sara grabs Marcos's hand and pulls him out of the chair. He swoops her up in his arms and runs toward the water. Sara's squeal breaks Samson out of whatever trance he was in. He stands up and wipes sand away from his shorts. He turns to walk back to the fire, but I notice the pause when he sees I'm sitting over here alone.

I keep my eyes on Sara and Marcos, if only because I

don't know what else to look at. I certainly don't want to look at Samson as he walks over here. I still feel embarrassed by the part of my conversation he overheard earlier. I don't want him to think I hate Sara, because I don't. I just don't know her all that well. But what he heard probably sounded worse than what it was.

He quietly takes a seat and stares at the fire, making no effort to speak to me. I look around us, at the incredible amount of space there is on this beach, and wonder how I can possibly feel like I'm suffocating right now.

I inhale a slow breath, then release it carefully before I speak. "I didn't mean what I said earlier. About Sara."

Samson looks over at me with a stoic expression. "Good."

That's all he says.

I shake my head and look away, but not before he sees me roll my eyes at his response. I don't know why, but even when he's defending his friends, he comes off as an asshole.

"What's wrong?" he asks.

"Nothing." I lean back in my chair and look up at the sky. "*Everything*," I whisper to myself.

Samson grabs a stick that's sitting in the sand by his chair. He starts poking at the fire but says nothing else. I lean my head to the right and look at the houses that line the beach. Samson's is by far the nicest one. It's more modern. It's stark white with deep black trim, boxy with lots of glass. But it seems cold compared to Alana and my father's house.

It also seems lonely, like he's the only one who lives there.

"Do you live in your house alone?"

"I don't really consider that my house, but yes, I'm the only one who stays there."

"Where are your parents?"

"Not here," he says.

His clipped responses aren't because he's shy. He's definitely not shy. I wonder if his conversations are like this with everyone or if it's just me.

"Are you in college?" I ask.

He shakes his head. "Taking a gap year."

I laugh under my breath. I don't mean to, but that answer is so out of touch with my reality.

He raises a brow, silently questioning why I'm laughing at his answer.

"When you're poor and you take a year off after high school, you're throwing away your future," I say. "But if you're rich and you take a year off, it's considered sophisticated. They even give it a fancy name."

He stares at me a moment but says nothing. I'd like to drill a hole in his head so his thoughts can pour out. But then again, I might not like them.

"What's the purpose of a gap year, anyway?" I ask.

"You're supposed to spend the year *finding yourself*." He says that last part with a hint of sarcasm.

"Did you? Find yourself?"

"I was never lost," he says pointedly. "I didn't spend my

gap year backpacking through Europe. I've spent it manning rent houses for my father. Not very sophisticated."

It sounds like he's a little resentful about that, but I'd give anything to get paid to live on a beach in a nice house. "How many houses does your family have here?"

"Five."

"You live in *five* beach houses?"

"Not all at once."

I think he might have just smiled a bit. I can't tell. Could have been a shadow from the fire.

Our lives are so incredibly different, yet here we are, sitting on the same beach in front of the same fire. Attempting to have a conversation that doesn't prove how many worlds apart we are. But we're so many worlds apart, we're not even in the same universe.

I wish I could be inside his head for a day. Any rich person's head. How do they view the world? How does Samson view me? What do rich people worry about if they don't have to worry about money?

"What's it like being rich?" I ask him.

"Probably not much different than being poor. You just have more money."

That is so laughable, I don't even laugh. "Only a rich person would say that."

He drops the stick back in the sand and leans back in his chair. He turns his head and makes eye contact with me. "What's it like being poor, then?"

I can feel my stomach drop when he throws my own

question back at me with a spin. I sigh, wondering if I should be honest with him.

I should. I've told too many lies in the past twenty-four hours, karma is sure to catch up with me. I give my attention back to the fire in front of us when I answer him.

"We didn't receive food stamps because my mother was never sober enough to make her appointments. We also didn't have a car. There are children who grow up never having to worry about food, there are children whose families live off government assistance for various reasons, and then there are children like me. The ones who slip through all the cracks. The ones who learn to do whatever it takes to survive. The kind who grow up not giving a second thought to eating a slice of bread they pulled out of a discarded loaf on the deck of a ferry, because that's normal. That's *dinner*."

Samson's jaw is hard as he stares back at me. Several beats of silence pass between us. He almost looks guilty, but then he glances away from me, giving his attention to the flames. "I'm sorry I said it wasn't much different. That was a shallow thing to say."

"You aren't shallow," I say quietly. "Shallow people don't stare at the ocean as deeply as you do."

Samson's focus returns to mine as soon as I say that. His eyes have changed a little—narrowed. Darkened. He runs a hand down his face and mutters, "Fuck."

I don't know why he says that, but it sends goose bumps

down my arms. It feels like it might have been a realization about me somehow.

I can't ask him about it because I spot the girl and guy walking out of the water toward us. Cadence and Beau.

When they get closer, I realize she's the girl Samson was kissing in his kitchen earlier. She's eyeing me as she makes her way over. The closer she gets, the prettier she gets. She doesn't sit in a chair; she sits right down on Samson's lap. She stares at me like she's expecting me to have a reaction to the fact that she's now using Samson as her personal chair, but I'm good at hiding what I'm feeling.

Why am I even feeling anything at all?

"Who are you?" Cadence asks me.

"Beyah. I'm Sara's stepsister."

I can tell by the way her eyes scroll over me that she's definitely a locker-room girl. She wraps an arm around Samson like she's staking a claim. Samson just looks bored, or lost in thought. Beau, who was just in the water with Cadence, sits down next to me.

His gaze starts at my feet and slowly slides up my body until he's finally looking me in the eyes. "I'm Beau," he says with an ambitious grin, reaching out a hand.

I shake it, but when I do, Sara reappears with Marcos from their swim. She groans when she sees Beau giving me attention. "Beyah is engaged to be married," Sara says. "Don't waste your time."

Beau looks down at my hand. "I don't see a ring."

"That's because the diamond is so big, it's too heavy for her to wear all day," Sara retorts.

Beau leans in toward me, staring at me with a smirk. "She's lying because she hates me."

"I can see that."

"Where are you from?"

"Kentucky."

"How long are you here for?"

"The summer, probably."

He grins. "Nice. Me too. If you ever get bored, I live over—" He lifts a hand to point toward wherever his house is, but he stops speaking because Sara is now standing in front of us.

She grabs my hand. "Come on, Beyah. Let's go home." I'm relieved. I didn't want to be here to begin with.

I stand up and Beau rolls his eyes, throwing up a defeated hand. "You're always ruining my fun, Sara."

Sara leans down and gives Marcos a kiss goodbye. I glance over in Samson's direction. All I can seem to focus on is the hand he has pressed against Cadence's thigh. I start to turn to walk with Sara, but right before I do, Samson makes eye contact with me. He stares so hard, I feel it pinching my chest. I look away and don't look back as I follow Sara.

"What's up with Beau?" I ask as we walk back toward the house.

"He's inappropriate in every way imaginable. Please don't give him any attention, it's the last thing he deserves."

It's hard to give anyone else attention when Samson is in my presence.

Sara and I walk past the dunes and everything in me wants to give one last glance back toward him, but I don't.

"What about the girl? Cadence?"

"Don't worry," Sara says. "She'll be gone tomorrow and Samson will be free."

I laugh. "I'm not waiting in that line."

"Probably for the best," Sara says when we reach her house. "Samson's leaving for the Air Force Academy at the end of the summer. As much as I was hoping I could set the two of you up, it would also suck if you fell for him right before he gets shipped away."

I pause on the stairs when she says that, but she doesn't notice because she's in front of me. But that takes me by surprise. He didn't mention what he was doing after his gap year was over. I don't know why, but I didn't expect it to be the military.

When we get inside the house, all the lights are out. "Want to stay up and watch a movie?"

"I'm exhausted. Maybe tomorrow night?"

She sits down on the sofa and grabs the remote. She leans her head back into the couch and looks at me upside down. "I'm glad you're here, Beyah." She powers on the TV and her attention is no longer on me, but her words make me smile.

I believe her when she says she's glad I'm here. That feels good. It's not often I feel like my presence is appreciated. Or even noticed.

When I get up to my room, I close and lock the door.

I walk over to the balcony doors and open them, wanting to listen to the sound of the ocean tonight while I sleep. But I also want to see what Samson is doing.

Marcos and Beau are still down at the fire. Cadence is walking away from the group in the opposite direction of Samson's house.

Samson is walking over the dune crossing, heading toward his house. Alone.

Why does that make me happy?

I don't want him to notice me up here, so I walk back into my room and close the balcony doors.

Before I crawl into bed, I take Mother Teresa out of the plastic sack she traveled in and prop the picture up on the dresser. It looks so out of place in this fancy room, but that makes me even happier that I brought it with me. I need a piece of home to remind me that this room and this house and this town are not my reality.

Nine

What the hell is that sound?

I put my hand over my ear, confused by the noise that's forcing me out of a perfectly deep sleep. It's coming from across the room. I open my eyes and lift my head off the pillow, and the sound gets louder. I glance outside and there's barely any light. The horizon is gray, like the world is still preparing to wake up.

I groan and toss the covers aside so I can locate the source of all the noise. It sounds like it's coming from the dresser, so I shuffle over to it.

It's my new phone. I wipe sleep from my eyes so I can read the screen. It's only 5:59 a.m.

An alarm is set on my phone. It reads: *Go watch the sunrise.*

That's all the alert says.

I cancel the alarm and the room falls silent again. I glance behind me, toward the balcony.

Samson.

It better be worth it.

I grab the comforter off my bed and wrap myself in it. I go out onto the balcony and look at Samson's balcony. It's empty.

I sit down in one of the chairs and pull the covers up to my chin. I stare out over the dark horizon. To the east, there's just the smallest sliver of sun peeking out over the ocean. To the north, the skies are dark and occasionally burst with lightning. It looks like a storm is rolling in, threatening to snuff out the light.

I sit on my balcony and stare at the sun as it slowly illuminates the peninsula. I listen to the sound of the waves as they wash onto the beach. Thunder rolls in the distance while seagulls begin to chirp nearby.

I'm in a complete trance for several minutes as the wind begins to pick up. As bright as the sunrise began, it slowly darkens as the storm moves closer. The skies swallow up every hue of color that was attempting to burst through, and after a while, everything is a muted gray.

That's when the rain starts. I'm protected by a roof over the balcony, and the wind isn't extreme right now, so I remain outside, watching as everything that started out hopeful just fifteen minutes ago slowly turns to gloom.

I wonder if Samson knew there would be a storm rolling in with the sunrise today. I glance over at his house and he's standing in his doorway, leaning against the door-frame, holding a cup of coffee. He isn't looking at the rain or the ocean or the sky.

He's looking at me.

Seeing him watching me stirs something inside me that I don't want to be stirred. I stare back at him for a moment, wondering if he wakes up every morning to watch the sunrise or if he just wanted to see what I would do about the alarm he set on my phone.

Maybe he actually appreciates the sunrise. Is he one of the few who doesn't take this view for granted?

I think there's a chance I might be wrong about him. I might have judged him a little too soon. But then again, what's it matter if I am wrong? Things between us are awkward and I don't see that changing unless one of us has a personality transplant.

I break our stare and walk back inside. I crawl back into bed.

I think I'll just stay here.

Ten

I've spent the majority of the last three days in my bedroom. The rain coupled with the week I've had made me not want to face the world at all. Plus, this bedroom is becoming my favorite place because I feel secure here, encased by these four walls. I have an unobstructed view of the ocean, a television I've finally figured out how to work, and my own bathroom.

I really could stay in this room for the rest of my time here and be content.

The issue is everyone *else* who lives in this house.

My father has checked on me multiple times. I told him I had a headache and my throat was sore and it hurt to talk, so he just pops in every now and then and asks if I'm feeling okay.

Sara has been bringing me things. Food, water, medicine I don't really need. At one point yesterday, she crawled into my bed and watched Netflix with me for an hour before leaving to go on a date with Marcos. We didn't speak much, but I surprisingly didn't mind her company.

She has a good energy. Sometimes I feel like a black hole around her. Like maybe I'm sucking all the life out of her by just being in her innocent presence.

I've kept track of Samson's routine more than I care to admit. I don't know why I'm so curious about him. His routine intrigues me, though.

I've left his alarm on my phone because the sunrises seem to have become a thing with us. He's out on his own balcony every morning. We watch the world wake up alone, yet together. Each time I make my way back into my bedroom, we make brief eye contact. He doesn't speak to me, though.

He's either not a morning person, or he'd rather appreciate the sunrise in silence. Either way, it feels intimate somehow. Like we have this secret daily meeting no one else knows about, even though we never speak during said meeting.

I usually go back to bed afterward, but Samson always leaves his house. I don't know where he goes that early each morning, but he's gone most of every day. And when he returns at night, his house is always dark. He only ever turns on the light to whatever room he's in, and then he turns out the light as soon as he leaves that room.

He seems to live with military precision already. The house is spotless, from what I can tell from my window.

Makes me wonder what kind of father he has. If he's going into the military, maybe he was raised in the military. Maybe that's why he seems so controlled and keeps his house so clean.

I really need to find something to occupy my brain if this is what I spend my time thinking about. Maybe I should get a job. I can't stay in this room forever.

I could buy a volleyball and a net and get some practice in, but that doesn't sound appealing at all. We've already been assigned workout routines and schedules from the coach, but I haven't even opened the email. I don't know why, but I have absolutely no desire to look at a volleyball until I'm in Pennsylvania. I've lived volleyball for the past five years of my life. I'm about to live it for the next four.

I deserve a month or two of not having to think about it.

The rain has stopped and the sun is out today. If I continue to pretend I'm sick for a fourth day in a row, my father might actually take me to a doctor. I don't really have an excuse to stay in my room much longer and it would be a good day to go out and job hunt. Maybe I could get a waitressing job and save up my tips for when I leave for college.

I'd give anything for another day like the three that came before this one, though. But it doesn't look like I'm gonna get it because someone is knocking at my bedroom door.

"It's me," Sara says. "Can I come in?"

"Sure." I'm already sitting up on the bed, leaning against

the headboard. Sara crawls onto the bed and sits next to me. She smells like cinnamon.

"You feeling better?"

I nod and force a small smile. "Yeah, a little bit."

"Good. The rain finally stopped. You want to have a beach day later?"

"I don't know. I was thinking maybe I should look for a summer job. I need to save up some money for college."

She laughs at that. "No. Enjoy your last summer before adulthood kicks in. Take advantage of all this," she says, waving her hand in the air.

She's so chipper. I'm still stuck in yesterday's mood. There's an obvious imbalance between us right now. She notices, because her smile disappears and she narrows her eyes at me.

"You okay, Beyah?"

I smile, but it takes too much effort and my smile falters with a sigh. "I don't know. This is all just . . . it's kind of weird for me."

"What?"

"Being here."

"Do you want to go back home?"

"No." I don't even know where home is right now, but I don't say that. I'm in limbo and it's a strange feeling. A depressing feeling.

"Are you sad?" she asks.

"I think so."

"Is there anything I can do about it?"

I shake my head. "No."

She rolls onto her side, holding her head up with her hand. "We have to get you out of this funk. Do you think some of it is because you feel like a stranger in this house?"

I nod. I do feel out of place here. "It probably contributes."

"Then we just need to fast-track our friendship." She rolls onto her back. "Let's get to know each other. Ask me some questions."

There actually is a lot I want to know about her, so I lean my head against the headboard and think of some. "Do you have a good relationship with your mother?"

"Yeah. I love her, she's my best friend."

Lucky. "Where is your dad?"

"He lives in Dallas. They divorced five years ago."

"Do you ever see him?"

Sara nods. "Yeah. He's a good dad. A lot like yours."

I somehow keep a straight face after that comment.

She's got two good parents and a stepfather who seems to know her better than he knows his own daughter. I hope she doesn't take that for granted.

Sara hasn't been through a lot of hardship. I can tell by looking at her. She's still full of hope. "What's the worst thing that's ever happened to you?" I ask her.

"My parents' divorce was really hard for me," she says.

"What's the best thing that's ever happened to you?"

She grins. "Marcos."

"How long have you two been together?"

"Since spring break."

"That's it?"

"Yeah, just a few months. But I would bet my life we're gonna get married someday."

"Don't do that."

"Don't marry him?" she asks, rolling onto her stomach.

"Don't bet your life on it. You've only known him a few months."

She grins. "Oh, I don't mean anytime soon. We'll wait until after college." She's still smiling dreamily when she says, "I'm transferring schools so I can be closer to him."

"Is he in college, too?"

"Yeah, he's a fashion major at U of H. Minoring in business."

"He's a fashion major?"

She nods. "He wants to start a clothing line called *His-Panic*."

"That explains the shirts."

"Yeah, it's pretty clever. He was born in Chiapas, so he plans to donate some of the income to help fight poverty there, if his clothing line ever takes off. He already has five thousand followers on Instagram."

"Is that good? I don't know a lot about social media."

"It's better than *not* having five thousand followers." She sits up on the bed and crosses her legs. She moves so much. I wish I had half her energy. "Can I ask you a question?"

I nod. "I've asked you about ten, so it's only fair."

"What makes you happy?" Her expression is full of genuine curiosity.

I have to look away before she sees the expression on my own face, because honestly . . . I don't know what makes me happy. I'm kind of curious about it, too. I've spent my whole life just trying to survive; I've never really thought about the things that lie beyond that.

Getting a meal used to make me happy. Nights when my mother didn't bring home strange men used to make me happy. Paydays at McDonald's used to make me happy.

I'm not sure why her question triggers so much in me, but I realize for the first time since I got here that the same things that used to make me happy aren't even issues in my life anymore.

What *does* make me happy?

"I don't know." I look out the window at the water and feel a sense of calmness come over me. "The ocean, I guess."

"Then you should enjoy the ocean while you have it. Don't get a summer job. You have the rest of your life to work. Make this summer all about you. It sounds to me like you deserve to be a little selfish for once."

I nod in agreement. "I do deserve it."

She smiles. "I'm glad you realize that." She pushes herself off the bed. "I promised Marcos I'd go with him to get his hair cut and grab a late lunch. You can come with us if you want."

"No, I need to shower. I might go for a walk on the beach later."

Sara backs out of my room. "Okay. We'll be back in a couple hours. Don't eat dinner, we're cooking out on the beach tonight."

Sara mentioned how there's a large part of Bolivar Peninsula referred to as Zoo Beach. Vehicles are allowed on the sand, as well as golf carts, so it's constant traffic and a constant party.

The area where Sara lives still sees some of that traffic, but it isn't nearly as busy as certain parts of the peninsula. But just a couple of miles down from Sara's house begins a whole different world. Not necessarily a better one. I guess that would depend on the mood you're in, but my mood right now certainly isn't loud music and toxic masculinity.

I turn around to walk back before I get too far into the crowded area. There are a couple of guys sitting on the back of their truck, coaxing a dog over with a hamburger.

The dog's rib cage is visible through his fur. I watch as the dog slowly makes his way toward the two guys in the back of the truck, as if he knows there's a price he'll have to pay for the food he's about to get.

I immediately empathize with the dog.

"That's it," one of the guys says, holding his hamburger out. "Just a little closer."

When the dog is within reach of him, the guy pulls his food away and the other guy quickly steps over the dog and captures it between his knees. They're laughing as he pulls a headband over the dog's eyes and lets him loose. The dog begins to stumble around, unable to see.

I rush over to the dog as he tries to claw the headband off with his foot. I remove it from around his head and he looks up at me, scared, then scurries off.

"Come on!" one of the guys says. "We're just having fun with him."

I throw the headband at them. "Stupid fucks." The dog is running away now. I walk over and grab the hamburger out of the guy's hand and follow after the dog.

"Bitch," I hear one of them mutter.

I walk back in the direction I came from, away from the crowd and toward the dog. The poor thing hides behind a blue trash can and hunkers down. I walk slowly toward him until I'm a few feet away and then I gently toss the burger in his direction.

The dog sniffs it for a second and then begins eating it. I continue walking, angry now. I don't understand humans sometimes. I hate it, because I find myself wishing that the entirety of humanity would suffer just a tiny amount more than they do. Maybe if everyone tasted a bit of what that dog has lived through, they would be more hesitant to be assholes.

I'm halfway home before I realize the dog has been following me. He must think I have more burgers.

I stop and the dog stops.

We stare each other down, sizing each other up.

"I don't have any more food."

I start walking again, and the dog continues to follow me. Every now and then he'll get sidetracked by something, but then he'll look up and find me and run to catch up with me. He's still on my heels when I finally reach the house.

I'm positive I'm not allowed to take a dog this filthy inside with me, but I can at least get him some food. When I reach the bottom steps, I turn and point at him. "Stay."

The dog sits right where I point. It surprises me. At least he listens well.

I grab some slices of turkey out of the refrigerator and fill a bowl of water and take it down to the dog. I sit on the bottom step and rub his head while he eats. I don't know if feeding him here at the house is a bad move. He'll probably hang around now that I've fed him, but maybe that's not such a bad thing. I could use the company of something that doesn't judge me.

"Beyah!"

The dog's ears perk up at the sound of my name. I look up and around, trying to locate the person who just yelled, but I don't see anyone.

"Up here!"

I look at the house catty-cornered to this one on the second row behind a vacant beachfront lot. There's a guy standing on the edge of an extremely high roof. He's so high up, it takes me a few seconds before I realize the guy is Samson.

He waves me over, and like an idiot, I look around to

make sure he's talking to me, even though he specifically said my name.

"Come here!" he yells.

Samson is shirtless. I feel as pathetic and as hungry as this dog when I immediately stand up.

I look down at the dog. "I'll be right back. Stay here."

As soon as I start to walk across the street, the dog follows me.

I walk into the yard that contains the house Samson is standing on top of. He's dangerously close to the edge of the roof now, looking down. "Take the stairs to the front door. Then take the first door on the left in the hallway. It leads to the roof access. I want to show you something."

I can see the sweat glistening on his skin from down here, so I look at my feet for a second, trying to figure out what to do. I haven't necessarily had the best interactions with him. Why would I expose myself to more of that?

"I'm scared of heights!" I say loudly, looking up at him.

Samson laughs. "You aren't scared of anything, get up here."

I don't like how he says that with such confidence, like he knows me. But he's right. I'm not scared of much. I turn to the dog and point next to the stairs. "Stay." The dog walks over to the spot I pointed at and sits. "Damn, dog. You are so smart."

I head up the stairs to the front door. *Should I knock?* I do, but no one answers.

I'm assuming Samson is the only one here or he would have come down to let me in himself.

I push the door open and feel extremely weird being in an unfamiliar house. I quickly head for the door on the left and open it. It's a stairwell that leads all the way up to a small, enclosed circular seating area at the top of the stairs. It's shaped like the top of a lighthouse and is situated in the center of the house. It's encased in windows with a 360-degree view.

It's stunning. I don't know why every house doesn't have one of these. I'd come up here every night and read a book.

One of the windows opens onto the roof and Samson is waiting for me, holding it open.

"This is really cool," I say, looking out. It takes me a moment to work up the courage to step onto the roof. I'm not actually afraid of heights like I said earlier, but this house is on stilts, and there are two floors on top of those stilts.

Samson takes my hand and helps me out and onto the roof before closing the window.

I inhale a shaky breath when I get situated because I didn't realize how high up we were until this moment. I don't dare look down.

Everything looks different from up here. Because of the height of this roof, all the other houses seem small in comparison.

There are loose shingles lying in a pile next to a toolbox at Samson's feet. "Is this one of your five rent houses?"

"No. Just helping my friend Marjorie. She's got a leak." The roof up here has two levels, one just a couple of feet higher than the other. Samson steps onto the second level and puts his hands on his hips. "Come here."

Once I'm standing next to him, he points in the opposite direction of the ocean. "You can see the sunset over the bay from up here."

I look in the direction he's pointing and the sky is ablaze on the other side of the peninsula. Reds and purples and pinks and blues, all swirled together.

"Marjorie has the tallest house in the neighborhood. You can see the entire peninsula."

I spin in a slow circle, admiring the view. The bay is lit up with splashes of colors so bright, it looks like a filter. I can see the entire beach as far as my eyes allow.

"It's beautiful."

Samson stares at the sunset for a moment, then hops down to the lower part of the split-level roof. He walks over to the toolbox, kneeling down next to it. He places a shingle on the roof and begins tacking it on.

Witnessing how he just moves about on this roof like he's on level ground makes me unsteady on my own feet. I sit down.

"That's all I wanted," he says. "I know you like the sunrises, so I wanted you to see the sunset from up here."

"Today's sunrise actually depressed me."

He nods, as if he knows exactly what I mean by that.

"Yeah. Sometimes things are so pretty, it makes everything else a little less impressive."

I watch him in silence for a while. He secures about five shingles in place while the sky eats up most of his light. He knows I'm watching him, but for some reason it doesn't feel embarrassing to stare at him this time. It's like he prefers me to be here than not. Kind of how it feels in the mornings when we sit on our respective balconies and don't speak.

His hair is wet from sweat, so it's a darker blond than normal. There's a necklace hanging around his neck and every now and then when he moves, I can see a flash of a tan line beneath it. He must never take it off. It's a piece of wood hanging from a thin black braided cord.

"Does your necklace have meaning?"

He nods but doesn't explain what that meaning is. He just keeps working.

"Are you going to tell me what it means?"

He shakes his head.

Okay, then.

I sigh. What am I even doing trying to have a conversation with him? I forgot what it's like.

"Did you get a dog today?" he asks.

"I went for a walk. He followed me home."

"I saw you feed him. He's not leaving now."

"I don't mind."

Samson eyes me for a moment, then wipes sweat away

from his forehead with his arm. "What are Sara and Marcos doing tonight?"

I shrug. "She said something about a cookout."

"Good. I'm starving." He goes back to tacking shingles onto the roof.

"Who is Marjorie?" I ask.

"She owns this house. Her husband died a couple of years ago, so I help her out every now and then."

I wonder how many people he knows in this neighborhood. Did he grow up in Texas? Where did he go to school? Why is he going into the air force? I have so many questions.

"How long have you had houses here?"

"I don't have houses here," he says. "My father does."

"How long has your *father* had houses here?"

Samson takes a second to answer. "I don't want to talk about my father's houses."

I chew on my lip. It seems like a lot of questions are off-limits with him. I hate it because it makes me even more curious. I don't come across people who hoard secrets like I do. Most people want a listener. Someone they can spill everything to. Samson doesn't want a listener. Neither do I. Which probably explains why conversations between us feel different than conversations I have with other people.

Our conversations feel splotchy. Like globs of ink and lots of white space.

Samson begins putting all his tools back in his toolbox. It's still light out, but it won't be for much longer. He stands up and comes back up to the top level, then sits down next to me on the roof.

I can feel the heat from his body, he's so close.

He rests his elbows on his knees. He really is a beautiful person. It's hard not to stare at people like him. But I think his charisma comes more from the way he carries himself than how he looks. He may have an artistic side.

There's definitely a quiet aspect to him that makes him seem introspective. Or maybe he's just guarded.

Whatever it is that makes him up as a whole, I find myself viewing him as a project I want to take on. A challenge. I want to crack him open and see what's inside him that makes him the only person on the planet I'm genuinely curious about.

Samson runs a thumb across his bottom lip, so naturally I'm already staring at his mouth when he begins to speak. "There was this fisherman who used to come around a lot," he says. "His name was Rake. He lived on his boat and would go up and down the coast from here to South Padre. Sometimes he'd anchor his boat right out there and swim up to the beach and join random people at their cookouts. I don't remember a whole lot about him, but I remember he used to write poems on scraps of paper and give them to people. I think that's what fascinated me the most about him. He was this fearless fisherman who wrote poetry." He smiles when he says that. "I remember thinking he was some kind of untouchable mythical creature." Samson's smile fades, and he pauses for a moment. "Hurricane Ike hit in 2008. It destroyed most of the island. I was helping with the cleanup and I found Rake's boat toward the end of the peninsula in Gilchrist. It was in shreds." He fingers his necklace, looking down at it. "I took a piece of the boat and made this necklace out of it."

He keeps his fingers on his necklace and looks back out at the ocean, sliding the piece of wood back and forth through the cord.

"What happened to Rake?"

Samson faces me. "I don't know. He wasn't technically a resident of the area, so he wasn't counted among the missing or dead. But he never would have abandoned that boat, even during a hurricane. I don't know that people actively searched for him, to be honest. I'm not even sure anyone noticed he was missing after the hurricane."

"You noticed."

Samson's expression changes when I say that. There's a sadness in him and a little bit of it seeps out. I don't like it because apparently sadness is what I connect with. I feel like he's tugging at my soul with that look.

Samson isn't at all who I thought he was when I met him. I don't know how to process that. Admitting he's nothing like I assumed he was makes me disappointed in myself. I've never looked at myself as judgmental, but I think I am. I judged him. I judged Sara.

I look away from Samson and stand up. I step down onto the lower level of the roof and turn around when I reach the window. We exchange a stare that lasts for about five silent seconds. "I was wrong about you."

Samson nods, holding my gaze. "It's okay."

He says that with sincerity, like he doesn't hold it against me at all.

I don't come across people very often who I think I can learn something from, but he might actually have me figured out more than I have him figured out. I find that attractive.

Which is why I exit the roof and walk down the stairs feeling a lot heavier than when I walked up them.

The dog is still in the same spot when I make it back outside. He's looking at me excitedly—his tail wags when I reach the bottom step. "Look at you, being all obedient." I bend down and pet him. His hair is all matted. The poor unloved thing reminds me so much of myself.

"Is that your dog?"

I follow the voice until I see a woman seated at a picnic table beneath the first level of the house. She's messing with a bag of something sitting on her lap. She's older, maybe in her seventies. She must be Marjorie.

"I don't know," I say, looking down at the dog. "We just met."

I walk closer to the picnic table. The dog follows me.

"You a friend of Samson's?" she asks.

"I don't know," I say, repeating myself. "We just met, too."

She laughs. "Well. If you figure him out, let me know. He's a mystery, that one."

I guess I'm not the only one who thinks that about him.

"He wanted me to see the view from your roof. It's gorgeous." Now that I'm closer, I can see she's cracking pecans. I lean against one of the stilts holding her house up. "How long have you known Samson?" I ask her.

She lifts her chin in thought. "Since the beginning of the year, I guess. I had a heart attack in February. Can't get around like I used to, so he comes over every now and then and I put him to work. He doesn't complain. He also doesn't charge me, so I'm not sure what he's getting out of it."

I smile. I like that he doesn't take money from her. Not that she can't afford to pay someone to help her. She's sitting in the tallest house in what's probably the nicest neighborhood on this peninsula. It's not the most modern. It's actually kind of dated, but it has character. It feels lived in, unlike a lot of these other houses, which are rent-ready and identical. "I really like your house," I say, looking around. "What do you call this level?"

"The stilt level," she says. She points above her head. "We consider that the first floor."

I glance around at the other houses. Some of them have enclosed their stilt levels. Some have made them parking spaces. I like Marjorie's. She's got a tiki bar, a picnic table, and a couple of hammocks hanging between some of the stilts.

"Some people like to turn their stilt levels into extra

rooms," she says. "The new idiots next door enclosed an entire guest room on their stilt level. Not too bright, but they didn't want my opinion. They'll figure it out soon enough. Some days the ocean is our neighbor, but some days the ocean is our roommate." She motions for me to come closer. "Here. Take these." She hands me a gallon-size bag of shelled pecans.

"You don't have to give me these," I say, trying to hand them back to her.

She waves me away. "Keep them. I have too many."

I have no idea what I'm going to do with a pound of pecans. I'll give them to Alana, I guess. "Thank you."

Marjorie nods her head at the dog. "Have you named him yet?"

"No."

"You should call him Pepper Jack Cheese."

I laugh. "Why?"

"Why not?"

I look down at the dog. He doesn't look like a piece of cheese. I'm not sure *any* dog looks like cheese. "Pepper Jack," I say, trying the name out on him. "Do you feel like a Pepper Jack?"

"Pepper Jack *Cheese*," Marjorie corrects. "He deserves the full name."

I like Marjorie. She's odd. "Thanks for the pecans." I look down at the dog. "Let's go home, Pepper Jack Cheese."

Eleven

I went to a small elementary school. That's where I met Natalie. It was only a few blocks from my house and it was small enough that there was only one teacher per grade. Your clique was the grade you were in. In elementary school, no one cared about money because we were too young to really know better.

Junior high and high school were different. They were much larger campuses, and by that age, money defined your clique. Unless you were exceptionally pretty. Or, in Zackary Henderson's case, famous on YouTube. He wasn't rich, but his social media status landed him in the rich crowd. Followers are considered a more valuable currency than cash to a lot of people my age.

I came from the worst part of town and everyone knew it. The kids in my neighborhood who were just as poor as me slowly began to dwindle. A lot of them followed in the same sad footsteps as their parents by turning to drugs. I never felt part of that crowd because I did whatever I could to be the exact opposite of my mother and the people like her.

It didn't matter at school, though. Natalie was my only friend until I joined the volleyball team as a freshman. A few of the girls on the team accepted me, especially after I became the best one on the team, but most of them resented me. They still treated me like I was less than them. And it wasn't necessarily typical bullying. No name-calling or being shoved around in the hallways. I think I might have been too intimidating to some of them to be bullied.

I would have fought back and they knew it.

It was more that I was avoided. Ignored. I was never included in anything. I'm sure a lot of that had to do with the fact that I was one of the few in my school who had no cell phone, no laptop, no home phone. No means of connecting outside of school hours, and that can be socially detrimental for anyone these days. Or maybe that's just my way of excusing being excluded for the better part of six years.

It's hard not to grow bitter when you spend so much time alone. It's especially hard not to grow bitter at class systems and people with money, because the richer they were, the more it seemed I didn't exist to them.

Which is why being here on this beach with the type of people I'm sure I would have been invisible to in high school is hard for me. I want to believe Sara would have treated me the same as she does now had I known her in high school. The more I get to know her, the less I see her as someone who would be intentionally shitty to anyone.

And Samson. How did he treat the underdogs?

Not everyone who had money was an asshole in my high school, but enough of them were that I think I might have just lumped them all together. Part of me wonders if things would have been different if I would have tried harder. Opened up more. Would I have been accepted?

Maybe the only reason I wasn't accepted is because I didn't want to be. It was easier to stay to myself. I had Natalie when I needed her, but she had a cell phone and other friends who kept her busy, so we weren't inseparable. I can't even say we were best friends.

I just know that I never did things like this. I never hung out in groups with people. When I was old enough to get a job, I worked as much as I possibly could. So bonfires and cookouts and spending time with people my own age is foreign to me. I'm trying to find a way to be at ease in this crowd, but it's going to take time. I've spent a lot of years becoming the person I am. It's hard to change who you are in a span of a few days.

There are about eight people around the campfire, but none of them are Samson. He came down and grabbed a burger but then went back to his house after he ate. The only two I know are Sara and Marcos, but they're sitting across from me, the fire separating us. I don't think they know the other people here all that well, either. I heard Marcos ask one of the guys where he's from.

This must be a beach thing. Hanging out with random people you barely know. Strangers gathering around a fire, asking one another superficial questions until they're drunk enough to pretend they've known each other their whole lives.

I think Sara can tell I'm folding in on myself. She walks over and sits down next to me. Pepper Jack Cheese is lying in the sand next to my chair. Sara looks down at the dog and scratches him on the head.

"Where'd you find this thing?"

"He followed me home earlier."

"Have you named him yet?"

"Pepper Jack Cheese."

She looks at me. "Seriously?"

I shrug.

"I kinda like it. We should give him a bath later. We have an outdoor shower on the stilt level."

"You think your mom would let me keep him?"

"Not in the house, but we could make him a spot outside. She probably won't even notice, honestly. They're barely here."

I've noticed that. They both get home late and tend to go to bed soon after. They leave early in the morning. "Why are they gone so much?"

"They both work in Houston. Traffic is terrible, so they

eat dinner together in the city on weeknights so they don't have to fight it. But they take off Fridays during the summer, so they both have three-day weekends."

"Why do they even bother driving here Monday through Thursday? Isn't their main house in Houston?"

"My mother would worry about me too much. She's not as strict as she used to be because I'm almost twenty, but she still wants to know I'm home in bed every night. And she loves the ocean. I think she sleeps better here."

"Do you guys only stay here in the summer?"

"We come here for holidays or a weekend getaway every now and then." She stops petting Pepper Jack Cheese and looks at me. "Where are you staying when you start classes in August? Are you moving back in with your mother?"

My stomach turns at that question. They all still think I'm going to some community college back in Kentucky. Not to mention I still haven't told anyone about my mother.

"No. I'll be—"

Marcos appears and pulls Sara out of her chair before I can finish my sentence. He swoops her up and she squeals and wraps her arms around his neck as he runs her out toward the water. Pepper Jack Cheese stands up and barks because of the commotion.

"It's okay," I say, putting my hand on his head. "Lie down."

He resumes his position in the sand. I stare up at Samson's house, wondering what he's doing. Does he have a girl with him? That would explain why he isn't out here social-izing.

I don't like being out here alone now that Sara and Mar-cos are in the water. I don't know any of these other people and they're really starting to get rowdy. I think I'm the only one not drinking.

I stand up and go for a walk to get away from the group before any of them decides to play spin the bottle or something else just as horrifying. Pepper Jack Cheese follows me.

I'm really starting to like this dog. His loyalty is nice, but his name is way too long. I might just call him P.J.

There's an abandoned, half-destroyed sandcastle a few yards away from the group. P.J. runs over to it and starts sniffing around it. I sit down next to the sandcastle and start rebuilding one of the walls.

Life is weird. One day you're staring at your dead mother and a few days later you're building a sandcastle on the beach by yourself in the dark with a dog named after a cheese.

"It'll be washed away by the tide in an hour."

I look up to see Samson standing beside me. I'm extremely relieved to see him here and that makes me feel strange. I'm starting to find an odd comfort in his presence.

"Then you better help me build a retaining wall."

Samson walks around the sandcastle and sits on the other side of it. He looks at the dog. "He likes you."

"I fed him. I'm sure if you gave him a burger, he'd follow you around, too."

Samson leans forward and begins piling sand up on his side of the castle. The sight of it makes me grin. A hot shirtless guy playing in the sand.

I steal glances at him every now and then, impressed by his focus.

"His name is Pepper Jack Cheese," I say, breaking a stretch of silence.

Samson smiles. "You met Marjorie?"

"How'd you know it was her idea?"

"She has two cats. Their names are Cheddar Cheese and Mozzarella."

I laugh. "She's interesting."

"Yeah, she is."

The tide pushes closer and some of the water spills into the area where we're working. Samson stops patting the walls with his hands. "You been in the water yet?"

"No. I'm kind of leery of it."

"Why?"

"Jellyfish. Sharks. All the things I can't see beneath the surface."

Samson laughs. "We hung out on top of a three-story house today. You're safer in the ocean than you were on that roof." He stands up and wipes sand from his shorts. "Come on."

He's walking into the water, not waiting on me. I look for Marcos and Sara, but they're a good ways down.

The ocean is massive, so I don't know why going into it with Samson seems intimate. I stand up and pull off my shorts, then toss them near Pepper Jack Cheese.

"Keep an eye on those," I say.

I walk into the water. It's warmer than I thought it would be. Samson is several feet ahead of me. I keep walking, surprised at how far out I have to go before the water even reaches my knees. Samson dives forward into a wave, disappearing under the water.

When the water is finally up to my chest, Samson reappears. He's two feet in front of me when he pops up out of the water. He brushes his hair back and looks down at me.

"See? Nothing scary."

He lowers himself until the water is up to his neck. Our knees accidentally touch, but he acts like he doesn't notice. He makes no move to back away, but I move the slightest bit to make sure it doesn't happen again. I don't know him all that well, and I'm not sure I want to give him that idea. He did just have a different girl on his lap the other night. I have no plans to be another lap trophy.

"Did Marjorie give you pecans today?" he asks. I nod and it makes him laugh. "I have so many fucking pecans," he says. "I just leave them on other people's porches now."

"Is that what she does all day? Crack pecans?"

"Pretty much."

"Where does she get them? She doesn't even have any trees."

"I have no idea," he says. "I don't know her all that well.

I only met her a few months ago. I was walking by her house and she stopped me and asked if I was going to the store anytime soon. I asked what she needed and she told me she needed batteries. I asked her what size and she said, 'Surprise me.'"

I smile, but it's not really because of what he said. It's because I like the way he talks. There's something about the way his bottom lip moves when he speaks that steals my focus.

Samson's gaze returns to my face, but he's not looking at my eyes. I notice him glance at my mouth and then look away again. He swims out a little farther.

The water is already up to my neck. I'm having to use my arms to keep myself in an area where I can touch.

"Sara said you've been sick the last few days," he says.

"I haven't been feeling well, but it's more of an emotional illness than a physical one."

"You homesick?"

I shake my head. "No. Definitely not homesick." He's in an uncharacteristically talkative mood, it seems. I take advantage of that. "Where do you go every day? What do you do besides help out old ladies for free?"

"I just try to be invisible," he says.

"What does that mean?"

Samson looks away from me, over to the full moon balancing right above the edge of the water. "It's a long explanation. I don't really feel like long explanations right now."

Not surprising. He seems to want to stay in the shallow end when it comes to conversations.

"I can't figure you out," I say.

His expression doesn't change at all, but his voice has a tinge of amusement to it when he says, "I didn't think you wanted to."

"That's because I thought I had you figured out. But I already told you I was wrong. You're layered."

"Layered?" he repeats. "Like an onion or a cake?"

"Definitely an onion. Your layers are the kind a person has to peel back."

"Is that what you're trying to do?"

I shrug. "I have nothing else to do. Maybe I'll spend my summer peeling back all your layers until you finally answer a question."

"I answered one. I told you about my necklace."

I nod. "That's true, you did give me that."

"Do you think you're easy to read?" he asks.

"I don't know."

"You aren't."

"Are you trying?"

He holds my stare for a moment. "If you are."

That response makes my knees feel like anchors. "I have a feeling we won't get far with each other," I say. "I like keeping my secrets. I get the feeling you do, too."

He nods. "You won't get past my first layer, I can promise you that."

Something tells me I will. "Why are you so private? Is your family famous or something?"

"Or something," he says.

He keeps moving closer to me. It makes me think this attraction might be mutual. That's hard for me to wrap my mind around. That a guy as good-looking and rich as him would find me interesting in any way.

It reminds me of how I felt the first time Dakota kissed me. Which is why I back away from Samson. I don't want him to say or do anything that might make me feel the way Dakota made me feel right *after* our first kiss.

I never want to feel that again, but I can't help but wonder if things would be different with Samson. What would he say after we kiss? Would he be as heartless as Dakota was?

We've somehow turned now and my back is toward the beach. It's like we're moving, but so slowly it isn't noticeable. There are drops of water on Samson's bottom lip and I can't stop staring at them.

Our knees brush again. This time I don't move away, but the connection only lasts for a second. I feel somewhat deflated when it passes.

I wonder how he feels. Probably not as confused about what he wants as I am.

"What's your reason for being secretive?" he asks.

I think about that for a moment. "I guess I've never had anyone I wanted to tell anything to."

There's an understanding in his eyes. He says, "*Same,*"

but it's almost a whisper. He sinks under the water and disappears. I hear him come up for air behind me a few seconds later. I spin around and he's even closer to me now. Our legs are definitely touching, but neither of us pulls away.

I'm not sure I've ever felt this—like my blood is zipping through my veins. My interactions with guys have always left me wanting more space between the guy and me. I'm not used to wishing there was *no* space between me and another person.

"Ask me some questions," he says. "I probably won't answer most of them, but I want to know what you want to know about me."

"Probably more than you'll give me."

"Try me."

"Are you an only child?"

He nods.

"How old are you?"

"Twenty."

"Where did you grow up?"

He shakes his head, refusing to answer that one.

"That wasn't even an intrusive question," I say.

"If you knew the answer, you'd realize it was."

He's right. This is going to be a challenge. But I don't think he realizes how competitive I can be. I did earn a full ride to Penn State thanks to my commitment to winning.

"Sara said you're going into the Air Force Academy?"

"Yes."

"Why?"

"It's a family tradition."

"Ah," I say. "A morsel. So your father was in the air force?"

"Yes. And my grandfather."

"How is your family so rich? The military doesn't pay that well."

"Some people go into the military for the esteem. Not the pay."

"Do you *want* to go to the air force or are you doing it because it's expected of you?"

"I want to go."

"That's good."

I don't know if it's him or the current, but he's even closer now. One of my legs is between his knees and my thigh occasionally brushes his. I might be doing it on purpose, which surprises me. Maybe he is, too.

"What's your favorite animal?" I ask.

"Whale."

"Favorite food?"

"Seafood."

"Favorite thing to do?"

"Swim."

I laugh. "These are typical beach-rat answers. I'll never get anywhere."

"Ask better questions," he says pointedly.

Another challenge. We stare at each other with heaviness while I think of a question I really want an answer to.

"Sara said you don't do relationships—that you only date girls who are here on vacations. Why is that?"

He doesn't answer. Another question that's off-limits, I guess. "Okay, too private. I'll think of an easier question."

"No, I'm going to answer that one," he says. "I'm just trying to figure out how." He lowers himself until the water is level with his chin. I do the same. I like that all we can focus on right now are each other's eyes. Although his aren't very telling.

"I don't trust easily."

I wasn't expecting that answer. I was expecting him to say he likes being single, or something equally stereotypical.

"Why? Did you get your heart broken?"

He presses his lips together while he ponders that question. "Yeah," he says flatly. "Crushed me. Her name was Darya."

The fact that he said her name out loud causes an unexpected, tiny sliver of jealousy to poke at me from the inside. I want to ask him what happened, but I don't really want the answer.

"What's it like?" I ask him.

"Having my heart broken?"

I nod.

He pushes a floating piece of seaweed away from us. "Have you never been in love?"

I laugh. "No. Not even close. I've never loved anyone, nor have I ever been loved *by* anyone."

"Yes you have," he says. "Family counts."

I shake my head again, because even if family counted, my answer would remain the same. My father barely knows me. My mother wasn't capable of loving me.

I look away from him and stare out at the open water. "I don't have that kind of family," I say quietly. "Not a lot of people have mothers like mine. I don't even remember her hugging me. Not once." I cut my eyes back to his. "Now that I think about it, I'm not even sure I've ever been *hugged*."

"How is that possible?"

"I mean, I've hugged people as a greeting. A quick hello or a quick goodbye hug. But I've never been . . . I don't know how to put it."

"Held?"

I nod. "Yeah. That's a better description, I guess. I've never been *held* by anyone. I don't know what that's like. I try to avoid it, actually. It seems like it would be weird."

"I guess it depends on who's holding you."

My throat feels thick. I swallow and nod in agreement but say nothing.

"It surprises me that you don't think your father loves you. He seems like a nice guy."

"He doesn't know me. This is the first time I've seen him since I was sixteen. I know more about you than I do about him."

"That's not very much."

"Exactly," I say, facing him full-on again.

Samson's knee brushes high up on my inner thighs this time and I'm glad he can't see anything from my chin down, because my body is covered in chills right now.

"I didn't think there were many people in the world like me," he says.

"You think we're alike?" I want to laugh at that comparison, but there's not an ounce of humor in his expression.

"I believe we have a lot more in common than you think we do, Beyah."

"You think you're as alone in this world as I am?"

He folds his lips together and nods his head, and it's the most honest thing I've ever seen. I never would have thought someone so well off could have a life as shitty as mine, but I can see it in the way he's looking at me. Everything about him suddenly seems familiar to me.

He's right. We are alike, but only in the saddest ways.

My voice comes out in a whisper when I say, "When I first met you on that ferry, I could tell you were damaged."

There's a flicker of something in his eyes as he tilts his head to the right. "You think I'm damaged?"

"Yes."

He moves even closer in the water, but there wasn't much space left between us to begin with. It's deliberate, and so much of me is touching so much of him now. "You're right," he says quietly, slipping a hand around the back of my left knee. "There's nothing left of me but a fucking pile of debris." He pulls me to him, wrapping both my legs around him. That's all he does, though. He doesn't try to kiss me. He just connects us together as if that's enough while our arms keep us both afloat.

I'm swiftly succumbing to him. I don't know in what way. All of them, maybe. Because right now, I need him to do something else. Anything else. Taste me. Touch me. Drag me under.

We watch each other for a moment and it's almost like looking into a broken mirror. He leans in slowly, but not toward my mouth. He presses his lips against my shoulder, so gentle it feels like a graze.

I close my eyes and inhale.

I've never felt anything so sensual. So perfect.

One of his hands disappears under the water and finds my waist. When I open my eyes, his face is just a couple of inches from mine.

We both look at each other's mouths for a brief second, and then it's like fire shoots down my entire leg.

"Fuck!"

Something just stung me.

Something just stung the shit out of me right when I was about to be kissed and if this isn't my damn luck. "Shit, shit, shit." I grip Samson's shoulders. "Something just stung me."

He shakes his head as if he's pulling himself out of a trance. He catches up to what just happened. "Jellyfish," he says. He grabs my hand and pulls me toward the shore, but my leg hurts so bad, it's difficult to walk.

"Oh my God, it hurts."

"Sara keeps a bottle of vinegar in their outdoor shower. It'll help the sting."

When he can tell I'm struggling to keep up, he bends down and scoops me up. I want to enjoy the fact that he's carrying me, but I can't enjoy anything.

"Where did it get you?" he asks.

"My right leg."

When the water is just below his knees, he's able to walk faster. He rushes me past the fire, toward the outdoor shower on Sara's stilt level. I hear Sara yell after us, "What happened?"

"Jellyfish!" he yells over his shoulder.

When we reach the shower, there's barely enough room for both of us inside. He sets me down and I spin around and press my hands against the shower wall. "It got the top of my thigh."

When he starts to spray the vinegar on my leg, it feels like tiny knives stabbing me in the fleshiest part of my thigh. I close my eyes, pressing my forehead against the wooden shower wall. I moan in agony. "Oh, God."

"Beyah," Samson says, his voice strained and deep. "Please don't make that noise."

I'm in too much pain to dissect that comment. All I feel is pain on top of more pain when the vinegar hits my skin. "Samson, it hurts. Please stop."

"Not yet," he says, spraying down my leg to ensure he gets all the sting. "It'll feel better in a second."

He's a liar, I want to die. "No, it hurts. Please stop."

"I'm almost finished."

He stops suddenly after saying that, but not by choice. Samson disappears in a confusing flash. I spin around and peek my head out just in time to witness my father punch Samson in the face.

Samson stumbles back and then falls over the concrete ledge of the foundation.

"She said stop, you son of a bitch!" my father yells at him.

Samson scrambles to his feet and backs away from my father. He holds his hands up in defense, but my father goes to hit him again. I grab my father's arm, but it does little to ease the impact of the second hit.

"Dad, stop!"

Sara appears and I look at her pleadingly for help. She runs over and tries to grab my father's other arm, but he's got Samson by the throat now.

"He was helping me!" I yell. "Let go of him!"

This prompts my father to release some of the pressure around Samson's throat, but he doesn't let go. Samson has blood running from his nose. I'm sure he could fight back, but he isn't. He's just shaking his head, staring at my father wide-eyed. "I wasn't— She got stung by a jellyfish. I was helping her."

My father looks over his shoulder, searching for me. When we lock eyes, I nod vigorously. "He's telling you the truth. He was spraying vinegar on my leg."

"But I heard you say . . ." My father closes his eyes when

he realizes it truly was a misunderstanding. He exhales deeply. "*Shit.*" He releases Samson.

There's blood running all the way down Samson's neck now.

My father puts his hands on his hips and tries to catch his breath for a few seconds. Then he motions for Samson to follow him. "Come inside," he mutters. "I think I broke your nose."

Twelve

Samson is leaning against the guest-bathroom counter, holding a rag to his nose to stop the bleeding. I'm sitting on a heat compress in the dry bathtub. The bathroom door is ajar, and even though Alana and my father are down the hall, we can hear every word they're saying.

"He's going to sue us," my father says.

Samson laughs quietly. "I'm not going to sue him," he whispers.

"He's not going to sue us," Alana says.

"You don't know that. We barely know him and I broke his nose," my father says.

Samson looks at me. "It's not broken. He doesn't hit that hard."

I laugh.

"I'm confused," I hear Alana say. "Why did you hit him?"

"They were in the outdoor shower. I thought he was—"

"We can hear you!" I yell. I don't want him to finish that sentence. This is already too embarrassing.

My father walks to the bathroom and opens the door all the way. "Are you on birth control?"

Oh my God.

Alana tries pulling him out of the bathroom. "Not in front of the boy, Brian."

Samson pulls the rag from his nose and narrows his eyes at me. "The *boy*?" he whispers.

At least he has a good sense of humor about this.

"Maybe you should go," I suggest. "This is getting too embarrassing."

Samson nods, but my father is back in the doorway. "I'm not saying you aren't allowed to have sex. You're almost an adult. I just want you to be safe about it."

"I *am* an adult. There's nothing *almost* about it," I say.

Samson is standing near my father, but my father is blocking the entire doorway as he speaks to me. He doesn't notice Samson attempting to squeeze by him to escape.

"This is my only way out," Samson says to my dad, pointing over his shoulder. "Please let me out."

My father realizes he's blocking him and quickly steps aside. "Sorry about your nose."

Samson nods and then leaves. I wish I could escape, but I'm pretty sure there are tentacles still embedded in my leg and it hurts to move.

My father returns his attention to me. "Alana can take you to get on the pill if you aren't already on it."

"We aren't . . . Samson and I aren't . . . *never mind*." I push myself out of the tub and stand up. "This is a really intense conversation and my thigh feels like it's melting off my body. Can we please do this later?"

They both nod, but my father follows after me. "Ask Sara. We're very open about this stuff if you ever want to talk about it."

"I'm aware of that now. Thank you," I say, heading up the stairs to my room.

Wow. So this is what it's like to have involved parents? I'm not sure I like it.

I walk straight to my bedroom window and watch as Samson enters his house. He turns on his kitchen light and then he leans over the counter and folds in on himself, pressing his forehead to the granite. He's gripping the back of his neck with his hands.

I don't know what to think of that. Is that a sign of regret? Or is he just overwhelmed because he got punched twice and refused to fight back? The way he's reacting right now fills me with so many questions. Questions I know he won't likely answer. He's a vault and I really wish I had a key.

Or some explosives.

I want an excuse to go over there so I can get a closer look at him and see what it is exactly that's bothering him so much. I need to know if it's because he almost kissed me.

Would he try it again if I gave him the chance?

I want to give him the chance. I want that kiss almost as much as I don't.

I do have his memory card. I could take it back to him. I haven't looked at the pictures yet, though. I really want to see them before I give it back to him.

Sara has a computer in her bedroom, so I fish the memory card out of my backpack and go to Sara's computer.

I wait several minutes for all the images to load. There are a lot of them. The first ones to load are all pictures of nature. All things he said he takes pictures of. Countless sunrises and sunsets. Pictures of the beach. But they aren't necessarily pretty pictures. They're soothingly sad. Most of them are taken with the focus zoomed in on something random, like a piece of trash floating in the water or seaweed piled up on the sand.

It's interesting. It's like he puts the focus on the saddest part of whatever is in view of his lens, but the picture as a whole is still beautiful.

The pictures he took of me begin to load. There are more than I thought there would be; he apparently started snapping pictures of me before I even moved to the back of the ferry.

Most of the pictures are of me on the side of the ferry, watching the sunset alone.

He put the focus on me in every picture. Nothing else. And based on all the other pictures he took, I suppose that means he thought I was the saddest thing in his frame.

There's one picture in particular that strikes me. It's zoomed in and the focus is on a small rip in the back of my sundress that I didn't even know was there. Even with his focus on something as sad as my dress, the picture is still striking. My face is out of focus, and if this were a picture of anyone else but me, I'd say it was a beautiful piece of art.

Instead, I'm embarrassed he paid such close attention to me before I even noticed he was there.

I scroll through every picture of me and notice there isn't a single picture of me eating the bread. I wonder why he didn't photograph that.

That says a lot about him. I regret reacting how I did when he tried to offer me money on the ferry that day. Samson may actually be a decent human and the pictures on this memory card back that up.

I remove it from the computer and even though I'm still in pain and kind of want to crawl in bed and go to sleep, I head downstairs, outside, and across the yard. Samson always uses his back door, so I head in that direction. I walk up the steps and knock.

I wait for a while, but I don't hear his footsteps and I can't see the kitchen from this point of view. I hear something behind me, though. When I turn around, P.J. is sitting at the top of the stairs watching me. I smile a little. I like that he's still around.

Samson eventually opens the door. He's changed clothes in the time I was watching him from my window to the point of me knocking on his door. He's wearing one of Marcos's *HisPanic* T-shirts, which seem to be the only shirts he wears, if he's wearing a shirt at all. I like that he's supportive of Marcos's vision. Their friendship is kind of adorable.

Samson is barefoot, and I don't know why I'm staring at his feet. I look back at his face.

"I was just bringing your memory card back." I hand it to him.

"Thanks."

"I didn't delete anything."

Samson's mouth curls up on the left side. "I didn't think you would."

He steps aside and motions for me to come in. I squeeze between him and the doorframe and enter his dark house. He flips on a light, and I try to hide my gasp—it's even bigger on the inside than it looks from the outside.

Everything is white and colorless. The walls, the cabinets, the trim. The floor is a dark wood—almost black. I spin around in a circle, admiring it for what it is but also recognizing how unlike a home it feels. There isn't any soul at all.

"It's kind of . . . sterile." As soon as I say it, I wish I hadn't. He didn't ask for my opinion on his house, but it's hard not to notice how unlived-in it feels.

Samson shrugs like my opinion of his house doesn't bother him. "It's a rent house. They're all like this. Very generic."

"It's so clean."

"People sometimes rent at the last minute. It's easier for me if I keep the houses rent-ready." Samson walks to his refrigerator and opens it, waving a hand inside. The refrigerator is mostly empty, aside from a few condiments in the door. "Nothing in the fridge. Nothing in the pantry." He closes the refrigerator door.

"Where do you keep your food?"

He motions toward a closet near the stairs that lead to the top floor. "We keep the stuff we don't want renters to have access to in that closet. There's a small fridge in it." He points to a backpack next to the door. "Everything else I own I keep in that backpack. The less I have, the easier it is for me to move between our properties."

I've seen him with the backpack a couple of times but thought nothing of it. It's kind of ironic that we both carry our lives around in a backpack, despite the vast difference of wealth between us.

I glance up near the door, at a picture on the wall. It's the only thing in the house that has any character. I walk over to it. It's a photo of a young boy, about three years old, walking on the beach. A woman is behind him, wearing a flowy white dress. She's smiling at whoever is taking the photo. "Is this your mother?" It reminds me of those perfect sample photos they place in frames before they're purchased.

Samson nods.

"So that's you? As a toddler?"

He nods again.

His hair is so blond in the picture, it's almost white. It's darkened since he was a child, but I'd still consider his hair blond. I don't know if it's this blond in the winter, though. It seems to be the kind of hair that changes color with the seasons.

I wonder what Samson's father looks like, but there aren't any photos of him. This is the only photo in this section of the house.

I have so many more questions as I stare at the picture. His mother seems happy. He seems happy. I wonder what happened to him to make him so private and withdrawn? Did his mother die? I doubt he'd elaborate on anything if I were to ask him.

Samson flips on more lights and leans against his kitchen counter. I don't know how he can appear so casual when all my muscles are tight with tension. "Your leg feel better?" he asks.

I can tell he doesn't want to talk about the picture or his mother or anything else that would be another layer deep. I walk into the kitchen and stand across from him, leaning against the large center island. It's the kitchen island Cadence was sitting on a few nights ago when I watched him kiss her.

I push that thought out of my head. "It feels a little better. I doubt I'll get in the water again, though."

"You'll be fine," he says. "Rarely happens."

"Yeah, that's what you said earlier, and then it happened."

He smiles.

It makes me want our moment back. I want to feel how I felt when he pulled me to him and kissed my shoulder. I don't know how to get there, though. It's so bright in here. The atmosphere is different than it was when we were in the water.

I think maybe I don't like his house. "How's your face?" I ask him.

He runs a hand across his jaw. "My jaw hurts worse than my nose." He lowers his hand and grips the counter at his sides. "That was nice of your dad."

"You think him attacking you was nice?"

"No. I thought the way he protected you was nice."

I hadn't really thought about that. My father didn't even think twice when he heard me asking someone to stop. But I'm not sure it's specifically because it was me. He would have protected anyone in that situation, I'm sure.

"Where do you go when this house gets rented out?" I ask, steering the conversation away from my father.

"We only keep four rented out at a time, so I always have somewhere to stay. This one is the most expensive, so it gets rented the least. I'm here seventy-five percent of the time."

I glance around me, trying to find something else like the picture that would give me a hint into his past. There's nothing. "It's kind of ironic," I say. "You have five houses, but none of them are actually your home. Your refrigerator is empty. You live out of a backpack. We surprisingly do live very similar lives."

He doesn't respond to that. He just watches me. He does that a lot and I like it. I don't even care what he's thinking when he stares. I just like that he finds me intriguing enough to stare at, even if his thoughts aren't entirely positive. It means he *sees* me. I'm not used to being seen.

"What's your last name?" I ask him.

He looks amused. "You ask a lot of questions."

"I told you I was going to."

"I think it's my turn now."

"But I've barely gotten anywhere. You're terrible at answering me."

He doesn't disagree, but he also doesn't answer my question. His eyes crinkle at the corners as he thinks of his own question. "What are you planning on doing with your life, Beyah?"

"That's a broad one. You sound like a school counselor."

He releases a small laugh and I feel it in my stomach. "What are you doing after the *summer* is over?" he clarifies.

I mull over that question. Should I be honest with him? Maybe if I'm honest with him, he'll be more open with me. "I'll tell you, but you can't tell anyone."

"It's a secret?"

I nod. "Yeah."

"I won't tell anyone."

I trust him. I don't know why because I don't trust anyone. I'm either a fool or deeply attracted to him and neither is really okay with me. "I have a full ride to Penn State. I move into my dorm August third."

His eyebrow lifts slightly. "You got a scholarship?"

"Yeah."

"What for?"

"Volleyball."

His eyes do this thing where they roll slowly down my body. Not in a seductive way, but in a curious way. "I can see that." When his eyes meet mine again, he says, "What part of that is a secret?"

"All of it. I haven't told anyone. Not even my father."

"Your own father doesn't know you received a scholarship?"

"Nope."

"Why haven't you told him?"

"Because it would make him feel like he did something right. And I had to work for the scholarship because he did everything wrong."

He nods, like he can empathize with that. I look away for a moment because my entire body heats up when I stare at him too much. I'm afraid it's obvious.

"Is volleyball your passion?"

His question makes me pause. No one has ever asked me that before. "No. I don't enjoy it all that much, to be honest."

"Why not?"

"I worked hard at it because I knew it was my only way out of the town I grew up in. But no one ever came to watch me play, so the actual sport started feeling depressing to me. All my other teammates had parents at every game cheering them on. I've never had anyone, and I think that prevented me from loving it as much as I could have." I sigh, spilling more of my thoughts out loud. "Sometimes I wonder if I'm doing the right thing by subjecting myself to four more years of it. Being on a team with people whose lives are so different from my own sometimes makes me feel even lonelier than if I weren't a part of a team."

"You aren't excited to go?"

I shrug. "I'm proud of myself for getting the scholarship. And I was excited to get out of Kentucky. But now that I'm here and I've gotten the first break from volleyball I've had in years, I don't think I miss it. I'm starting to wonder if I should just stay here and get a job. Maybe I'll take a *gap year*." I say that last part with a hint of sarcasm, but it's starting to sound very appealing. I've spent the last several years working my ass off to get out of Kentucky. Now that I'm out, I feel like I need to take a breather. Reassess my life.

"You're thinking about giving up a scholarship to a great school just because the sport that got you there sometimes makes you lonely?"

"It feels more complicated than you make it sound," I say.

"You want to know what I think?"

"What?"

"I think you should wear earplugs at the games and just pretend people are out there cheering you on."

I laugh. "I thought you were going to say something profound."

"I thought that *was* profound," he says, grinning. I notice when he smiles that his jaw is beginning to bruise. But his smile fades and he tilts his head a little. "Why were you crying on your balcony the night you got here?"

I stiffen at his question. It's a jarring jump from talking about volleyball. I don't know how to answer that. Especially in a room this bright. Maybe if it didn't feel like an interrogation room, I'd be more at ease. "Can you turn off some of these lights?" I ask him.

He looks confused by my request.

"It's too bright in here. It's making me uncomfortable."

Samson walks over to the light switches and turns all of them off except for one. The lights that trim the cabinets stay on, so it's significantly darker and I relax almost immediately. I can see why he keeps it dark in this house. The assaulting lights and all the white paint make it feel like a psychiatric ward.

He returns to his spot against the counter. "Is that better?"

I nod.

"Why were you crying?"

I blow out a rush of air, then just spit it out before I change my mind and decide to lie to him. "My mother died the night before I came here."

Samson doesn't react to that at all. I've come to realize that maybe his lack of reaction is *how* he reacts.

"That's also a secret," I say. "I haven't even told my father yet."

His expression is solemn. "How'd she die?"

"Overdose. I found her when I got home from work."

"I'm sorry," he says with sincerity. "Are you okay?"

I lift a shoulder in uncertainty, and when I do, it feels like some of those feelings that forced me into tears on the balcony attempt to seep back in. I wasn't prepared to talk about this. I don't want to talk about it, honestly. It's not really fair that I don't know how to not answer his questions, but he doesn't open up about anything.

I feel like a waterfall around him, just spilling myself and my secrets out all over the floor.

Samson's expression turns empathetic when he sees my eyes rim with tears.

He pushes off the counter and begins to walk toward me, but I stand up straight and immediately shake my head. I press a hand against his chest, stopping him from touching me.

"Don't. Don't hug me. It'll just feel patronizing now that you know I've never been hugged like that."

Samson shakes his head gently as he stares down at me. "I wasn't going to hug you, Beyah," he whispers. His face is so close to mine, his breath grazes my cheek when he speaks. I feel like I'm about to slide to the floor, so I grip the edge of the counter behind me.

He dips his head until his lips catch mine. His mouth is soft, like an apology, and I accept it.

His tongue coaxes my mouth open and I welcome him by fisting both of my hands in his hair, pulling him even closer. Our chests meet and our tongues slide against each other, wet and warm and soft.

I want this kiss, even if it's only happening because he's drawn to sad things.

He tugs me away from the counter and into him, and then in one swift move, he lifts me and I'm sitting on his island and he's standing between my legs. His left hand slides down my leg until his fingers are brushing my outer thigh.

I'm full of things I'm not usually filled with. Warmth and electricity and light.

It scares me.

His kiss scares me.

I'm not impenetrable against his mouth. I'm vulnerable, and I feel my guard lowering. I'd give him all my secrets right now and that isn't me. His kiss is potent enough to turn me into a girl I don't recognize. I love it and I loathe it.

As much as I try to remain focused on what's happening between us, it's hard for the image of what happened between him and Cadence not to flash through my head. I don't want to be just another girl he kisses on his kitchen island.

I'm not sure I can handle being a throwaway to Samson like I was to Dakota. I'd rather not be kissed at all than allow that to happen again, only to look out my bedroom window tomorrow night and see someone else in this same spot, feeling the same things he's making me feel right now.

The same things Dakota made me feel right before he

pulled away and ruined the next few years of my life with one gesture.

God, what if Samson pulls away and looks at me like Dakota looked at me that first night in his truck?

The thought makes me nauseated.

I need air. Fresh air. Not air from his lungs or this sterile house.

I end the kiss abruptly, without warning. I push against Samson and slide off the island, leaving him confused. I avoid his eyes as I walk straight for his door. I go outside and grip the balcony railing, gasping for air.

I've been through enough in my life that I don't want a guy to change the things I like about myself the most. I've always been proud of my impenetrable resolve, but he somehow infiltrates me like I'm full of holes. Dakota never reached this far inside me.

I hear Samson walk outside. I don't turn around to face him. I just inhale another deep breath and then close my eyes. I can feel him next to me, though. Quiet, brooding, sexy, secretive—all my favorite ingredients in a guy, apparently. *Why did I stop the kiss, then?*

I think maybe Dakota ruined me.

When I open my eyes, Samson's back is against the railing. He's staring down at his feet.

Our eyes meet and it's like I can see my own fears looking back at me. We don't break our gaze. I've never stared at someone without speaking as much as I've looked at him. We do a lot of looking and not much talking, but they both feel equally productive. Or unproductive. I don't even know what to think of what's been developing between us. Some moments, it feels like something huge and important, and other times it feels like less than nothing.

"That was a really bad moment to choose to kiss you," he says. "I'm sorry."

I think a lot of people might agree with him, that kissing a girl right after—or *because*—she tells you her mother died might be poor timing.

Maybe I'm fucked up, but I thought it was perfect timing. Until it wasn't.

"That's not why I came outside."

"What is it, then?"

I blow out a quiet rush of air while I work out how to answer that. I don't want to bring up how I fear that deep down, he's no better than Dakota. I don't want to bring up Cadence or the fact that he's only with girls who are here for the weekend. He doesn't owe me anything. I'm the one who showed up at his front door wanting this to happen.

I shake my head. "I don't want to answer that."

He turns around until we're both leaning over the railing. He picks at a piece of chipped paint, pulling at it until it reveals an inch of bare wood. He flicks the chipped paint over the railing and we watch as it flutters to the ground.

"My mother died when I was five," he says. "We were swimming about half a mile from here when she got caught in a rip current. By the time they pulled her out of the water, it was too late."

He glances at me, probably to gauge my reaction. But he's not the only one who can hide his emotions well.

I get the feeling he hasn't told a lot of people that. A secret for a secret. Maybe that's how this will go. Maybe that's how Samson's layers are peeled back—by peeling my own layers back first.

"I hate that for you," I whisper. I keep my arms folded over the railing, but I lean slightly toward him. I press my mouth against his shoulder. I kiss him there, just like he did me in the water.

When I pull away, he lifts a hand to the side of my face. His thumb brushes my cheekbone, but then he dips his head to try to kiss me again and I immediately pull away from him.

I wince because I'm embarrassed by my own indecisiveness.

He pushes off the railing and runs a hand through his hair, and then looks at me for guidance. I know I'm throwing all kinds of mixed signals his way, but it's a reflection of what's going on inside me. I feel stirred up and confused, like my current feelings and past experiences were just thrown together in a blender and turned on high.

"I'm sorry," I say, frustrated with myself. "I haven't had the best experience with guys, so I just feel . . ."

"Hesitant?" he suggests.

I nod. "Yeah. And confused."

He begins picking at the same spot on the wood. "What's been your experience with guys?"

I laugh half-heartedly. "*Guys* is overshooting it. There was only one."

"I thought you said you've never had your heart broken."

"I haven't. It wasn't that kind of experience."

Samson gives me a sidelong glance, waiting for me to elaborate. There's no way I'm elaborating on that.

"Did he force you to do something you didn't want to do?" Samson's jaw is hard when he asks that, like he's already angry on my behalf.

"No," I say quickly, wanting him to get that thought out of his head. But then I think back on my life in Kentucky and the times I spent with Dakota, and now that I'm no longer in that situation, I look at it differently.

Dakota never forced me to do anything. But he certainly didn't make it easy for me. We were in no way equals when it came to who got taken advantage of.

Thinking about it is stirring up dark thoughts. Dark feelings. Tears begin to sting my eyes, and when I suck in a breath to fight them back, Samson notices. He turns and presses his back against the railing so he can see my face better.

"What happened to you, Beyah?"

I laugh, because it's absurd I'm even thinking about this right now. I'm good at not thinking about it most of the time. I feel a tear skate down my cheek. I quickly wipe it away. "This isn't fair," I whisper.

"What?"

"Why do I end up wanting to answer every single question you ask me?"

"You don't have to tell me what happened."

I make eye contact with him. "I want to, though."

"Then tell me," he says gently.

My eyes focus on everything but him. I look at the roof of the balcony, then at the floor, then at the ocean over Samson's shoulder.

"His name was Dakota," I say. "I was fifteen. A freshman. He was a senior. The guy every girl in the school wanted to date. The guy every other guy wanted to be. I had a mild crush on him like everyone else. Wasn't anything serious. But then one night he saw me walking home after a volleyball game, so he offered me a ride. I told him no because I was embarrassed for him to see where I lived, even though everyone knew. He convinced me to get in the truck, anyway." I somehow bring my gaze back to Samson's. His jaw is hard again, like he's expecting this story to go the way he assumed earlier. But it doesn't.

I don't know why I'm telling him. Maybe I'm subconsciously hoping that after he hears this, he'll leave me alone for the rest of the summer and I won't have this intense and constant distraction.

Or maybe I'm hoping he'll tell me that what I did was okay.

"He drove me home and for the next half hour, we talked. He sat in my driveway and didn't judge me. He listened to me. We talked about music and volleyball and how he hated being the son of the police chief. And then . . .

he kissed me. And it was perfect. For a moment, I thought maybe the things I assumed people thought of me weren't true."

Samson's eyebrows draw apart. "Why just for a moment? What happened after he kissed you?"

I smile, but not because it's a fond memory. I smile because the memory makes me feel ignorant. Like I should have expected it. "He pulled two twenties out of his wallet and handed them to me. Then he unzipped his jeans."

Samson's expression is vacant. To most people, they would assume that was the end of the story. They would assume I threw the money back at Dakota and got out of the truck. But I can tell by the way Samson is looking at me that he knows that's not where the story ends.

I fold my arms across my chest. "Forty dollars was a lot of money," I say as another tear slides down my cheek. It curves at the last minute and lands on my lip. I can taste the saltiness of it as I wipe it away. "He gave me a ride home at least once a month after that. He never spoke to me in public. But I didn't expect him to. I wasn't the kind of girl he could parade around town. I was the kind of girl he wouldn't even tell his closest friends about."

I wish Samson would say something, because when he just stares at me, I keep rambling. "So to answer your question, no, he didn't force me to do anything. And to be honest, he never even threw it in my face. He was actually a decent guy compared to—"

Samson immediately interrupts me. "You were fifteen the first time it happened, Beyah. Do not call that guy *decent*."

The rest of my sentence gets stuck in my throat, so I swallow it.

"A decent guy would have offered you money with no return expectations. What he did was just . . ." Samson looks like he's filled with disgust. I'm not sure if that's aimed at Dakota or me. He runs a frustrated hand through his hair. "That day on the ferry when I handed you money . . . that's why you thought . . ."

"Yeah," I say quietly.

"You know that's not what I was doing, right?"

I nod. "I know that now. But even knowing that . . . I still feared it when you kissed me. That's why I came outside. I was scared you would look at me like Dakota did. I'd rather not be kissed at all than risk feeling that worthless again."

"I kissed you because I like you."

I wonder how true that is. Are his words accurate or convenient? Has he said them before? "You like Cadence, too?" I ask him. "And all the other girls you've made out with?"

I'm not trying to throw it in his face. I'm genuinely curious. What do people feel when they kiss other people as often as he does?

Samson doesn't look like he takes offense to my question, but it does look like I've made him uncomfortable. His posture stiffens a bit. "I'm attracted to them. But it's different with you. A different kind of attraction."

"Better or worse?"

He thinks on this for a moment and settles on, "Scarier."

I release a quick laugh. I probably shouldn't take that as a compliment, but I do, because that means he's getting a taste of my own fear when we're together.

"Do you think the girls you're with enjoy being with you?" I ask. "What are they getting out of it by just having a weekend fling?"

"The same thing I get from them."

"Which is what?"

He's definitely uncomfortable now. He sighs and leans over the railing again. "Did you not like it when we kissed earlier?"

"I did," I say. "But I also didn't."

I find a comfort in his nonjudgmental presence, and it's confusing, because if I'm comfortable around him and I'm attracted to him, why did I start to panic when he was kissing me?

"Dakota took something you're supposed to enjoy and he made you feel ashamed of it. It's not like that for all girls. The girls I've been with—they enjoy it as much as I do. If they didn't, I wouldn't allow it to happen."

"I enjoyed it a little bit," I admit. "Just not the whole time. But that's not your fault, obviously."

"It isn't yours, either," he says. "And I won't kiss you again. Not unless you ask me to."

I don't say anything. I don't understand why that feels like both a punishment and a chivalrous gift.

He smiles gently. "Won't kiss you, won't hug you, won't make you get back in the ocean."

"My God, I'm just a ball of fun," I say, rolling my eyes.

"You probably are. Hell, I might be, too. We just have too much piled on top of us to know what we're like when we're not under pressure."

I nod in complete agreement. "Sara and Marcos are fun. But me and you? We're just . . . depressing."

Samson laughs. "Not depressing. We're deep. There's a difference."

"If you say so."

I don't know how we possibly ended this night and this conversation with both of us smiling. But I'm afraid if I don't walk away now, one of us will say something to ruin this moment. I back a step away from him. "See you tomorrow?"

His smile falters. "Yeah. Good night, Beyah."

"Good night."

I slip away from him, toward the stairs. Pepper Jack Cheese stands up and follows me down. When we reach the stilt level of my house, I spin around and look up at him. Samson hasn't gone back inside yet. He's leaning over the balcony, watching me. I walk backward a couple of feet, until I'm under the house and can't see him anymore.

When he's out of my line of sight, I stop walking and lean against a pillar. I close my eyes and run my hands down my face. There's no way I can be around him all summer and not want to be consumed by him. But I also don't want to be consumed by someone I'm just going to have to say goodbye to eventually.

I might feel invincible sometimes, but I'm not Wonder Woman.

Alana is awake and in the kitchen when I walk back into the house. She's at the counter, leaning over a bowl of ice cream. She takes a spoon out of her mouth and smiles at me. "Feeling better?"

"Yeah. Thank you."

"What about Samson? Is he okay?"

I nod. "He's fine. He said Dad doesn't hit all that hard."

Alana laughs. "I'm surprised your father hit him. I didn't know he had it in him." She points at her ice cream. "You want a bowl?"

Ice cream actually sounds like heaven right now. I need something to cool me down. "I'd love some."

Alana pulls a bowl out of the cabinet and I take a seat at the bar. She takes ice cream out of the freezer and begins scooping it into the bowl. "I'm sorry if we embarrassed you earlier."

"It's okay."

Alana pushes the bowl of ice cream across the counter. I take a bite and it's so good, I want to groan. But I stay quiet and eat it like ice cream has always been something I had access to. In reality, we never had it at our house. I learned not to keep much frozen stuff, because when the power gets cut due to lack of payment, cleaning out a freezer of melted and rotten food is never fun.

"Can I ask you something?" Alana says.

I nod but keep the spoon in my mouth. I'm nervous for whatever it is she's going to ask me. I just hope she doesn't ask me about my mother. Alana seems nice and I'm not sure I can lie to her, but I certainly don't want to tell her the truth right now.

"Are you Catholic?"

That's not what I was expecting her to ask. "No. Why?"

She flicks a hand toward the ceiling. "Saw the picture of Mother Teresa in your room."

"Oh. No. It's just . . . it's more like a souvenir."

She nods, and then says, "So you aren't religiously opposed to birth control?"

There it is. I look away from her, down to my ice cream. "No. But I'm not currently taking it. I'm not . . . you know."

"Sexually active?" She says it so casually.

"Yeah. Not anymore, anyway."

"Well," she says. "That's good to hear. But if you think you might find yourself in a situation this summer where that might change, it wouldn't hurt to be prepared. I can make you an appointment."

I take another bite of my ice cream to stall my response. She can probably see the flush in my cheeks.

"It's nothing to be embarrassed about, Beyah."

"I know," I say. "I'm just not used to talking about things like this with people."

Alana casually drops her spoon in her empty bowl and walks it to the sink. "Your mother never talks to you about this stuff?"

I stab at my ice cream. "No."

She turns around and looks at me quietly for a moment. "What's she like?"

"My mother?"

Alana nods. "Yeah. Your father never knew her that well and I've been curious. She seems to have done a good job with you."

I laugh.

I wish I wouldn't have laughed because I can tell my reaction just filled Alana with a dozen more questions. I take a bite of my ice cream and shrug. "She's nothing like you."

I meant that as a compliment, but Alana seems confused by my answer. I hope she didn't take it as an insult, but I don't really want to get into it even deeper or I'll end up telling her the truth. I want to save the news about my mother for my father. I feel like I should tell him before I tell Alana.

I definitely should have told him before I told Samson. But I can't seem to control my secrets around Samson for some reason.

I push the half-eaten bowl of ice cream away from me. "I do want to get on the pill. Not that Samson and I are . . ." I look up at the ceiling and blow out a breath. "You know what I mean. I'd like to be safe, just in case." *God, this is hard to talk about. Especially with a woman who is essentially a stranger to me.*

Alana smiles. "I'll set up an appointment tomorrow. No biggie."

"Thank you."

Alana turns around to wash my bowl. I use the moment to escape to privacy upstairs. I'm about to walk into my bedroom when I hear Sara say, "Hold up, Beyah. I need a detailed report."

I pause and look into her bedroom. Her door is open, and she and Marcos are sitting on her bed. She looks at Marcos and waves him away. "You can go home now."

He looks like he isn't used to being dismissed. "Okay, then." He stands up but leans over and kisses Sara. "Love you, even though you're kicking me out."

She smiles. "Love you, too, but I have a sister now, so you have to share me." She pats the mattress where Marcos was sitting and looks at me. "Come here."

Marcos salutes me as he's walking out of Sara's bedroom.

"Close the door," Sara says to Marcos.

I walk to her bed and sit on it. She pauses the television and then repositions herself on the bed so that she's facing me.

"How'd it go?"

I lean against the headboard. "Your mother trapped me in the kitchen with ice cream and then talked to me about my sex life."

Sara rolls her eyes. "Never fall for the ice-cream trick. She uses it on me all the time. But I'm not referring to that and you know it. I saw you walking over to Samson's house earlier."

I debate telling Sara that we kissed, but that seems like something I should keep private for now. At least until I figure out if I want it to happen again.

"Nothing happened."

She deflates, falling onto her back. "Ugh. I wanted juicy details."

"There are none. Sorry."

"Did you even try to flirt with him?" she asks, sitting back up. "It doesn't take much for Samson to put his mouth on a girl. If it has boobs and it's breathing, it's good enough for him."

My stomach catapults to the floor with that comment. "Is that supposed to make me want him more? Because it doesn't."

"I'm exaggerating," she says. "He's hot and he's rich, so girls just tend to throw themselves at him and sometimes he catches them. What guy wouldn't?"

"I don't throw myself at people. I avoid people."

"But you went to his house."

I raise an eyebrow but say nothing.

Sara smiles, like that's enough for her to work with. "Maybe we should go on a double date tomorrow night."

I don't want to encourage her, but I'm also not sure I'm opposed to that idea.

"I take your silence as a yes," she says.

I laugh. Then I groan and cover my face with my hands. "Ugh. This is all so confusing." I drop my arms and slide down until I'm staring up at her ceiling. "I feel like I'm giving it too much thought. I'm trying to think of all the reasons why it isn't a good idea."

"Name a few," Sara suggests.

"I'm not good at relationships."

"Neither is Samson."

"I'm leaving in August."

"So is Samson."

"What if it hurts when we end things?"

"It probably will."

"Then why would I want to subject myself to that?"

"Because most of the time, the fun you have that leads to the pain is worth the pain."

"I wouldn't know. I've never had fun."

"Yeah, I can tell," she says. "No offense."

"None taken."

I turn my head and look at Sara. She's on her side, her head held up by her hand. "I've never had feelings for anyone before. If that happens, how bad is it going to hurt when summer is over?"

Sara shakes her head. "Stop it. You're thinking too far

ahead. Summers are for thinking about today and today only. Not tomorrow. Not yesterday. *Today*. So what do you want *right now*?"

"Right now?" I ask.

"Yes. What do you want *right now*?"

"Another bowl of ice cream."

Sara sits up and grins. "Dammit, I love having a sister."

And I love that Sara didn't even flinch when I mentioned ice cream. Maybe I'm not as bad for her as I thought. I might not be as bubbly and as happy as she is, but knowing she's starting to enjoy food and doesn't seem as worried about her weight as she did when I arrived makes me think I might actually have something to offer in this friendship.

This is a new feeling—the idea that maybe I'm worth having around.

Thirteen

The alarm on my phone goes off before the sun is even up.

I should probably cancel the damn thing, but there's something exciting about watching the sunrise and getting a possible glimpse of Samson while it happens.

I crawl out of bed wearing the T-shirt I slept in last night. I pull on a pair of shorts just in case Samson is awake and on his balcony outside.

I've been awake for ten seconds and I've already thought of him twice. Denying him last night doesn't seem to be working out for me.

I unlock my balcony door and slide it open.

Then I scream.

"Shh," Samson says, laughing. "It's just me."

He's sitting on the wicker outdoor couch with his legs propped up in front of him on the railing. I press my hand to my chest and blow out a calming breath.

"What are you doing here?"

"Waiting for you," he says casually.

"How did you even get over here?"

"I jumped." He holds up his arm, showing me his elbow. It's smeared with blood. "It was farther than it looked from my railing, but I made it."

"Are you insane?"

He shrugs. "I wouldn't have fallen very far if I didn't make it. I would have just landed on the balcony roof below us."

That's true. He wouldn't have fallen to the ground because of the way this house sits, but still. There's about three feet with nothing below him when he's in the air between houses.

I sit down next to him. The seat is meant for two, but it's still small, so our sides touch. I think that was his goal, though, or he would have chosen any of the single chairs on the balcony.

I lean my head against the back of the chair. I end up somehow leaning even more into him than I had intended, and my head is now resting against his upper arm, but it doesn't feel unnatural.

We're both staring out over the water at the small sliver of sun peeking up at the world.

We spend the next several minutes in silence, watching the sunrise together. I have to say, it feels better watching it with Samson on my balcony than when he's on his own.

Samson rests his chin on top of my head. It's a tiny move, but even that slight and silent display of affection feels like an explosion somehow. I don't know how everything inside of me can feel so loud while this part of the world is still asleep.

The sun is three-quarters of the way visible now. The bottom half still looks like it's dipped in the sea.

"I need to leave; I'm helping a guy repair a dune crossing on the island. We want to get it done before it gets too hot. What are your plans?"

"I'll probably go back to bed and sleep until noon. I think Sara wants to go to the beach after that."

He moves his arm from the back of the chair. My eyes crawl up his body as he stands. Before he leaves, he looks down at me and says, "Did you tell Sara we kissed?"

"No. Is it something we're trying to hide from them?"

"No," he says. "I was just curious if you told her. Didn't know if Marcos was going to bring it up today. I wanted our stories to align."

"I didn't tell her."

He nods and heads toward the railing, but then turns back again. "I don't care if you tell her. That's not why I asked."

"Stop worrying about my feelings, Samson."

He pushes the hair back from his forehead. "I can't help it." He walks backward, slowly.

"What are you doing? Are you about to jump again?"

"It's not that far. I'll make it."

I roll my eyes. "Everyone is still asleep. Just go downstairs and use the front door before you break your arm."

He looks at the blood covering his elbow. "Yeah, maybe I should."

I stand up and walk into my bedroom with him. We're heading for the door when he pauses and looks at the picture of Mother Teresa on my dresser.

"Are you Catholic?" he asks.

"No. Just oddly sentimental."

"I wouldn't have taken you for sentimental."

"That's why I prefaced it with *oddly*."

He laughs and follows me out the door. When we make it to the bottom of the stairs, we both pause.

My father is standing in the kitchen in front of a coffeepot. He drags his eyes to the stairwell and sees me standing here with Samson. I suddenly feel like a child who has been caught in a lie. I've never really had to deal with parental punishment before. My mother didn't pay enough attention to me to care, so I don't know what's about to happen. I'm a little nervous, considering my father does not look pleased. He looks past me, at Samson.

"Yeah, this isn't okay," my father says.

Samson steps in front of me and holds up his hands in defense. "I didn't stay the night. Please don't punch me again."

My father looks at me for an explanation.

"He just got here fifteen minutes ago. We watched the sunrise on the balcony together."

My father focuses his attention on Samson now. "I've been in this kitchen for a lot longer than fifteen minutes. If you just got here fifteen minutes ago, how did you get in?"

Samson scratches the back of his neck. "I, uh... jumped?" He lifts his arm to show my father his bloody elbow. "Barely made it."

My father stares at him for a moment, then he shakes his head. "You're an idiot," he mutters. He fills his coffee cup and then says, "Either of you want some coffee?"

Huh. He got over that fast.

"I'm good," Samson says, easing his way toward the door. He looks at me. "See you later?"

I nod and Samson lifts a brow, sending me a look. I'm smiling and staring at the door for several seconds after he leaves. My father clears his throat and it sucks me back into the moment. I look at him, hoping that's the end of this conversation. "I'll take some coffee," I say, trying to divert his attention to something else.

My father grabs a mug out of the cabinet and pours me a cup. "You take it black?"

"No. As much cream and sugar as you can fit in there." I sit in one of the chairs at the kitchen bar while my father mixes my coffee.

He slides it toward me and says, "I don't know how I feel about what just happened."

I stare at my coffee as I sip from it, just so I don't have to stare at my father. When I set the mug back on the counter, I cup my hands around it. "I'm not lying to you. He didn't spend the night."

"Yet," my father says. "I was a teenager once. His bedroom balcony and yours are feet apart. Today might have just been a sunrise, but you're here for an entire summer. Alana and I don't allow Sara to have boys spend the night. It's only fair if the same rules apply to you."

I nod. "Okay."

My father is looking at me like he's not sure if I'm agreeing to appease him or if I'm actually agreeing. To be honest, I don't even know.

He leans against the counter and takes a sip of his coffee. "Do you always wake up this early?" he asks.

"No. Samson wanted me to watch the sunrise, so he set an alarm on my phone."

My father waves toward the door Samson walked out of earlier. "So is he . . . Are you two dating?"

"No. I'm moving to Pennsylvania in August, I don't want a boyfriend."

My father narrows his eyes at me. "Pennsylvania?"

Shit.

That slipped out.

I immediately look down at my coffee. My throat feels thick with nerves. I blow out a slow breath. "Yeah," I say. I leave it at that. Maybe he won't pry.

"Why are you moving to Pennsylvania? When did you decide this? What's in Pennsylvania?"

I grip my mug even tighter. "I was going to tell you. I just . . . I was waiting for the right moment." *I'm lying. I had no intentions of telling him, but I'm in it now.* "I got a volleyball scholarship to Penn State."

My father stares at me blankly. No surprise, no excitement, no anger. Just a blank, unreadable stare before he says, "Are you serious?"

I nod. "Yeah. Full ride. I move in on August third."

Still, his expression is blank. "When did you find out?"

I swallow and take a slow sip of my coffee, trying to decide if I should tell him the truth. It might just make him angry. "Junior year," I say quietly.

He chokes on air.

He looks very surprised. Or offended. I can't tell.

He quietly pushes off the counter and walks to the windows. He stares out at the ocean with his back to me. After about thirty seconds of silence, he turns and faces me again. "Why didn't you tell me?"

"I don't know."

"Beyah, this is huge." He's walking toward me now. "You should have told me." Before he reaches me, he pauses. I can see confusion seeping in. "If you got a full ride last year, why did your mother tell me you needed tuition for community college?"

I blow out a steady breath, gripping the back of my

neck. I press my elbows against the counter and give myself a moment to figure out how to respond to that.

"Beyah?" he asks.

I shake my head, needing him to be quiet for a second. I squeeze my forehead. "She lied to you," I say. I stand up and walk my cup to the sink. "I didn't even know she asked you for tuition money. She didn't know about the scholarship, either, but I can guarantee whatever you sent her for tuition was never meant for me to begin with."

I pour my coffee into the sink and rinse the cup out. When I turn around and face him, he looks dejected. Confused. His mouth opens like he's about to say something, but then he closes it and shakes his head.

I'm sure it's a lot to process for him. We don't talk about my mother. This is probably the first time I've ever spoken negatively about her to him. And while I would love to tell him just how much of a mother she never was, it's six thirty in the morning and I can't have this conversation right now.

"I'm going back to bed," I say, heading toward the stairs.

"Beyah, wait."

I pause on the second step and slowly turn to face him. He's standing with his hands on his hips, looking at me intently. "I'm proud of you."

I nod, but as soon as I turn around and walk back up the stairs, I feel a ball of anger tightening inside me.

I don't want him to be proud of me.

It's precisely why I didn't tell him.

And even though it seems like he's trying to make an

effort with me now, I can't help but feel full of resentment that I went most of my life without him in it.

I will not allow his words to make me feel good, nor will I allow them to excuse his second-rate parenting.

Of course you're proud of me, Brian. But you should only be proud of me because I miraculously survived childhood all on my own.

Fourteen

I couldn't go back to sleep after Samson left this morning, no matter how hard I tried. Maybe it was the conversation with my father that made sleep difficult.

Sara set up loungers and an umbrella on the beach after lunch and I must have finally fallen asleep in my lounger at some point, because I just woke up. There's drool on my arm.

I'm on my stomach, facing away from Sara's lounge chair, when I open my eyes. I wipe my arm and push myself up enough so that I can roll over onto my back.

When I get situated, I look over at Sara, but it's not Sara I'm looking at.

It's Samson.

He's asleep in her lounge chair.

I sit up and look out at the water. Sara and Marcos are on paddleboards a good ways out in the ocean.

I grab my phone and look at the time. It's four o'clock. I slept for an hour and a half.

I lie back down and glance over at Samson while he sleeps. He's on his stomach, his head resting on his arms. He's got a ball cap on turned backward and he's wearing a pair of sunglasses. No shirt, but that's not a bad thing.

I roll onto my side and rest my head on my arm, and I stare at him for a while. I know very little about the pieces that make him up as a whole, but I feel like I know what kind of person all those pieces have made him.

Maybe you don't have to know a person's history to realize who they are in the present. And who I've started to realize he is on the inside makes him even more attractive on the outside. Attractive enough that I think about him almost every waking second.

I find myself focusing my attention on his mouth. I don't know why I freaked out while he was kissing me last night. Maybe because I'm still trying to wrap my head around the fact that this past week has been real.

It's a lot at once and it seemed to all culminate and scream at me during our kiss last night. It makes me wonder if he kissed me again tonight, would I react the same way? Or would I allow myself to actually see it through and enjoy the entire kiss like I enjoyed the first few seconds of it?

I stare at his lips, convincing myself that it's worth a second try. And a third and maybe a fourth. Maybe if I kiss him enough, it'll eventually only feel perfect.

"You realize my eyes are open, right?"

Shit.

I thought he was asleep. I cover my face with my hand. There's no hiding my embarrassment.

"Don't worry," he says, his voice hoarse, like it's scratching its way up his throat. "I've been staring at you the whole time you've been sleeping." He reaches out and touches my elbow with his finger. "How'd you get this scar?"

"During a volleyball game." His lounge chair is only about a foot from mine, but it seems like a mile away when he stops touching my arm.

"How good was your team?"

"We won our state championship twice," I say. "Did you play any sports in high school?"

"No. I didn't go to a typical school."

"What kind of school did you go to?"

Samson shakes his head, indicating he's not going to answer that.

I roll my eyes. "Why do you do that? Why do you ask me questions and then I ask you the same thing and you refuse to answer?"

"I've told you more than I've told anyone. Ever," he says. "Don't be greedy."

"Then stop asking me questions you aren't willing to answer yourself."

He grins. "Stop answering my questions."

"You think me knowing where you went to high school is somehow more personal than you having your tongue in my mouth? Or me telling you about Dakota? Or you telling me about your mother?" I pull my arms up behind my head and close my eyes. "Your logic is quite stupid, Samson."

There's really no point in trying to have a conversation with him if all he's going to do is dance around every topic like he's some kind of ballerina.

"I went to boarding school in New York," he finally says. "And I hated every second of it."

I smile, feeling like I won this battle somehow, but inside I'm kind of saddened by that answer. Boarding school doesn't sound fun. No wonder he didn't want to talk about it. "Thank you."

"You're welcome."

I swivel my head and look at him. He's removed his sunglasses and the reflection of the sun makes his eyes look almost clear. It doesn't seem like someone with eyes as transparent as his could be as closed off as he is.

We stare at each other, much like we always do, but it's different this time. Now we know what each other tastes like. He knows my darkest secret, yet he's still looking at me like I'm the most interesting thing on this peninsula.

He drops his gaze and looks down between our chairs. He drags a finger in the sand. "How do you spell your name?"

"B-e-y-a-h."

I watch as he writes my name in the sand. When he finishes, he drags a finger across it and strikes it out, then wipes his whole hand across it until my name disappears.

I don't know how I could possibly feel that beneath my skin, but I did.

Samson glances toward the water. "Sara and Marcos are coming back." He puts his shades on and then hops up.

I keep my hands behind my head, pretending to be relaxed, despite feeling like I've just been electrocuted. Samson walks to Sara, who is struggling with her board. He takes over and drags it the rest of the way out of the water for her.

Sara pulls at her ponytail when she reaches me and takes a seat on the lounge chair Samson was just lying on. She squeezes water out of her hair.

"You have a good nap?" Sara asks.

"Yeah. I can't believe I fell asleep."

"You snore," she says, laughing. "Did you ask Samson if he wants to double-date tonight?"

"No. It didn't come up."

Marcos and Samson are walking the paddleboards toward us. "Samson, we're all going on a double date," Sara says to him. "Be ready at six."

Samson doesn't miss a beat in his response. "Who's my date?"

"Beyah. Idiot."

Samson looks at me like he's considering it. "Is this like a friend date?"

"It's food," Marcos says. "Don't let Sara put a label on it."

"We doing seafood?" Samson asks him.

"Would you even allow us to eat anything else?"

Samson looks back at me. "You like shrimp, Beyah?"

"I don't know. I don't think I've ever had it."

Samson tilts his head. "I can't tell if you're being sarcastic."

"I'm from Kentucky. We don't have a lot of affordable seafood restaurants."

"You've never even been to a Red Lobster?" Marcos asks me.

"Y'all forget things like Red Lobster are fancy to a lot of people."

"I'll order for you, then," Samson says.

"How very chauvinistic of you," I tease.

Sara pulls on her bathing suit cover-up and stands. "Come on, let's go get ready."

"Now? We aren't leaving for another two hours."

"Yeah, but we have a lot to do to get you ready."

"Like what?"

"I'm giving you a makeover."

I shake my head. "No. Please, no."

She nods. "Yes. I'm doing your hair, your nails, your makeup." She grabs my hand and pulls me out of the lounger. She points at all the stuff we brought to the beach earlier. "You two strapping men take care of this, will ya?" We get halfway to the house before she says, "He's into you. I can tell. He doesn't look at other girls like he looks at you."

I don't respond to her because I get a text in the middle of her comment. I rarely get texts. Not many people have my phone number.

I look at my phone as Sara starts walking up the stairs. The text is from Samson.

Look at us going on a spontaneous date. Maybe we ARE fun.

"You coming?" Sara asks.

I wipe the grin off my face and follow her inside.

Fifteen

They're all staring at me, waiting for me to take a bite. Even our waiter.

Talk about pressure.

"Dip it in cocktail sauce first," Marcos suggests.

Samson pushes the cocktail sauce away from me. "Are you crazy? That'll make her puke." He pushes tartar sauce toward me. "Here, use this."

Sara rolls her eyes as she stacks up three of the menus. She and Marcos just ordered, but Samson and I haven't yet because he wanted to make sure I liked shrimp first. The waiter was amused I'd never had shrimp, so he brought me a piece to try and now he's sticking around to watch my reaction.

It's grilled shrimp without a shell or a tail. I'm not a huge fan of fish, so I'm not expecting much, but the pressure is real as I dip it into the tartar sauce.

"Y'all are acting like her reaction is going to be life or death," Sara says. "I'm getting hangry."

"It'll only be life or death if she's allergic to shellfish," the waiter says.

I pause before taking the bite. "What exactly falls under the definition of shellfish?"

Samson says, "Lobster. Shrimp. Things in shells."

"Crab. Crawfish. Turtles," Marcos says.

"Turtles aren't a fish," Sara says, rolling her eyes.

"It was a joke," Marcos says.

"Have you ever had lobster or crab?" Samson asks me.

"I've had crab."

"You should be fine, then."

"For Pete's sake, just eat it before I do," Sara says. "I'm starving."

I bite down on the shrimp, only eating half of it. Everyone is watching me chew, even Sara. It's got a decent flavor. It's not the greatest thing I've ever had, but it's good. "Not bad." I pop the rest of it in my mouth.

Samson smiles and hands the menu to the waiter. "We'll both have the shrimp platter."

The waiter writes it down and walks away. Sara scrunches her nose up. "He really did just order for you. I can't tell if that's cute or disgusting."

"I tried ordering for you once and you elbowed me in the side," Marcos says.

Sara nods. "Yeah, you're right. It's disgusting." She

takes a sip of her drink. "I feel like doing something touristy this weekend."

"Like what?" Marcos asks.

"The water park? Or a duck tour?" She looks at me and Samson. "You two want to come?"

"I'm free after lunch every day. Except tomorrow. I'm finishing Marjorie's roof."

Well that kind of melts my heart a little.

"Shawn?"

All four of us look in the direction of the voice. A guy is approaching our table, looking at Samson. The guy is tall and skinny with arms covered in tattoos. I'm staring at one on his forearm of a lighthouse when I feel Samson stiffen.

"Holy shit," the guy says. "It *is* you. How are you, man?"

"Hey," Samson says. He doesn't sound very excited to see this guy. Also . . . *why did the guy call him Shawn?*

Samson taps my leg, wanting out of the booth. I stand up to let him out and he gives the guy a hug. I take my seat and the three of us aren't even hiding the fact that we're eavesdropping on their conversation.

"Dude," the guy says to Samson. "When did you get out?"

Get out?

Samson looks over at our table. There's a discomfort to him now. He puts his hand on the guy's back and walks him away from the table so we can't hear what they're saying.

I look at Sara and Marcos to see what their reactions

are. Marcos is taking a drink, but Sara's head is tilted in curiosity as she stares at Samson. She falls back against the booth and says, "That was weird. Why did that guy call him Shawn?"

Marcos shrugs.

"Maybe Samson is his middle name," I say, more to myself than to Sara or Marcos. I wonder why I didn't demand he tell me his full name last night when I asked. This is weird, knowing I didn't even know the guy's first name. But I guess he doesn't know that my last name is Grim. Or maybe he does, since I have the same last name as my father.

"Why did that guy ask him when he got out?" Sara says. "Got out of where? Jail? Prison?"

Marcos shrugs again. "Could have been referring to rehab."

"He was in *rehab*?" Sara asks.

"I have no idea, I've known the guy as long as you have," he says.

Samson reappears at our table moments later, sans friend. I stand up and he slides back into the booth. He says nothing. Offers no explanation. That doesn't matter because Sara won't let this slide. I can tell by the way she's staring at him.

"Why did that guy call you Shawn?"

Samson stares at her a moment, then releases a quiet laugh. "What?"

She waves her hand toward the direction the guy went. "He called you Shawn! And then he asked you when you got out. Where have you been? Jail?"

For some reason, Samson looks at me. I say nothing because I'm waiting for the same answers as Sara.

He looks back at Sara and says, "That's my name. Shawn Samson." He waves a hand at Marcos. "He called me Samson when we met, and it just stuck with you guys. Everyone else calls me Shawn."

Marcos brings his straw to his mouth. "Sounds vaguely familiar, now that I think about it."

Shawn? His name is *Shawn*?

I'm so used to calling him Samson, I'm not sure I can call him Shawn.

"Okay," Sara says. "But where'd you *get out* of? Jail? Were you in jail?"

Samson sighs and I can tell he doesn't want to talk about it.

"Leave him alone," Marcos says, also recognizing Samson's discomfort.

Sara waves a defensive hand toward me. "I'm trying to set my stepsister up with him, I think we deserve to know if he's some kind of criminal."

"It's fine," Samson says. "He was talking about getting out of the city. We went to boarding school together and he knew how much I hated New York."

I can see the slow roll of his throat after he says that, as if he's swallowing a lie. What are the chances he'd run into a guy from New York on a peninsula in Texas?

Very slim, but is it really Sara's business? Is it mine? None of us owe one another our past.

I don't know why I feel protective of him right now, but I know he hates talking about himself. Maybe that's something Sara doesn't know about him.

I'll get the truth out of him later. But right now, I just want the awkwardness to disappear, so I say, "I've never been to New York. Texas is only the third state I've ever been to."

"Seriously?" Sara says.

I nod. "Yep. Only ever left Kentucky when I'd fly to Washington to see my father. I had no idea Texas was this hot. I'm not sure I like it."

Marcos laughs.

The waiter shows up with the appetizers Sara ordered. He takes my glass to get me a refill and Samson reaches for a piece of calamari, popping it into his mouth. "You ever tasted calamari, Beyah?"

I take a piece from him. "Nope."

Marcos rolls his head. "It's like you were raised on a different planet."

Sara doesn't wait for me to start eating this time. She makes herself a plate of appetizers and begins eating. This small moment may not seem like a big deal to anyone at the table, but I'm relieved to know Sara isn't putting as much pressure on herself as she was the night I showed up.

Sara starts asking me questions about what else I've never tried, and the conversation moves from being only about Samson to being unrelated to Samson.

After a few minutes, Samson reaches under the table and grabs my hand. He gives it a squeeze before releasing it. When I look at him, he's saying a silent *thank you*.

I barely know the guy, but I can somehow communicate better with him by not using words than I've ever been able to communicate verbally with anyone else.

He gives me one look and it's proof that I don't need to know more. Not right now, anyway.

I'll peel his layers back on his time.

Sixteen

There weren't two seats next to each other when we made it to our nightly bonfire, so Samson is sitting across from me.

Sadly, Beau is the one next to me.

I've noticed Samson eyeing Beau every time he speaks to me. I'm trying to make it very clear that I'm not interested, but Beau isn't taking the hint. Guys like him never do. They're used to getting what they want, so they can't recognize when what they want doesn't want them. It's an unfathomable thought to Beau, I'm sure.

"Oh, God," Sara mutters.

I glance at her and she points a hand at the dune crossing about fifty feet from our site.

Cadence is walking over the dune.

"I thought she left," I say.

"I thought so, too," Sara says.

I watch with a knot in my stomach as Cadence approaches us. Samson's back is to her, so he doesn't know she's walking up.

When she reaches him, she wraps her hands around Samson's head and covers his eyes. He pulls her hands away and leans his head back, looking up at her.

Before he can even react, she says, "Surprise!" Then she leans down and kisses him on the mouth. "We came back for another week."

The blood in my body feels like it just turned to lava.

Samson's eyes immediately find mine when she pulls away. I'm not displaying the jealousy on my face, but it sure is running through my body.

Samson stands up and turns to Cadence. I can't hear what he says to her, but he glances at me for a split second before he puts his hand on Cadence's lower back and points at the water. They start walking in that direction and all I can do is look down at my lap.

I hope he's walking away from all of us so he can let her down gently. Or ungently, I don't care.

Not that he owes me anything. I'm the one who stopped the kiss last night.

"You okay?" Sara asks, noticing the change in my demeanor.

I blow out a steady breath. "What are they doing?"

"Who? Cadence and Samson?"

I nod.

"Walking," she says. She narrows her eyes at me in suspicion. "What's up with the two of you?"

I shake my head. "Nothing is up."

Sara leans back in her chair. "I know you're private about a lot of things, Beyah. I can deal with that, but if Samson kisses you this summer, will you *please* just give me a sign? You don't even have to say it out loud. Just high-five me or something."

I assure her with a nod, then glance over at Samson and Cadence. They're standing at least two feet apart. Her arms are folded tightly over her chest. She looks angry.

I train my gaze back on the fire, but a few seconds later, there's a collective gasp.

"Holy shit," Marcos says, laughing. I look at him, but he's looking at Samson, who is now walking back to the fire. He's alone, rubbing his cheek.

"She slapped him," Sara whispers. When Samson reaches his seat, she says, "What did you say to her?"

"Nothing she wanted to hear."

"Did you just turn her down?" Beau asks. "Why the fuck would you do that? She's hot."

Samson looks at Beau with a deadpan expression. He waves in the direction Cadence just stomped. "She's fair game, Beau. Shoot your shot."

Beau shakes his head. "Nah, I'm only interested in this shot right here," he says, indicating a hand toward me.

"Not gonna happen, Beau," I say.

Beau grins at me, and I have no idea how my flat-out refusal of him makes him think I mean anything other than the words I'm speaking to him. He stands up and grabs my hand. He tries to pull me up, but I don't budge.

"Come swimming with me," he says.

I shake my head. "I've told you no twice already."

He tries to pick me up, but I kick him in the knee just as Samson jumps out of his seat and stalks over to us. He stands between us, facing Beau. "She said no."

Beau looks at Samson, and then around him, at me. He flicks a finger between us. "Oh. I get it. You two are a thing now."

"It has nothing to do with me," Samson says. "I've listened to her ask you to leave her alone several times. Take a fucking hint."

Samson is angry. I don't know if it's stemming from jealousy or the simple fact that Beau is an asshole.

I expect that to be the end of it, but Beau apparently doesn't like being yelled at. He swings at Samson, hitting him in the face. Then Beau puts up both fists like he's ready for a fight, but Samson brings a hand up to his jaw and stares hard at Beau. "Are you fucking serious?"

"Yeah, I'm fucking serious," Beau responds, still in his fighting stance.

Marcos is standing now, ready to defend Samson, but Samson doesn't look like he cares to entertain Beau.

"Go home, Beau," Marcos says, stepping between Beau and Samson.

Beau looks at Marcos. "How do you say *asshole* in Mexican?"

The only thing I hate more than a douche is a *racist* douche. "It's Spanish, not Mexican," I say. "And I think *Beau* is the correct translation for *asshole*."

Samson lets out a small laugh when I say that. It pisses Beau off.

"Fuck you, you little rich prick. All of you can go to hell." Beau's face is red with rage.

"We're in hell every time you show up," Sara says flatly.

Beau points at Sara. "Fuck you." He points at me. "And fuck *you*."

I guess that's where Samson draws the line. He doesn't hit Beau, but he moves toward him fast enough to make Beau jump back. Then Beau spins around and grabs his stuff from his chair and leaves.

It's a beautiful sight.

Samson falls into the chair, gripping his jaw. "I've been slapped by a girl and punched by two guys since you showed up."

"Then stop taking my side."

Samson looks at me with a small grin, almost as if he's saying, *That's not gonna happen.*

"You're bleeding." I grab a nearby towel and wipe his jaw. He's got a small gash across his jawbone. Beau must have been wearing a ring. "You should put a bandage on that."

Samson's eyes change as he stares back at me. "I have

some at the house." He pushes out of his chair and walks around the fire, heading home.

He doesn't even invite me or wait on me, but I could tell from his expression he wants me to follow him. I press a palm against my neck, feeling the heat rising to my skin. I stand up. I glance at Sara before I walk away.

"Remember," she whispers. "A signal. A high five."

I laugh and then follow Samson to his house. He's several yards ahead of me, but he leaves his door open when he goes inside, so he knows I'm following him.

When I reach the top of the stairs, I blow out a calming breath. I don't know why I'm nervous. We kissed last night. The hardest part is over.

I close the door when I walk inside. Samson is at the sink, wetting a paper towel. I walk into the kitchen and notice he didn't turn any of the lights on. The only lights in the house are coming from the appliances and the moon shining through the windows.

I lean against the counter to get a look at his cut. He tilts his head so that I can inspect it. "Is it still bleeding?" he asks.

"A little." I pull back and watch him as he presses the wet napkin against his jaw again.

"I don't have any bandages," he says. "I was lying."

I nod. "I know. You don't have shit in this house."

His mouth twitches like he wants to smile, but there's something heavy weighing his smile down. Whatever that heaviness is weighs *me* down.

He pulls the napkin away and tosses it on the counter, then he grips the edges of the counter like he's having to hold himself back.

He's not going to make the first move this time, no matter how much he seems like he wants to. And as nervous as I am, I want to experience a whole kiss with him, from beginning to end.

Samson's stare is like a magnetic pull, coaxing me toward him. I step closer, my movements timid. No matter how nervous I seem, he doesn't push it. He just waits. My heart is pounding in my chest when it's clear to both of us that I'm about to kiss him.

It feels different than last night. It feels more significant since we've both spent the last day thinking about it and have obviously come to the conclusion that we both want it to happen again.

We maintain eye contact as I lift onto my toes and lightly press my lips to his. He inhales while my mouth is still against his, as if he's summoning up patience that no longer exists inside of him.

I pull back a fraction, needing to see his reaction. His pointed gaze and parted lips are a promising hint for whatever might happen next. I don't feel like I'll end up running out of this kitchen again now that I've spent the last twenty-four hours regretting that move.

Samson lowers his forehead to mine. I squeeze my eyes shut when he wraps a hand around the back of my head. He keeps his forehead pressed against mine and I imagine his eyes are closed, too. It's like he wants to be close to me, but he knows he can't hug me and he doesn't know if he should kiss me.

I tilt my head back on instinct, wanting his lips against mine again. He accepts the silent invitation by kissing the corner of my mouth, then the center of it. He releases a shaky breath, like he's savoring what's coming.

The hand he has wrapped in my hair angles my head back even more, and then he kisses me with confidence.

It's slow and deep, like he might not survive if he doesn't swallow a little bit of my soul in this kiss. He tastes like saltwater and my blood feels like the sea, raging and crashing through my veins.

I want to live in this feeling. Sleep in it. Wake up in it.

I don't want the kiss to end yet, but when he starts to slow it down, I like how he does it. Gradual, careful, difficult, like he's coming to a halt about as slow as a train could.

When we're no longer kissing, he releases me, but I don't move away. I'm still pressed against him, but he's gripping the counter again on either side of himself rather than gripping me. I appreciate that he isn't wrapping me in his arms right now.

Kissing I've proved I can handle tonight. Being held is something I'm not quite ready for, and he already knows how I feel about it.

I press my forehead against his shoulder and close my eyes.

I can hear his breaths, labored and deep as he rests his head lightly against mine.

We stay like this for a while and I don't know what to feel or what to think. I don't know if it's normal to feel a thousand pounds heavier after you kiss someone.

I feel like I'm doing this all wrong, but at the same time, it feels like maybe Samson and I are the only people who are doing this right in the whole world.

"Beyah," he whispers. His mouth is right over my ear, so when he says my name, goose bumps run down my neck and arms. I keep my forehead pressed against him and my eyes closed.

"What?"

There's a pause that feels way longer than it actually is. "I'm leaving in August."

I don't know what to say to that. It was only four words, but he drew a very deep line in the sand with those four words. A line I knew would eventually come.

"Me too," I say.

I lift my head and my eyes are drawn to his necklace. I touch it, running my finger across the wood. He's looking down at me like maybe he wants to kiss me again. I would take a thousand more of those tonight. I didn't feel anything negative this time. It was all good, yet chilling. It's as if he kissed me backward, from the inside out—the same way I think he looks at me sometimes. Like he sees the inside of me before he notices what's outside.

He tilts my chin up with a finger and presses his lips to mine again, this time with his eyes open, soaking me in. He pulls back, but not very far. All his words seem to seep into my mouth when he speaks. "If we do this, it stays in the shallow end."

I nod, but then I shake my head. I don't know if I'm agreeing or disagreeing. "What do you mean by shallow end?"

His stare matches the tightness in my chest. He slides his tongue over his top lip like he's thinking of how to elaborate on his thoughts without hurting my feelings. "I just mean . . . if this becomes a thing. A summer thing. That's all I want it to be. I don't want to leave here in August in a relationship."

"I don't want that, either. We'll be on two different sides of the country."

He slides the backs of his fingers down my arm. When he slides them back up again, he doesn't stop at my shoulder. His fingers glide up my collarbone until he's touching my cheek.

"People sometimes still drown in the shallow end," he whispers.

That's a dark thought. One I think he probably meant to keep to himself. But here I am, pulling back those layers whether he likes it or not.

So many layers.

I don't know how kissing him felt like I bypassed every

layer and burrowed right into his core, but it did. It's like I see the real him, despite all the unknown that still surrounds him.

"Who was that guy at dinner?" I ask.

He swallows hard, glancing away, and it makes me want to run a soothing hand down his throat. "I don't want to lie to you, Beyah. But I also can't be honest with you." I have no idea what that means, but the thing about Samson is, he doesn't seem to be the type to want attention or manufacture drama. So by saying something like this, it makes me think it's even worse than how he's presenting it.

"What's the worst thing you've ever done?" I ask him.

He brings his eyes back to mine with another predictable shake of his head.

"It's that bad?"

"It's bad."

"Worse than what I did with Dakota?"

Samson presses his lips into a thin, irritated line and then dips his head, looking at me with intensity. "There are two different kinds of wrong. The wrong that stems from weakness and the wrong that stems from strength. You made that choice because you were strong and needed to survive. You didn't make that choice because you were weak."

I grasp on to every word of that because I want to make it my truth.

"Will you just answer one question for me?" I ask. He

doesn't say yes but he also doesn't say no. He just waits for my question. "Was it an assault of any kind?"

"No. Nothing like that."

I'm relieved by that. He can tell. He brushes my hair over my shoulders with both hands and then presses his mouth against my forehead. He kisses me there, then leans his head against mine. "I'll tell you the day before you leave for college."

"If you're eventually going to tell me, why can't you just tell me right now?"

"Because I want to spend the rest of the summer with you. And if I tell you, I don't think you'll want that."

I'm not sure what he could possibly tell me that would make me not want to speak to him, but I know if I dwell on it, I'm just going to stress over it.

I'll wait.

At the rate our conversations have been going, I'll get it out of him before August.

But for now, I just nod because it's nothing he wants to tell me tonight. And if there's one thing I can do right now, it's show him the same patience he showed me last night.

He kisses me again. It's a quick kiss. A goodnight kiss.

I don't say anything as I pull away from him and walk toward the door because all my words feel too big for my voice. It's hard just walking out his door right now. I can't imagine what August 3 will feel like.

P.J. is waiting outside the door when I close it. He follows me loyally down the stairs and to the house. When I reach the top of the stairs, he walks to his dog bed I've made for him out of a few towels and lies down.

Thankfully, no one is in the living room when I enter the house. I lock the door and sneak up the stairs. Before I open my door, I glance at Sara's bedroom door.

I think I want to tell her we kissed. It's a weird feeling, wanting to open up to another girl. I never even told Natalie about the thing between Dakota and me. I was too ashamed to tell her.

I knock softly on Sara's door, not wanting to wake up anyone else in the house. Sara doesn't say anything. She's probably still at the beach.

I push her door open to check and see if she's in her bed, but as soon as I peek my head inside, I pull the door shut.

Marcos was on top of her. He was clothed, but still. I wasn't expecting that.

I walk to my room, but then remember what Sara said at the beach about just giving her a silent sign.

I walk back into her room. She and Marcos stop kissing and look at me. I reach the bed and hold up a hand to get a high five from her.

She laughs and high-fives me. "Hell yes!" she whispers as I leave her room.

Seventeen

The last few days have been the least stressful days of my life. It's like spending time with Samson releases some kind of hormone from my brain that's been missing for nineteen years. I feel happier. I don't feel like I'm on the verge of breaking all the time.

I'm sure it's more than just Samson. It's a combination of all the things I've never had before. Decent shelter that isn't rotting from the inside by termites. Three meals a day. A constant friend who lives right across the hall. The ocean. The sunrise.

It's almost too much good happening at once. I'm overdosing on good things, which only means I'll eventually have to go through withdrawal when summer ends. But like Sara said, summers are for focusing on today and today only. I'll worry about the painful part of summer on August 3.

Samson decided a ladder would be safer and easier to

reach my balcony in the mornings than jumping proved to be. I'm sitting in my usual seat on my balcony eating grapes I just took from the refrigerator when I hear him raising the ladder. My favorite part of our morning routine is when he reaches the top of the ladder and smiles at me. Although last night might have been better than our mornings together. He talked me into getting back in the ocean and we kissed without that kiss being interrupted by a searing pain.

Kiss is putting it mildly.

We made out. As much as a person can make out in the ocean without putting hands inside bathing suits and swim trunks. But that's the only physical time we've really gotten outside of these last few mornings. I'm kind of uncomfortable with public displays of affection in front of other people, and we're always with Sara and Marcos.

Samson reaches the top of the ladder and we both smile at each other. "Morning."

"Hey." I pop another grape into my mouth. After he climbs over the railing, he bends down and gives me a quick kiss, then sits next to me.

I take a grape out of the bag and bring it to his lips. He barely parts them with a grin, forcing me to shove my finger into his mouth as he takes the grape. He circles his lips around my finger for a second, then pulls away slowly. He starts to chew the grape. "Thank you."

Now I want to feed him grapes all day.

He wraps an arm over the back of the chair and I lean

against him, but not close enough that he would take it as a sign to pull me to him. We watch the sunrise in silence, and I think about the turn my life has taken since I arrived.

I thought I knew who I was, but I had no idea people could become different versions of themselves in different settings. In this setting, where everything feels good and perfect, I'm actually at peace with my life. I don't fall asleep bitter every night. I don't even actively hate my father like I used to. And I'm not so much a disbeliever in love anymore. I'm not a skeptic here because I'm able to look at life through a different lens.

It makes me wonder what version of myself I'll be when I get to college. Will I be happy there? Will I miss Samson? Will I continue to thrive or will I wilt back into my old self?

I feel like a flower being taken out of the shadows and put into the sun. I'm blooming for the first time since I broke through the earth's soil.

"What are today's plans?" Samson asks.

I shrug. "I think it's clear by now that I have absolutely no plans until August third."

"Good. Want to rent a golf cart and take a tour of the beach this afternoon? I know a really secluded spot."

"Sure. Sounds fun." Especially since he said the word *secluded*. That sounds like an invite to finally be able to spend some alone time with him.

The sun is up now and this is usually when Samson leaves so I can go back to sleep, but instead of standing up, he slides me onto his lap so that I'm straddling him. He leans his head back against the chair, resting his hands on my hips. "We should start watching the sunrise in this position."

"I would block your view," I say.

He brings a hand up to my face, and his fingertips against my jaw feel like tiny little fires against my skin. "You're prettier than the view, Beyah." He slips his hand behind my head and brings me to his mouth.

Both of his arms wrap around me and he pulls me closer, but I shift a little so that he'll be reminded not to do that. I don't like it when both of his arms go around me while we kiss because it makes me think of being held, and being held is something more personal to me than kissing or even sex.

I like kissing Samson. I like spending time with him. But I don't like the idea of sharing something so intimate with someone who doesn't want to share more than a few weeks of themselves with me.

His hands fall to my hips like I've trained them to do over the last few days. He kisses my jaw, then the side of my head. "I have to go," he says. "I have a lot to do today."

Every day he's always doing something different. Helping someone repair a roof, rebuilding a dune. Most of it seems like busywork. I don't know that he actually takes money for the work he does.

I slide off him and watch as he heads back toward the ladder.

He doesn't make eye contact with me as he descends

the ladder and disappears. I lean my head against the back of the chair and pop a grape into my mouth.

I'm sure he wants more than I'm giving him physically, but I can't give him more if he insists on staying in the shallow end. Hugs and being held might seem like shallow-end stuff to him, but to me, those things are buried somewhere in the Mariana Trench.

I'd rather have casual sex with him than let him hug me.

That's probably proof that I have some deep shit that needs unpacking by a therapist. But whatever.

Ocean therapy has worked wonders for me so far and it's free.

Secluded was an understatement.

He brought us so far down the beach, the houses aren't clustered in neighborhoods anymore. They're sparse and scattered. There are no people. Just the dunes behind us and the ocean in front of us. If I were going to choose a place to build a house, this would be it.

"Why aren't there very many houses here? Does the land flood too easily?"

"There used to be a lot of houses here. Hurricane Ike leveled everything." Samson takes a drink of water. He brought sandwiches, water, and a blanket. He's considering this our first official date, since hanging out with Sara and

Marcos doesn't really count. He even pulled up to my stairs earlier in the golf cart to pick me up.

"Do you think it'll ever be the same as before the hurricane?"

He shrugs. "Maybe not like it was before. The whole peninsula became gentrified in the rebuild, but it's thriving more than I thought it would. It's still a work in progress, though. It'll take more than just a few years to even come close to what it was like before." He points to a spot behind us. "That's where I found Rake's boat. There are probably still pieces of it buried behind the dune. They haven't done much work in this area since the hurricane."

I feed a piece of my bread to P.J. He rode in the back of the golf cart all the way here. "You think this dog belonged to one of the people whose houses were destroyed?"

"I think you're the only person that dog has ever belonged to."

I smile when he says that, even though I know I'm not the first person P.J. has ever loved. He knows commands, so someone spent time training him in the past.

I've always wanted a dog, but I never had enough food to feed one. I'd take in strays, but they eventually left me for other families who fed them more often.

"What are you going to do with him in August?" Samson asks, leaning across me to scratch P.J. on the head.

"I don't know. I'm trying not to think about it."

Samson's eyes meet mine in that moment, and there's a flash of contemplation that passes between us.

What will I do with the dog?

What will we do about *us*?

What's goodbye going to feel like?

Samson stretches out in the sand. I'm sitting cross-legged, so he lays his head in my lap and stares up at me thoughtfully. I run a hand through his hair, trying not to think about anything beyond or before this moment.

"What do other people think of you?" Samson asks.

"That's an odd question."

Samson looks at me expectantly, like he doesn't care that it's an odd question. I laugh, looking out at the water while I think.

"I'm not meek, so sometimes my attitude can be misconstrued as being bitchy. But I was lumped in with my mother back home. When you're judged based on the person who raised you, you can't be neutral about who you are. You either let it consume you and you become who others think you are, or you fight it with everything in you." I look down at him. "What do you think people think of you?"

"I don't think people think of me at all."

I shake my head in disagreement. "I do. And do you know what I think?"

"What do you think?"

"I think I want to get back in the ocean with you."

Samson grins. "We're pretty far from the vinegar."

"Then make it worth it in case I get stung again."

Samson hops to his feet and then pulls me up. I slip off my shorts as he removes his shirt. He holds my hand as we work our way through the waves and away from the shore. When the water is up to my chest, we stop walking and face each other, lowering ourselves until the water is up to both of our necks.

We close the gap between us until we're kissing.

Every time we kiss, it's as if we leave more of ourselves inside the other. I wish I knew more about relationships and love and all the things I used to think I was too good for, or maybe not good *enough* for. I want to know how to make this feeling last. I want to know if a guy like Samson could ever fall in love with a girl like me.

A wave crashes over us, forcing us apart. The water completely soaks my hair. I'm wiping it out of my eyes, laughing, when Samson makes his way back to me. He wraps my legs around his waist but keeps his hands on my hips.

There's a flicker of happiness in his eyes.

It's the first time I've seen it.

I've been here almost two weeks and this is the first time he's looked completely at ease. It makes me feel good that he seems to find that with me, but I'm sad it's not something he feels all the time.

"What kind of things make you happy, Samson?"

"Rich people are never content," he says instantaneously. It's sad he didn't even have to think about it.

"So the saying is true? Money doesn't buy happiness?"

"When you're poor, you have things to reach for. Goals that excite you. Maybe it's a dream house or a vacation or even a meal at a restaurant on a Friday night. But the more money you have, the harder it is to find things to be excited about. You already have your dream house. You can go anywhere in the world anytime you want to. You could hire a private chef to make you every food you ever crave. People who aren't rich think all those things are fulfilling, but they aren't. You can fill your life with nice things, but nice things don't fill the holes in your soul."

"What fills the holes in a soul?"

Samson's eyes scroll over my face for a few seconds. "Pieces of someone else's soul."

He lifts me slightly so that less of my skin is beneath the water. He drags his mouth across my jaw, and when his lips find mine, I'm hungry for them. Starving.

I feel him harden, even though we're in the water. Yet still, all we do is kiss. This kiss lasts for several minutes. It's both not enough and more than enough.

"Beyah," he whispers against my mouth. "I could stay here forever, but we should probably head back before it gets dark."

I nod, but then I kiss him again because I don't really care if it gets dark. Samson laughs, but he quickly shuts up and returns the kiss with even more urgency.

I wish there were more parts of him I could reach. I can't stop running my hands over his chest and his shoulders and his back. They end up in his hair as his mouth makes its way down my chest. I feel his warm breath against my skin, right between my breasts. He lifts a hand to the back of my neck and I feel him touch the knot on my bathing suit top.

Then he looks me in the eyes, silently asking for permission. I nod, and he slowly pulls at the string until it's untied.

The straps to my bathing suit fall down, and Samson leans forward, kissing the top of my breast. He slowly begins to work his mouth down until he takes my nipple in his mouth.

I suck in a shaky breath. The sensation of his tongue against my skin sends chills down my body. I close my eyes and press my cheek against the top of his head, never wanting him to stop.

But he does, thanks to the sound of an engine in the distance.

He immediately pulls away when we both hear it. There's a truck down the beach headed in this direction.

Samson lifts the straps of my bikini and reties them around my neck. I groan, and maybe even pout. We make our way back to the shore, even though the truck turned around and headed back in the other direction before it reached us.

We're both quiet as we pack up our things into the golf cart. The sun is beginning to set on the other side of the peninsula, casting a red and purple glow across the sky. The wind from the ocean has picked up and I look over at Samson for a moment. He's facing the breeze, his eyes closed. There's a calmness about him right now, and that calmness spreads to me.

His moods are contagious. I'm glad he seems to only have one or two. I've never felt as stable as I have since I started spending all my hours with him.

"Have you ever closed your eyes and just listened to the ocean?" he asks. He opens his eyes and turns to face me.

"No."

He faces the water again and closes his eyes. "Try it."

I close my eyes and blow out a breath. Samson's hand finds mine and we just stand there together, in silence, facing the water.

I listen for what he's hearing.

Seagulls.

Waves.

Peace.

Hope.

I don't know how long we stand here because I become consumed by the meditation. I don't know that I've ever stood in one spot with my eyes closed and just let go of my thoughts.

I let them go. All of them.

Eventually, it's like the world grows completely silent.

I'm pulled out of that silence when I feel Samson kiss the back of my head. I open my eyes and inhale a deep breath.

And that's the end of that. Dinner, a make-out session, and a stress reliever. What a date.

"Where's your dog?" he asks as we start to climb into the golf cart.

I look around but don't see Pepper Jack Cheese any-where. I call for him, but he doesn't come running. My heart picks up a little and that doesn't go unnoticed.

Samson calls for him.

I start to get worried because we're a long way from our houses, and if we don't find him, he may not be able to make his way back.

"Maybe he's behind the dunes," Samson suggests. We both make our way over to the high rows of sand. Samson grabs my hands and helps me up the dune. When we reach the top and look on the other side of it, I'm immediately relieved to see P.J.

"Oh, thank God," I say, scaling down the other side of the dune.

"What's he doing?" Samson asks, walking behind me. P.J. is about ten feet away, digging furiously in the ground.

"Maybe he found some crabs."

When we reach him, I freeze. Whatever he found, it's not a crab. It looks like . . . "Samson?" I whisper. "What is that?"

Samson drops to his knees and starts wiping dust off what looks like bones in the shape of a hand.

I pull P.J. away, but he fights to get out of my grip. Sam-son is now digging, moving sand away, revealing more and more of what is obviously a human arm.

"Oh my God," I whisper. I cover my mouth with my hand. P.J. slips out of my grip and gets away from me. He rushes back to Samson's side, but Samson pushes him away. "Sit," he commands the dog.

P.J. sits but whimpers.

I lower myself to my knees next to Samson and watch as he continues to uncover more of the bones.

"Maybe you shouldn't touch it," I suggest.

Samson says nothing. He just keeps digging until he reaches the shoulder joint of the skeleton. There's still a shirt attached to it. It's a red-checkered shirt, faded and torn. Samson touches a piece of it and it falls apart in his hands.

"Do you think it's an entire body?"

Samson still doesn't answer me. He just falls back onto his haunches and stares at the ground.

"I'll go get my phone and call the police." I start to get up, but Samson grabs my wrist. I look at him and his eyes are pleading.

"Don't."

"*What?*" I shake my head. "We have to report this."

"Don't, Beyah," he says again. I've never seen his expression so unyielding. "This is the guy I was telling you about. Rake. I recognize his shirt." He looks back down at what he's just uncovered. "The police will just throw him in an unmarked grave."

"We still have to report this. It's a body. A missing person."

He shakes his head again. "He wasn't a missing person.

Like I told you, no one even noticed he was gone." I can already tell by Samson's demeanor that I'm not changing his mind. "He would want to be in the ocean. It's the only place he belongs."

We're both quiet for a while as we think.

For whatever reason, I don't feel like this is my decision. But I sure as hell don't want to be here a second longer.

Samson stands up and disappears back over the dune. I have no intention of being left alone with human remains, so I follow after him.

Samson walks toward the water, and when he's a few feet away from it, he just stops. He clasps his hands behind his head. I stop walking because it looks like he needs a minute to process this.

He stares at the water for what seems like an eternity. I just pace behind him, torn between doing what I know is right or leaving this decision completely up to Samson. He's the one who knew the guy. I didn't.

After a while, I finally break the silence. "Samson?"

He doesn't face me. His voice is resolute when he says, "I need you to take the golf cart back to the house."

"Without you?"

He nods, still facing the other direction. "I'll meet up with you later tonight."

"I'm not leaving you out here. It's too far to walk in the dark."

He turns now, and when he does, he looks like a completely different person than he did ten minutes ago. His features are hardened, and there's something newly broken inside him.

He walks toward me and takes my face in his hands. His eyes are red, like he's on the verge of breaking down. "*Please*," he says. "Go. I need to do this alone."

There's an ache in his voice. A pain I'm unfamiliar with.

An agony I expected to feel after finding my mother dead, but instead I was left empty and numb.

I have no idea why he needs this, but I can see his need for me to leave this up to him is greater than my need to disagree with him. I just nod, and my voice releases in a whisper when I say, "Okay."

For the first time in my life, I actually feel an overwhelming need to hug someone, but I don't. I don't want our first hug to be attached to such an awkward moment. I climb into the golf cart.

"Take P.J. with you," he says. I wait while he walks back over the dune to get him. When he returns with P.J., he puts him in the passenger seat of the golf cart. Samson grips the top of the golf cart and his tone is flat when he says, "I'll be okay, Beyah. I'll see you later tonight." He pushes away from the golf cart and walks back toward the dune.

I drive home, leaving Samson with something I know he'll never explain to me, and likely won't speak of again.

Eighteen

I'm worried about Samson, obviously. But the longer I sit here and wait for him, I wonder if that worry should be mixed in with anger.

It wasn't fair of him to ask me to leave that situation, but the look in his eyes made it seem like throwing Rake's remains into the ocean was way more important to him than reporting it was to me.

I've seen some disturbing shit in my life. A few bones being moved from a dune and into the ocean is surprisingly not that jarring to me. I don't know what that says about me. Or Samson, for that matter.

Even though I'm not angry at him, I am concerned. My stomach is in knots. It's been almost four hours since I got home. I tried to pass the time by showering, eating dinner, and having mindless conversation with my father and

Alana. But my mind is still back with Samson on the other side of that dune.

I'm sitting out by the bonfire now, staring at Samson's dark house. Waiting.

"Where is Samson?" Sara asks.

Great question. "Helping someone. He'll be back soon." I take a drink of water, washing the lies out of my mouth. Part of me wants to tell Sara the truth, but I know better. How would I even come out and say, *Hey, Sara, there are human remains down the beach and Samson is digging them up and throwing all the bones into the ocean?*

Yeah, she wouldn't be able to handle something of that magnitude.

"You know," Sara says, staring at me with hope in her eyes. "You never gave me details about the kiss. What was it like?"

I get the feeling she'd probably prefer a stepsister who will gossip with her at night while they brush each other's hair. I'm sad she didn't get that. Instead, she got me. No-fun Beyah.

"The kiss was actually kind of depressing."

"What? Why?"

"I'm not saying it was bad. He's a great kisser. He's just . . . he's so serious all the time. So am I. It's difficult to share a fun, sexy kiss when there's nothing fun about either of us." I sigh and rest my head against the chair. "Sometimes I wish I could be more like you."

Sara laughs. "If you were more like me, Samson wouldn't look at you the way he does."

That makes me smile. Maybe she's right. Some people just fit together. I wouldn't fit with Marcos and she wouldn't fit with Samson.

I just wish our fall and winter fit as well as our summer.

Sara holds both hands up in the air when the song on the Bluetooth changes to a new song I've never heard. "I love this song!" She jumps up and starts dancing. Marcos gets up and dances with her. It's not a slow song, so they're stomping and spinning around like their lives weigh nothing.

I watch them dance until the song is over and Sara falls back into her chair, out of breath. She reaches down for a bottle of liquor stuck in the sand. "Here," she says, handing it to me. "Alcohol makes everyone fun."

I bring it to my mouth and pretend to take a drink. I'd rather be boring than become my mother, so I have no desire to actually swallow it. But I pretend to for Sara's sake. I've already been enough of a downer tonight, I don't want to deny the alcohol and make her feel guilty for drinking. I hand the bottle back to her, just as something behind her catches my eye.

Finally. It's been four hours.

Samson will have to walk past us to get to his house. He's covered in sand. He looks tired. He even looks a little bit guilty when we make eye contact. He looks away quickly but then spins as he walks past us. He lifts his eyes again while he walks backward. He nudges his head toward his house and then spins around and disappears into the darkness.

"You're being summoned," Sara says.

I remain seated for a moment, not wanting to appear too eager to follow him. "I'm not a dog."

"Are you two fighting?"

"No."

"Then go. I like it when Marcos summons me. It always means good things." She looks at Marcos and says, "Hey, Marcos. Summon me."

Marcos nods his head once, and Sara jumps out of her chair and walks over to him, falling dramatically into his lap. The chair falls over and spills them out onto the sand. Marcos is still holding his beer up in the air. He didn't even spill a single drop.

I leave them alone and start walking toward Samson's house. I can hear the outdoor shower running when I get close. I walk onto the concrete foundation of the stilt level of his house. I haven't spent any time down here, but it's nice. Aside from the shower, there's a bar and a couple of tables. I don't know why we never spend time here instead of at the beach every night. Samson has the kind of house that would be good for parties, but he doesn't seem like the type who would want to host one.

I don't see Samson's shorts as I approach the shower, which means he's still dressed. There isn't a door to the shower. The walls are made of wood and there's an opening and a left turn I have to make before I see him.

His back is to me. His palms are pressed against the wood and the shower spray is falling over the back of his neck. His head is hanging between his shoulders.

"I'm sorry," he says quietly. He turns and pushes the wet hair off his forehead.

"For what?"

"For putting you in this position. For expecting you to keep secrets when I don't tell you any of mine."

"You never asked me not to tell anyone. You just asked me not to call the police."

He wipes his hand over his face and leans back into the stream of water. "Did you tell anyone?"

"No."

"Are you going to?"

"Not if you don't want me to."

"I'd rather it stay between us," he says.

I silently agree. It's not that hard for me to keep secrets. I'm a pro at it.

I kind of like that Samson is a closed book. You can't really dislike a book you haven't read yet. But I think I'm able to be patient with him because he told me he'd eventually tell me all his truths. Otherwise, I might not find him worth the effort.

"I feel like there's more to the story with Rake," I say. "Will you explain it with all the other answers you owe me on August second?"

He nods. "Yeah. I'll tell you then."

"I'm going to start keeping a list of all the questions I want answers to."

His lip twitches, like I amuse him. "And I'll answer them all on August second."

I take a step toward him. "You promise?"

"I swear."

I lift one of his hands. He's got dirt beneath all his fingernails. "Did you dig up all of it?"

"Yes."

"And you're sure it was Rake?"

"Positive."

He looks and sounds exhausted. Maybe even sad. I really do think Rake was a bigger part of his life than he's letting on. I glance at his necklace, then look back at his face. He's staring down at me, the small streams of water sliding down his face.

My clothes are starting to get wet from the spray, so I take off my shirt and toss it over the wall of the shower. I leave on my shorts and bikini top and help Samson clean his fingernails. He stands patiently as I get all the dirt out from beneath each nail and then wash his hands with soap.

When I'm finished, Samson pulls on my hand and tugs me until I'm standing under the water with him. He kisses me, and I move with him as he backs himself against the wall, pulling me out of the stream of water.

It's a lazy kiss. His hands are resting on my hips while

gainst the wall of the shower and lets me direct
moment.

I lean against him, pressing my breasts against his bare
chest, wrapping my left hand around the back of his neck.
*I shouldn't have told Sara it was a depressing kiss. That's such a
terrible description of what this is.*

Durable is a better word.

All of our kisses feel important, like they'll stay with
me forever. They aren't small displays of affection that happen in passing. There's something bigger behind them than
attraction. Right now that bigger thing is sadness, and I
want to take that away from him, even if it's just for a few
minutes.

I drag my right hand down his chest until my fingers
meet the elastic band of his shorts. I dip my hand inside,
and right when I do, Samson inhales sharply. We stop kissing while I touch him for the first time. His eyes are focused
hard on mine, like he's silently saying I don't have to do this
but also begging me not to stop.

I wrap my hand firmly around him and his head falls
back with a sigh. "Beyah," he whispers.

I kiss his neck and slowly begin to move my hand up
and down the length of him. There's more to him than
there was to Dakota. It doesn't surprise me. There's more
to Samson in almost every aspect compared to anyone else
I know.

I use my left hand to lower his shorts enough so that
he's not confined inside them. We stand in this position

for a couple of minutes, at least. Me touching him. Samson breathing heavier and deeper, gripping my hips tighter with every stroke. I watch his face the whole time, unable to look away. Sometimes he looks at me and other times he squeezes his eyes shut like it's all too much.

When he begins to clench all the muscles in his body, he suddenly brings a hand up to my hair and pulls gently, tilting my head back so that his mouth can fit against mine. He takes two quick steps, pushing me against the opposite shower wall while he kisses me with more strength than every other kiss that came before this one.

My hand is still gripping him, and it's like he can't even breathe and kiss me at the same time because he breaks apart and presses the side of his head to the side of mine. His mouth is over my ear when he breathes out a guttural "*Fuck.*"

Chills roll down my body as he begins to shudder beneath my touch. I continue to stroke him until I feel the sticky warmth of him on the palm of my hand, and he eventually sighs, burying his face against my neck.

He takes a moment to catch his breath, and then he reaches for the showerhead. He pulls it between us, washing himself and my hand, and then he lets it fall to the floor before kissing me again.

He's breathing like he just ran a marathon. At this point, I might be breathing like that, too.

When he finally pulls away and looks down at me, some of the weight has lifted from behind his eyes. That's all I wanted. For him to feel better about whatever happened to him out there tonight.

I kiss him tenderly on the corner of his mouth, preparing to say good night, but he runs his fingers through my wet hair and whispers, "When are you going to let me hold you?"

His eyes are pleading, like he needs a hug more than he needed what I just gave him.

I'd probably let him hug me right now if I wasn't so afraid it would make me cry. It's like he can see the war in my eyes, so he just nods and kisses the side of my head.

"Good night," I whisper.

"Good night, Beyah." He turns off the shower and I grab my shirt, pull it back on, and walk away from his house.

Nineteen

All five of Samson's houses were rented for the July 4 week-end, so he's staying with Marcos.

It's been a week since he found Rake. We haven't talked about it. There's less than a month left until August 2, and I'll get all my answers then. I'm not looking forward to it. August 2 to me just means the eve of the day we'll be saying goodbye to each other.

I'm just trying to focus on today.

And today, the beaches are so crazy, we don't even want to be out there. We're on Marcos's balcony. It's a few rows back from the beach, which is why we're here. There is so much music and noise and more drunk people than you could find in any bar in Texas, so none of us has the urge to hang out closer to those crowds.

We ate dinner with Marcos's family tonight. He's got two little sisters and there was so much activity and conversation and food. Samson looked like he was right at home with Marcos's family, and it made me wonder what he's like when he's around his own family.

Do they have family meals together, like my father and Alana like to do? Would they accept me if they ever met me? Something tells me they wouldn't or he wouldn't be so secretive about them.

I felt accepted tonight, though. Accepted and well fed. My goal to gain weight this summer has been crushed. I'm not sure I can even fit into the one pair of jeans I bought when I got here. I've worn mostly shorts and my bathing suit this whole summer.

The sun just set, but the fireworks started before that. They're picking up now that it's finally dark, and they're coming from all over the peninsula.

"The Galveston fireworks will start in a few minutes," Sara says. "I wish we could see them from here."

"Marjorie's roof would have a good view," Samson says.

"You think she'd let us use it?" I ask.

Samson shrugs. "Depends on if she's awake or not."

Marcos stands up. "No one can sleep through this noise."

We all make our way to Marjorie's, along with P.J., who was waiting beneath Marcos's house.

Marjorie is sitting on her porch when we reach her street, watching all the commotion on the beach. She sees us approaching and says, "I figured you'd be here sooner than this." She waves a hand toward her front door. "Be my guest. Leave Pepperjack Cheese with me, I'll make sure the fireworks don't scare him off."

"Thanks, Marjorie," Samson says.

Once we're inside, he waits for Sara and Marcos to climb the stairs first, then me. When we reach the roof entrance, Sara is on her hands and knees as she crawls out the opening. Marcos tries to help her, but she shakes her head. "It's too high. I can't move."

Samson laughs. "Try to get to the center of the roof. You'll only see the sky instead of the ground."

Sara crawls to the center of the roof. We all follow and I sit down next to her. Samson sits next to me.

"How do you walk around up here?" Sara asks him.

"I don't look down," Samson says.

Sara covers her face for a minute as she tries to lessen the dizziness. "I had no idea I was afraid of heights."

Marcos wraps an arm around her. "Come here, babe." She moves closer to Marcos, and seeing him hold her like that makes me very aware that Samson and I aren't even touching. I glance at him, but he's looking at fireworks that are being shot from somewhere down the beach.

"Is Marjorie lonely?" I ask him.

He looks at me and smiles. "No. She has a son. He's a lawyer in Houston. He comes to visit her a couple times a month."

That makes me feel good.

Samson sees the relief on my face, and then he leans toward me and gives me a quick peck. "You're sweet," he whispers. Then he grabs my hand, threading his fingers through mine, and we watch the fireworks in silence.

The more time that passes, the more there are. We can see them all around us, in the bay, coming from Galveston. Somehow, there are even fireworks being shot from way out in the ocean.

Marcos looks at Sara and says, "This would have been a great marriage-proposal moment with all these free fireworks in the background. Too bad we just met over spring break."

"Bring me back here next year," she says. "I'll pretend I forgot this conversation."

They make me laugh.

After a few more minutes, Sara tells Marcos she needs to get down because she's feeling nauseated. They leave, but Samson and I stay on Marjorie's roof.

I find myself watching him more than I'm watching the fireworks. He looks enamored of everything.

"I've never seen Darya look this beautiful," Samson whispers.

Wait. *What?* Darya is the name of the girl he said broke his heart.

"Look how the fireworks reflect off her," he says, pointing out at the ocean. I look at where he's pointing, then back at him, confused.

"Are you calling the *ocean* Darya?"

"Yeah," he says, matter-of-fact. "Darya means *the sea.* It's what Rake used to call her."

"You told me Darya was the ex-girlfriend who broke your heart."

Samson laughs. "I told you Darya broke my heart, but I never said I was talking about a girl."

I try to think back on that conversation. This whole time, he was talking about the *water*? "How does an ocean break a heart?"

"I'll tell you on—"

"August second," I finish with a roll of my eyes. I adjust myself and reach into my pocket for my phone. "I'm taking notes. You owe me a lot of explanations."

Samson laughs. "Can I see the list?"

I hand him my phone after I add the last one. He starts reading off the list.

"*Why don't you like talking about your father's rental houses? Who was the guy that interrupted our dinner? What's the worst thing you've ever done? Why don't you like talking about your family? What's the whole story behind Rake? How many girls have you had sex with?*" He pauses and looks at me for a beat, then goes back to the list. "*What's your full name? How did the ocean break your heart?*"

He stares at my phone for a moment, then hands it back to me.

"Ten," he says. "But I really only remember nine. My memory of one of the girls is fuzzy."

Ten. That's a lot in comparison to me, but not much compared to what I assumed his past was like. He could have said fifty, and I don't know that I would have been surprised. "Ten isn't very many."

"Compared to your one it is," he says teasingly.

"I just thought there were more. The way Sara talked about you, it seemed like you slept with a different girl every week."

"I rarely slept with them. I have no idea how many I've made out with, though. Please don't ask me that question on August second, because I won't be able to answer it."

A huge blast of fireworks begins shooting off straight in front of us. Samson's attention gets pulled away from me, but I continue to stare at him.

"Sometimes I wonder if I even want all the answers to my questions. I think the mystery that surrounds you might be one of my favorite things about you. While simultaneously being one of my *least* favorite things about you."

Samson doesn't look at me when he says, "You want to know what my favorite thing about you is?"

"What?"

"You're the only person I've ever met who would probably like me more if I were poor."

That's the honest truth. "You're right. Your money is definitely my least favorite thing about you."

Samson presses a kiss to my shoulder. Then he looks back out over the water. "I'm glad you showed up this summer, Beyah."

"Me too," I whisper.

Twenty

I don't like birth control. I've been on it almost a week now and I feel like it's messing with my emotions. I'm starting to feel things even more than I did after showing up here. There are moments I severely miss my mother. Moments I convince myself I'm falling in love with Samson. Moments I feel excited to have a conversation with my father.

I don't know who I'm becoming, but I'm not sure I like it. I doubt it really has anything to do with the birth control, but it feels good to have something to blame.

Samson has been gone most of the day. Sara and I spent time without him and Marcos on the beach. It's past time for dinner and we're hungry, so we start packing up just as three guys begin to set up a volleyball net on the beach between our house and Samson's. When Sara and I drop our chairs in the storage compartment on the stilt level, I look back at them.

There's a weird pinch in my chest, like volleyball is something I miss.

I never thought that would happen.

"I'm going to ask if I can play with them," I say. "You want to play?"

Sara shakes her head. "I want to shower. I have sand in my crack." She heads for the stairs. "Have fun, though. Kick some ass."

When I reach the guys, they're just about to start a game of one-on-one.

One of them is sitting on the invisible sideline while the other two are in position to start their game. "Hey," I say, interrupting them. All three of them turn and look at me. Now that I'm closer, I'm a little bit intimidated. I might make a fool of myself now that I've seen the size of these guys. "Need one more?"

The three of them look at one another. There's a smirk on the tallest one's face when he says, "You sure about that?"

The smirk annoys me. "Yeah. I'll even make it fair and team up with the worst one out of the three of you."

They laugh. Then two of them point to the guy still sitting down. "He's the worst out of the three of us."

The guy in the sand concurs. "It's true. I suck."

"Great. Let's play." P.J. is standing next to me, so I walk him over to a spot where he'll be out of the way and tell him to sit.

The guys introduce themselves to me before we start.

The one on my team is named Joe. The tallest one is Topher and the other one is Walker. Walker serves the ball right to me and I easily bump it over the net.

Walker sets the ball for Topher and he attempts to spike it right at me. Before he knows it, I'm up at the net successfully blocking it.

"Impressive," Topher mutters after I get my first point.

I get three hits in before Joe even touches the volleyball.

I haven't worked out in a while, so I notice myself getting winded quicker than I normally would. I'll blame that on the birth control, too. And the sand. I've never played on sand before.

They score two more points before Joe and I finally side-out. I'm about to serve the ball when I see Samson standing on his balcony.

He's staring down at me, watching us. I wave, but he doesn't wave back.

Is he jealous?

He pushes off the balcony and walks back inside his house.

What the hell?

It actually pisses me off. Samson knows I play volleyball. I should be able to play an innocent game without him assuming I'm flirting with any of these three guys.

My anger fuels my serve and I hit the ball harder than I mean to. Luckily, it's in, landing right on the line.

This is what I was worried about. The more time I spend with Samson, pieces of him might come to light that

I don't necessarily like. Jealousy is definitely something I don't like.

We finish a short rally before I steal a glance at his balcony. He still hasn't come back out.

I put all my anger and energy into the game. I lunge for the volleyball and fall to my knees. I fall three more times before Joe even touches the ball again. I'm going to be the color of an eggplant by the end of this game.

We score a point on them and tie it up four to four. Joe walks over and high-fives me. "This might be the first game I ever win," he says.

I laugh in response, but my smile fades when I see Samson walking down his stairs. If he comes over here and makes a scene, I'm going to be so angry.

He is. He's coming this way.

And he's carrying a . . . *chair.*

"Heads up," Joe yells. I look up and see the ball flying at me, just barely out of reach. I go for the dig and receive a mouthful of sand when I hit the ground, unintentionally shanking the ball.

"Get up, Beyah!" I hear Samson yell.

I jump to my feet and look in his direction. He's walking over to us, holding his chair. He drops it in the sand next to P.J. about five feet from the net and takes a seat in it, sliding his sunglasses from his eyes to his head. Then he cups his hands around his mouth. "Go, Beyah!" he yells.

What is he doing?

The ball goes to Joe this time and he finally sets the ball

perfectly at the net for me. Little do they know, I was the best outside hitter on my team.

I spike it directly between Topher and Walker. When it hits the sand and we get a point, Samson jumps out of the chair.

"Yes!" he yells. "More of that, Beyah!"

My mouth falls open when it hits me. Samson remembered what I told him—that no one has ever come to any of my games.

He came out here to cheer for me.

"Who the hell is that dude?" Joe says, staring at Samson.

Samson climbs up into the chair and starts chanting. "Beyah! Beyah!"

It might possibly be the cheesiest thing I've ever seen. One guy, alone in an invisible audience, yelling at the top of his lungs for a girl he knows has never been yelled for.

It's the most touching thing anyone has ever done for me.

Topher serves the ball and I'm shocked I'm able to hit it back through the cloud of tears in my eyes.

Fucking emotions. I'm blaming this moment on the birth control, too.

For a long stretch of time, Samson doesn't shut up. I think he's annoying the three guys I'm playing with, but I'm not sure I've ever smiled this much in my life. I smile through all the falls and all the points and all the times I get the breath knocked out of me. I smile because I've never enjoyed a game of volleyball this much. I smile, because Samson has made me realize just how much I miss it. I'm buying a volleyball today. I need to start practicing again.

Not that I'm as terrible as Joe. He's doing his best, but I'm single-handedly keeping us in this game. At one point, he's so out of breath, he just steps aside and leaves me to do all the work for a good thirty seconds.

I'm somehow miraculously one point ahead when the game almost reaches the final point. If I can get one more, I win.

I notice Samson is quiet as I lift the ball to serve it. He's staring intently at me, like he's really into this. All he does is give me the smallest of smiles and a cheesy thumbs-up and I suck in a breath, serve the ball, and pray it hits the sand on the other side of the net.

It's short. Both Topher and Walker dive for it, but I know neither will be able to reach it. *ACE!* When the ball falls to the sand with a thud, Samson jumps out of his chair. "You did it!"

I stand here in shock.

I did it. I would say *we did it*, but Joe really wasn't a lot of help. I high-five him and then receive the handshakes the other two offer me.

"You're really good," Topher says. "Want to go another round?"

I glance over at Samson and shake my head. I work to catch my breath and say, "Not tonight. But I'm around if you guys come back tomorrow."

I wave goodbye to them and then run over to Samson. He meets me with the biggest smile on his face. I throw my arms around his neck and he picks me up and swings me around. When my feet are back on the sand, he doesn't release his hold on me.

"You're a fucking legend," he says. He wipes dirt from my face. "A filthy legend."

I laugh and Samson pulls me to him. He presses his cheek to the top of my head and squeezes me.

I realize at the same time he does what's happening between us. I can feel his whole body take a pause, like he's not sure if he should release me or hold me tighter.

My face is pressed against his shirt.

I pull my arms from around Samson's neck and slip them around his waist. I close my eyes, absorbed in the closeness of him.

I feel his own grip tighten around me, and he lets out a sigh as he runs a hand down my back. He adjusts himself just a little so that I somehow fit against him even better.

And then we just stand this way while the world moves around us. Him holding me. Me allowing it.

Me *wanting* it.

I had no idea how good it would feel. Any of this. All the moments I spend with him are charged and exciting and I feel them right in the center of my chest. It's like he wakes up a part of me that's been asleep for nineteen years. I appreciate so many things I didn't think I would ever be able to appreciate.

I like being kissed by someone who actually respects me. I love that he's so proud of me, he picked me up and swung me around. He went out of his way to scream like an idiot on the sidelines of a silly beach volleyball game just to make me feel good.

At some point during this hug, I started crying. It's not a noticeable cry, but I can feel the wetness sliding down my cheeks.

I honestly don't feel like we're close enough, even though we can't possibly get any closer. I want to melt into him. Become a piece of him. I want to see if I make the inside of his chest feel as alive as he makes mine.

It's as if he can tell I don't want him to let go. He lifts me until my legs go around his waist, and then he walks me straight to his house, away from the beach, away from the guys.

When we reach his stilt level, he lowers me to my feet. I reluctantly pull back to look up at him, but with the sun setting and being under the first floor of his house, I can't see him as well as I wish I could. There's very little light left, which is casting a shadow over his eyes. He takes both of his thumbs and brings them to my cheeks, wiping them dry. Then he kisses me.

We taste like a mixture of tears and grains of sand.

I pull away. "I need to rinse off. I have sand everywhere."

"Use the outdoor shower," he says, motioning toward it.

I don't let go of his hand as we walk toward the shower.

My whole body is sore and I'm still a little out of breath. Samson takes off his shirt and drops it to the ground before walking into the shower. He turns on the water and steps out of the way so that I can stand beneath the stream. I open my mouth to rinse some of the sand out of it. Then I drink some of it.

I take the showerhead off the holder and wash the sand from myself. Samson leans against the wall and watches me the whole time.

I like how he watches me. Even though it's dark, especially in this shower, he looks like he's soaking up every inch of me.

When I'm finished rinsing off, I replace the showerhead. Out of the corner of my eye I see Samson move. Then I feel him behind me. He snakes an arm around me, pressing his palm flat against my stomach.

I lean my head back against his shoulder and tilt my face toward him. Samson brings his mouth down on mine.

We remain in this position while we kiss—my back against his chest, him wrapped around me from behind. His hand slides up my stomach and disappears beneath my bikini top.

He cups my breast, and I suck in more of his air in a gasp. Then his other hand begins trailing down my stomach. When he reaches the edge of my bikini, he dips his thumb inside, pulling away from my mouth. He looks in my eyes and gets his answer.

I do not want him to stop.

My lips are parted as I anticipate whatever it is he's about to do.

He watches my face as his hand disappears between my legs. I arch my back and moan, and that move puts even more pressure behind his touch.

I've imagined what this would feel like since the night he first kissed me. His actual touch puts my imagination to shame.

It doesn't take long for my entire body to react. It's embarrassingly quick before I'm trembling beneath his fingers. I reach for his legs behind me and grip his thighs. He falls against the wall, pulling me with him, never stopping the rhythm of his hand. Luckily, when it gets to be too much, he covers my mouth with his and muffles all my noises.

When it's over, he's still kissing me. He pulls his hand from between my legs and spins me until I'm against his chest.

I'm completely out of breath as I fall against him, my arms limp and my legs sore. I sigh heavily.

"I want to get a tattoo," Samson says.

I laugh against his chest. "*That's* what you're thinking about right now?"

"That was my second thought," he says. "I didn't say the first one out loud."

"What was the first one?" I look up at him.

"I think it's obvious."

I shake my head. "It's not. I'm afraid you're going to have to say it out loud."

He dips his head and brings his lips to my ear. "I can't fucking wait for our first time," he whispers. Then he turns off the water and walks out of the shower like that thought was never whispered aloud. "You want one?" he asks.

I'm kind of in shock, I think, so I take a few seconds to respond to him. "Want what?"

"A tattoo."

I never thought I'd want one until this moment. "Yeah. I think I do."

Samson peeks his head back into the shower and smiles. "Look at us, deciding to get spontaneous tattoos. We are definitely fun people, Beyah."

Twenty-One

"I have an idea," Marcos says with a mouthful of food. "My friend Jackson."

Tonight is baptismal dinner night. Breakfast again. We haven't been talking about anything specific, so none of us knows what Marcos is referring to. He's met with blank stares, so he points across the table toward Samson. "Jackson has dark blond hair. Blue eyes. Your face structures are different, but it's a tattoo shop, I doubt they really look at your ID too hard."

Oh. That. Samson can't find his wallet and it's been three days since he suggested getting a tattoo.

You can't get a tattoo without identification, and even though he's torn his house upside down for the better part of three days looking for it, he hasn't had any luck. He thinks the last renters might have found it and taken it. He said it's always in his backpack, but we both looked in the backpack and it wasn't there. Everything else he owns was, though. I don't know how he carries it around so casually; the thing weighs fifty pounds.

Samson chews on Marcos's suggestion, then shrugs. "Worth a shot."

"Tattoo shop?" my father asks. "Who's getting tattoos?"

Sara immediately points at me and Samson. "Those two. Not me."

"Thank God," Alana mutters.

Not that I'm much more than her husband's daughter, but that comment stings. It doesn't bother her if I get one, but she's obviously relieved her daughter isn't getting one.

My father looks at me and says, "What are you getting?"

I point to the inside of my wrist. "Something right here. I don't know what yet."

"And when are you going?"

"Tonight," Marcos says, holding up his phone. "Jackson just said we could swing by and borrow his driver's license."

"Nice," Samson says.

"Do you know what you're getting, Samson?"

"Not yet," he says, shoveling a forkful of eggs into his mouth.

My father shakes his head. "Both of you are getting something inked onto your bodies for the rest of your lives in a matter of hours, and neither of you knows what you're getting?"

"We have to take the ferry to get there," Samson says.

"That's plenty of time to think about it." Samson scoots his chair back and stands up. He's got a slice of bacon in his hand as he walks his plate to the kitchen. "We should probably get going. Ferry line might be long with it being the end of the weekend."

"Beyah," my father says, his voice pleading. "Maybe you should think about this for a few weeks."

What a parental thing to say. I think I like it. "Trust me, Dad. I'll have much bigger regrets in life than a tattoo."

His expression falters when I say that. I meant it as a joke, but he looks genuinely concerned about my decision-making abilities now.

The tattoo shop is empty, and I think that worked to our advantage. When the guy took Samson's fake driver's license, he looked at Samson, then back at the driver's license. He shook his head but said nothing. He just disappeared behind a door to make copies of our paperwork.

When Marcos returned to the car earlier with Jackson's driver's license, I couldn't stop laughing. He's a good fifty pounds lighter than Samson and at least five inches shorter. Marcos told Samson if the tattoo shop doesn't believe it's him, he should just say he's been lifting.

They didn't even question it. I'd be offended if I were Samson.

"They must be desperate for business," I whisper. "He didn't even question you."

Samson slides a photo album full of ideas for tattoos in front of me. He grabs one for himself and we start flipping through the pages.

"I want something delicate," I say, scrolling through pictures of hearts and flowers, but nothing tugs at me.

"I want the opposite of delicate," Samson says.

What is the opposite of delicate? I flip toward the back of the book and come across tattoos that seem like they would be more up Samson's alley than mine, but none of them seem like something he would like. When I get to the last page, I close the book and try to focus.

Delicate to me means dainty, soft, fragile. So, the opposite would be what? Strength? Durability? Maybe even threatening?

I know immediately after that thought what he should get. I open my phone and search for pictures of hurricanes. I scroll through several before I find one I think he would love.

"I found one I think you should get."

Samson doesn't even look up from his book when he says, "Okay." He continues scrolling while he flips his left arm over and says, "I want it right here." He points at a spot on the upper inside of his forearm. "Go show it to the guy so he can start getting it ready."

"You don't want to see it first?"

Samson's eyes slide over to mine. "Do you think I'll love it?"

I nod. "I do."

"Then it's the tattoo I want." He's so matter-of-fact about it, like there's no question at all that this tattoo is more about me than anything else. I can't help but kiss him.

There are two tattoo artists working tonight, and even though we're both getting a tattoo, I still haven't found what I want. Samson is in the chair, the tattoo gun pressed to his arm. His head is tilted away from it so that he doesn't see it before it's finished.

He's scrolling through his phone, trying to help me find something.

"What about a sunrise?" he asks.

That's not a bad idea, so I look through a few. I ultimately decide against it. "That seems like it would take a lot of ink and would look better if it were bigger. I want to start small."

I've flipped through every book they have. I'm starting to think my father was right. Maybe I have to give this more thought.

"I have an idea," Samson says. "We should look up meanings and see what kind of symbols they correlate to."

"Okay."

"What do you want it to symbolize?" he asks.

"Maybe something that means luck. I could use some better luck in my life."

He starts scrolling through his phone while I go to check the progress of his tattoo. Even though I chose a hurricane for him, it's not with typical black ink. I chose a tattoo that resembles what it would look like on a radar screen, with reds, yellows, blues, and greens. It's not necessarily a watercolor tattoo, but the colors all swirled together against faded black edges sort of make it look that way.

It's turning out even better than I hoped.

"Found yours," Samson says. He goes to hand me his phone so I can see what he picked out for me, but I don't take it.

"I trust you," I say. It's only fair.

"You shouldn't."

His expression after he says that sends a swirl of unease through me. He's right. I shouldn't trust someone I hardly know anything about. I was just agreeing to let him do what I'm doing—choosing his tattoo blindly. But I feel like between the two of us, I'm oddly the more trustworthy one. I grab his phone to look at it. "What is it?"

"A pinwheel."

I look at the photo. It's delicate. Colorful. And he doesn't even know I've chosen a hurricane for him, so we would both have tattoos that resemble a pattern of rotation. "It says pinwheels are supposed to turn around bad luck."

"It's perfect," I whisper.

Sara and Marcos have been outside since we filled out the paperwork for the tattoos, which was a good two and a half hours ago, but they haven't come inside to complain about the wait. I'm sure they've found something to keep themselves occupied.

My tattoo is finished. It's perfect. The tattoo artist lined the outside with a thin line of black ink and then filled it with color, but the colors bleed outside of the lines like dripping paint. I got it on my left wrist. I showed Samson and then took a picture before I let the guy cover it up with a bandage.

Samson's tattoo artist wipes his down one final time. Samson hasn't peeked once. "All done," the guy says.

Samson sits up in the chair without looking down at the tattoo. He stands up and walks to the bathroom, then summons me to follow him with a nod.

He wants to look at it with no one else around. I don't blame him. He might hate it and that wouldn't just make me feel bad, it would make the tattoo artist feel bad.

I walk into the bathroom with him and close the door behind me. It's a small bathroom, so we're standing really close together. "Are you nervous?"

He says, "I wasn't. But now that it's done, I am."

I smile, and then I start anxiously bouncing on my toes. "Look at it, I'm dying."

Samson looks down at his tattoo for the first time. It's about the size of a fist, right beneath the inside crease of his elbow. I'm staring at his face, waiting for his reaction.

He has no reaction.

He just stares at it.

"It's Hurricane Ike," I explain, running my finger across it. "I used a radar photo of when it was right over Bolivar Peninsula and had him turn it into a tattoo."

The only thing I get from Samson is a sigh. And I can't even tell if it's a good sigh.

I feel anxious now. I was so convinced he would like it; I didn't think about what it might mean if he didn't.

Samson slowly lifts his eyes. There's no give in his expression that would hint at what he's thinking.

But then he grabs my face and kisses me so sudden and so hard, I fall against the bathroom door. *I think this means he likes it.* He lowers his hands to my thighs and slides me up the door until I'm wrapped around him, like he's trying to tie us in a permanent knot.

He's kissing me with a freshly dug-up feeling he's never kissed me with before. I'm not sure any other response to seeing his tattoo would have been an appropriate one now that I've been met with *this* response.

He moves against me in a way that makes me moan, but as soon as I do, he pulls his mouth from mine like that moan was a big red stop sign. He drops his forehead to mine and his words are full of emotion when he says, "I'd take you right here if you didn't deserve better."

I'd let him.

Twenty-Two

"No." My father's response is absolute.

"Please? I'm nineteen."

"She's on the pill," Alana says.

I set my fork down and press a hand to my forehead. I don't know why I even asked him if I could stay the night with Samson. I should have just snuck out and come home before he woke up. But I'm trying not to break any of his rules.

Sara finished eating before this discussion started, but she looks like she's enjoying it. She's seated at the table with her knee pulled up to her chest, watching this conversation like we're playing it out on a television. All she needs is a bag of popcorn.

"Does your mother let you spend the night with guys?" my father asks.

I laugh half-heartedly at that. "My mother didn't care

where I spent the night. I *want* you to care. I would just also appreciate it if you trusted me."

My father runs a hand down his face like he doesn't know what to do. He looks to Alana for answers. "Would you allow Sara to spend the night with Marcos?"

"Sara and Marcos spend the night together all the time," Alana says.

I glance at Sara just as she perks up in her chair. "We do not."

Alana rolls her head. "I'm not ignorant, Sara."

There's a look of complete surprise on Sara's face. "Oh. I thought you were."

I laugh at that, but no one else does.

With that news, my father somehow seems even more torn.

"Listen, Dad," I say as gently as possible, "I wasn't really asking you for permission. I was more or less telling you I'm staying at Samson's house tonight as a courtesy because this is your house and I'm trying to be respectful. But it would make this a lot easier if you would just say okay."

My father groans, falling back into his chair. "I'm so glad I punched that damn kid when I had the chance," he mutters. Then he waves toward the front door. "Fine. Whatever. Just be home before I wake up so I can pretend tonight never happened."

"*Thank* you," I say, pushing back from the table. Sara immediately follows me out of the kitchen and up the stairs. When we get to my room, she falls onto the bed.

"I can't believe my mother knows Marcos sleeps over sometimes. I thought we were really sneaky about it."

"You might be sneaky, but you certainly aren't quiet."

She laughs. "I can't let Marcos find out she knows. He likes the forbidden aspect of it all."

I text Samson to let him know I'm definitely staying over, and then I open my closet door and stare into it. "What the hell do I wear?"

"I don't think it matters. The goal is to end up in nothing by the end of the night, right?"

I can feel my skin begin to tingle with nervousness. I've had sex plenty of times, but never in a bed. Never fully naked. And definitely never with someone I care about.

Samson texts me back a fireworks emoji. I roll my eyes and slip my phone back into my pocket.

"Have you guys not had sex yet?" Sara asks.

I decide not to change clothes. I just throw a fresh T-shirt and a clean pair of underwear into my backpack. "Not yet."

"Why not?"

"There hasn't been a lot of opportunity for that," I say. "We're always with you and Marcos. And when we're alone, we just . . . we've done other things. Just not *that*."

"Marcos and I have sex all the time. We even had sex while y'all were getting tattoos."

I look at her and wince. "In the back seat?"

"Yep. Twice."

Gross. Samson and I had to ride home in that back seat.

"Are you going to give me all the details tomorrow? Or am I just getting another lame high five?"

Sara's been patient with me considering how little I share about certain aspects of my life, and how blunt I am in other areas. "I'll tell you everything," I say, right before walking out of my bedroom. "Promise."

"I want every detail! Take notes if you have to!" Luckily, my father and Alana are no longer in the kitchen, so I slip out of the house without having to continue to discuss the fact that I'm having sex with my neighbor tonight. I am definitely not used to having a family who discusses every single thing out in the open like they do.

Samson is waiting at the bottom of the stairs.

"Desperate much?" I tease.

He kisses me and takes my backpack. "Eager."

We begin walking toward Samson's house. P.J. is following us, but Samson doesn't have a dog bed for him. "P.J., go home." I point to the stairs. P.J. pauses for a moment. I repeat myself, and then he finally turns and goes back up our stairs.

Samson slips his hand through mine and holds it until we're in his house. He locks the front door behind him, sets the code on the alarm, and then kicks off his shoes.

I look around, wondering where this is going to happen. *How* it's going to happen. It feels a little weird knowing what's coming. I prefer spontaneity over plans when it comes to sex. Dakota treated me like I was on a strict rotating schedule.

"You thirsty?" Samson asks.

I shake my head. "I'm fine."

He tosses my backpack against the wall next to his backpack. He grabs my hand and twists my wrist so that he can see my tattoo. It's been a week since we got them and both of ours healed well. It kind of makes me want another one, but I feel like I need to wait until I have a reason. Getting one with Samson felt important. I'll wait for another important life moment before getting a second one.

"It turned out really good," he says, running his finger over it.

"You never actually said if you liked yours."

"I told you I loved it the night I got it. I just didn't say it with words." He slides his fingers through mine and leads me up a set of stairs. When he opens the door to his room, he lets me walk in first.

The balcony doors are open and there's a breeze blowing the sheer curtains into the room. The bed is perfectly made, and I still can't get over how clean he keeps everything. Samson flips on a lamp by the bed.

"It's pretty," I say, walking toward the balcony. I step outside and glance over at my bedroom. I accidentally left the light on, so I have a clear view of my bed. "You can see straight into my room."

Samson is next to me now. "Yeah, I know. You don't leave that light on nearly enough."

I look at him and he's grinning. I shove him playfully

in the shoulder and walk back into the bedroom. I make my way over to the bed and sit on the edge of the mattress.

I remove my shoes and then lie down on his bed and watch him. He walks slowly around the bed, staring at me from every angle.

"I feel like I'm being circled like I'm prey," I say.

"Well, I don't want to be the shark in this scenario." Samson plops down next to me on the bed, holding his head up with his hand. "There. Now I'm plankton."

"Better," I say, smiling.

He brushes a strand of hair over my ear with a thoughtful expression on his face. "Are you nervous?"

"No. I feel comfortable with you."

That sentence causes concern to briefly fall over his features—almost as if he finds it uncomfortable that I feel comfortable with him. But the look disappears as soon as it appeared.

"I saw that thought," I say quietly.

"What thought?"

"The negative thought you just had." I bring a finger to the spot between his eyebrows. "It was right here."

He's quiet as he digests my words. "For someone who doesn't know a lot about me, you sure know a lot about me."

"All the stuff you've kept secret from me isn't really stuff that counts."

"How do you know if you don't know what secrets I'm keeping from you?" he asks.

"I don't have to know anything about your past to know you're a good person. I can tell by your actions. I can tell by the way you treat me. Why would it matter what kind of family you have, or how rich you are, or what the people in your past meant to you before I showed up?" That negative thought is back, so I take my finger and smooth out the wrinkles in his forehead. "Stop," I whisper. "You're too hard on yourself."

Samson falls onto his back and brings his hands to his chest. He stares at the ceiling for a moment, so I scoot closer to him and lift my head up, resting it on my hand. I touch his necklace, then walk my fingers up his neck and begin tracing his lips.

He tilts his face toward mine. "Maybe we shouldn't do this?"

His words are more of a question, so I immediately shake my head. "I want to."

"It's not fair to you."

"Why? Because I don't know everything about you?"

He nods. "I'm worried you wouldn't be saying yes right now if you knew the whole truth about me."

I press my lips to his, but only briefly. "You're being dramatic."

"I'm actually not," he says. "I've just lived a dramatic life and you might not like it."

"Same thing. We're both dramatic because we have dramatic parents and dramatic pasts. We could be having dramatic sex right now if you'd stop feeling so guilty."

He smiles. I sit up and take off my shirt. The worry in his eyes disappears as he slides me onto him so that I'm straddling him. He already feels ready, but he brings a hand up and traces a finger slowly over the lace edges of my bra like he's in no hurry at all.

"I've only ever had sex in Dakota's truck," I say. "This will be my first time in a bed."

Samson drags his finger down my stomach, stopping at the button on my shorts. "This will be my first time with a girl I have feelings for."

I try to stay as stoic as him when he makes that declaration, but his words move through me so hard, I frown.

He brings his hand up to my mouth, sliding his fingers across it. "Why did that make you sad?"

I debate shaking my head to avoid answering that question, but if there's one thing I've learned this summer, it's that secrets aren't really as valuable as I used to think they were. I go with honesty. "When you say things like that, it makes me dread when we have to say goodbye. I wasn't expecting to end the summer with a broken heart."

Samson tilts his head, looking at me with complete candor. "Don't worry. Hearts don't have bones. They can't actually break."

Samson rolls me onto my back and takes off his shirt, and that's enough to appease me for about two seconds, but then my thoughts are right back to where they were before he got half naked.

He lowers himself on top of me, but before we kiss

again, I say, "If there's nothing inside a heart that can break, why does it feel like mine is going to snap in half when I move? Does your heart not feel like that?"

Samson's eyes scroll over my face for a moment. "Yeah," he whispers. "It does. Maybe we both grew heart bones."

As soon as he says that, I grip the back of his neck and pull him to my mouth. I want to catch as many of those words as possible and trap them inside me. His sentence lingers in pieces, like his words are floating around us, between us, and absorbing into me as we kiss.

He might be right. Maybe we did grow heart bones. But what if the only way of knowing you grew a heart bone is by feeling the agony caused by the break?

I try not to think about our impending goodbye, but it's hard to experience something that feels this perfect without being acutely aware it's about to be taken away.

Samson sits up on his knees. He fingers the button on my shorts until it pops open. He keeps his eyes on mine as he pulls down the zipper and begins to slide my shorts off me. I lift my hips and then my legs to help him get rid of them. He throws them aside and then takes a moment to soak up the sight of me. I like seeing myself through his expressions. He makes me feel prettier than I probably am. He pulls the covers over us and lies down next to me while he removes his own shorts. It's not uncomfortable in any way, so I have absolutely no hesitation when I remove my bra and panties. There's a level of ease with him, like we've done this with each other a dozen times, but I'm filled with the anticipation of someone who has never experienced this at all.

When we're completely naked under the covers, we face each other, both of us on our sides. Samson brings a hand to my cheek and rests it there softly. "You still seem sad."

"I am."

He runs his hand down my neck and over my shoulder. His eyes follow his hand, so he isn't looking directly at me when he says, "Me too."

"Then why do we have to say goodbye? I can go to college and you can go to the Air Force Academy, but we can stay in touch and visit each other and—"

"We *can't*, Beyah." His eyes are back on mine when he says that, but then they flicker away and fixate on something else. "I'm not going to the air force. I was never going to the air force."

His words and the expression on his face make my heart feel like it's already starting to fracture. I want to ask him what he means but I'm too scared to know the truth, so the question never forms.

Samson sighs heavily and leans toward me. His grip on my arm tightens as he presses his lips to my shoulder. I squeeze my eyes shut when I feel his breath against my skin. I want so much from him right now. I want his honesty, but I also want his silence and his touch and his kiss. Something tells me I can't have all of it. It's either this moment or the truth.

He tucks his face in the crook of my neck. "Please don't

what I mean by that, because if you do, I'll be honest with you. I can't lie to you anymore. But I want this night with you more than I've ever wanted anything in my life."

His words roll over me like a wave, crashing against me with so much force, I wince. I run my hand through his hair and tilt my face until we're looking at each other. "I know we agreed to talk about it all on August second, but if I give you tonight, will you be honest with me when we wake up tomorrow? I don't want to wait until August anymore."

Samson nods. He doesn't even say yes out loud, but I believe him.

I believe him because he looks like he's scared he might lose me. And he might. But he has me tonight and that's all I really care about.

I kiss him to let him know the truth can wait until tomorrow. Right now, I just want to feel what I've always deserved to feel during sex—like my body is respected and my touch has more than just a monetary value.

Samson pulls away long enough to grab a condom out of the bedside table drawer. He puts it on beneath the covers and then rolls back on top of me. He's patient as he kisses me, waiting for just the right moment to push himself inside me.

When it finally happens, he's staring down at me, watching the expression on my face. I gasp, holding in all my breaths until we're as connected as we can possibly be. He sighs shakily. Then, as he begins to pull out of me as slowly as he entered me, he rests his mouth against mine.

I moan when he pushes into me again, amazed at how new Samson makes this feel for me. There isn't even a piece of me that doesn't want to be here right now, and that makes all the difference in the world.

Samson rests his head against mine. "Does this feel okay?"

I shake my head. "It's so much better than okay."

I feel his laugh against my neck. "I agree." His voice sounds strained, like he might be holding back because he's scared I'll break.

I press my mouth to his ear, dragging my fingers through his hair. "You don't have to be careful with me." I wrap my legs around him and kiss his neck until his skin breaks out in chills against my tongue.

My words make him groan, and then it's like he suddenly comes to life. His mouth finds mine and he kisses me like he's hungry and touches me like his hands are starving.

It somehow gets better with every passing minute. We find a rhythm with our bodies, a tempo with our kiss, and a cadence in our collective moans. It becomes everything I've never experienced during sex.

It becomes love.

Whatever tomorrow brings with his truth, I already know it won't change what I feel for him, even though he's convinced it will. I'm not sure he knows how much he means to me. Knowing I'm finally going to learn the full truth about him doesn't feel threatening.

Samson makes me wonder if there's a difference between

a liar and a person who tells lies to protect someone from the truth.

Samson doesn't feel like a liar to me. He feels protective, not dishonest.

And in this moment, Samson is being more honest than he's ever been, and he's not uttering a single word.

I've never felt more appreciated than I feel right now. Not only appreciated, but savored. Respected. Wanted.

Maybe even loved.

Twenty-Three

"I'm so sorry."

Samson's words feel like concrete moving through me. I haven't even opened my eyes yet, but his voice sounds more regretful than any sound I've ever heard.

Is it a dream?

A nightmare?

I reach toward his pillow and open my eyes, but find nothing. I fell asleep wrapped around him, but now he's gone and my arms are empty. When I roll over and look toward his bedroom door, I see him. His hands are behind his back. There's a police officer gripping his arm, shoving him out of the bedroom.

I sit up immediately. "Samson?"

It isn't until I say his name that I see another officer on the other side of the bed, her hand on her hip, touching her gun. I pull the covers up over my chest. She can see the fear in my eyes, so she raises a hand. "You can get dressed, but move slowly."

My pulse is racing as I try to make sense of what's happening. The officer reaches to the floor and tosses me my shirt. My hands are shaking as I try to put it on under the covers. "What's going on?"

"I need you to come downstairs with me," the officer says.

Oh my God, what is happening? How can the night go from us making love to Samson being handcuffed? This has to be some kind of mistake. Or a cruel joke. It can't be real.

"We didn't do anything wrong." I get out of the bed and look for my shorts. I can't even remember where they are, but I don't have time to look for them. I need to stop them from taking Samson.

I rush to the door and the officer says, "Stop!"

I pause and look back at her.

"You need to finish getting dressed. There are other people downstairs."

Other people?

Maybe there was a break-in. Maybe they're confusing Samson for someone else. Or maybe someone found out what he did with Rake's remains.

Is that what this is about?

That thought makes me panic, because I was there. I saw what he did and I failed to report it, which makes me just as guilty as Samson.

The officer exits the bedroom while I'm pulling on my shorts. She waits and then walks behind me while I head for the stairs. When I emerge into the living room, there are two more police officers standing in Samson's living room.

"What is happening?" I whisper to myself. I look outside and the sun hasn't even risen yet, which means it's still the middle of the night. Samson and I fell asleep after midnight.

I glance at the clock on the wall. It reads two thirty in the morning.

"Have a seat," the female officer says.

"Am I being arrested?"

"No. We just have some questions."

I'm scared now. I don't know where they took Samson. "I want my father. We live in the house next door. Can someone please tell him what's going on?"

She nods at one of the officers and he exits the house.

"Where is Samson?" I ask.

"Is that the name he gave you?" The officer pulls out a notepad and writes something down.

"Yes. Shawn Samson. This is his house and you just took him out of his own bed in the middle of the night."

The front door opens and a different officer walks in, followed by a man holding a child. The man is followed by a woman. It must be his wife, because she clings to him as soon as they get inside.

Why are there so many people here?

The woman looks familiar, but I can't place her. She looks like she's been crying. The man is eyeing me suspiciously as he hands his child over to his wife.

"How long have you been staying here?" the officer asks.

I shake my head. "I don't. I live next door."

"How are you and the young man acquainted?"

I feel dizzy and scared, and I wish my father would hurry up. I don't like these questions. I want to know where Samson is. Do I need a lawyer? Does Samson?

"How did you get in?" This question comes from the man who was holding the child.

"Get in?"

"Our *house*," he says.

His house?

I look at his wife. I look at the child. I immediately look at the picture frame by the door. That picture is of her. And the little boy in the picture is in her arms.

"This is your house?" I ask the man.

"Yes."

"You own it?"

"Yes."

"Is Samson your son?"

The man shakes his head. "We don't know him."

I look back at the picture. The one Samson said was of him and his mother. *Did he lie about that, too?*

I'm shaking my head in complete and utter confusion when my father rushes through the door. "Beyah?" He glides across the room but comes to a halt when one of the officers puts a hand on his shoulder and steps between us.

"Can you wait outside the door, please?"

"What happened?" my father asks. "Why are they being arrested?"

"Your daughter isn't being arrested. We don't believe she had a part in this."

"A part in *what*?" I ask.

The female officer inhales a slow breath like she doesn't want to say what she's about to say. "This house belongs to this family," she says, motioning in the direction of the man, woman, and child. "Your friend didn't have permission to be here. He's being charged with breaking and entering."

"Son of a *bitch*," my father says through clenched teeth.

I can feel tears burning behind my eyes. "That can't be right," I whisper. This is Samson's father's house. He even set the alarm last night. You can't break into a house when you know the alarm code. "This has to be some kind of mistake."

"It's not a mistake," the officer says. She puts her notepad in her back pocket. "Do you mind coming with us to the station? We'll need to file a report and we have a lot of questions."

I nod and stand up. They might have questions for me, but I certainly don't have answers.

My father steps forward, waving a hand in my direction. "She had no idea this wasn't his house. I'm the one who allowed her to stay here last night."

"It's just a formality. You're welcome to meet us at the station, and if everything checks out, she'll be free to leave with you."

My father nods. "Don't worry, Beyah. I'll be right behind you."

Don't *worry*?

I'm fucking terrified.

Before I exit the house, I grab both Samson's and my backpacks, which are still sitting by the door, and hand them to my father. "Can you put my stuff in the house?" I don't tell him one of the backpacks belongs to Samson.

He grabs both of them and looks me firmly in the eyes. "Don't answer any questions until I get there."

Twenty-Four

The room is so small, I feel like there isn't enough air for the four of us.

My father is sitting next to me at this tiny table, so I'm leaning to the right to try to preserve my own space bubble. My elbows are digging into the table and my head is in my hands.

I'm worried.

My father is just angry.

"Do you know how long he's been staying at that house?"

I learned the female officer's name is Officer Ferrell. I don't know the man's name. He hasn't said much. He's just taking notes and I don't really feel like looking up at anyone.

"No."

"Beyah just moved here in June. But Samson has been

in that house since at least spring break. That's when I met him, anyway."

"You don't know the owners?" the officer asks my father.

"No. I've seen people there, but I just assumed they were renters. We live in Houston most of the year, so I don't know many of the neighbors in our area yet."

"Do you know how Samson bypassed the alarm?" This question is directed at me.

"He knows the code. I saw him enter it last night."

"Do you know how he got the code?"

"No."

"Do you know of any other houses he's stayed in?"

I know he has other houses, but I have no idea where they are. "No."

"Do you know where he stays when the owners occupy the house?"

"No." I don't know how many different ways I can say no, but I haven't known answers to hardly any of their questions.

I don't know where Samson is from. I don't know the name of his father. I don't know his birthday, where he was born, where he grew up, whether his mother is actually alive or dead. The more questions they ask me, the more embarrassed I become.

How can I know nothing about him, yet feel like I know him so well?

Maybe I don't know him at all.

That thought forces me to lay my head on my arms. I'm

tired and I want answers, but I know I won't get any until I get to speak to Samson. The only answer I really want to know is whether or not he actually grew a heart bone. If he did, is his breaking right now?

Because mine is.

"She really doesn't know anything else," my father says. "It's late. Can you guys just call if there are more questions?"

"Sure. Let me check on something real quick before you leave. We'll be right back."

I hear both officers leave the room, so I finally lift my head and then lean back in the chair.

"You okay?" my father asks.

I nod. If I say I'm not okay, he'll want open dialogue. I'd rather not speak.

The door is open, which gives me a good view of the activity outside this room. There's a man who is obviously strung out on something being detained in a room across the hall. The whole time we've been in this room, we could hear him making unintelligible noises for no reason. Every time he would do it, I would flinch.

I should be used to that behavior because it was so common in my house. My mother mumbled to herself all the time. Especially in the past year. She'd talk to people who weren't even there.

I almost forgot what it's like to live with an addict. It makes me sad seeing that man here. Jail isn't going to help him with his addiction, just like it never helped my mother.

If anything, it made it worse. Being locked up and released over and over is a cycle that gets stronger with every arrest. My mother was arrested several times. I'm not exactly sure what she was arrested for, but it was always drug related. Possession. Intent to purchase. I remember a neighbor coming to get me in the middle of the night and taking me to her house to sleep a few times.

My mother needed more help than I was capable of giving her. I tried on more than one occasion, but I was in over my head. Looking back now, I wish I'd done more. Maybe I should have reached out to my father.

I don't think she would have been a bad person if she wasn't sick. And that's what addiction is, right? It's an illness. One I'm susceptible to but determined never to catch. I wonder what she could have been like had she not been addicted to drugs. Was she like me in any way whatsoever?

I glance over at my father. "What was my mother like when you met her?"

He looks jarred by that question. He shakes his head. "I don't really remember. I'm sorry."

I don't know why I expected him to remember. It was a one-night stand when he wasn't much older than me. They were both probably drunk. I sometimes want to ask him how they met, but I'm not sure I want to know. I'm sure it was at a bar and there isn't a romantic moment he would be able to recall.

I wonder how my father turned out somewhat normal

while my mother turned out to be the worst version of herself she could be. Is it strictly because she was an addict? Was it an imbalance of nature vs. nurture?

"Do you think humans are the only species that get addicted to things?" I ask my father.

"What do you mean?"

"Like drugs and alcohol. Do you think animals have any vices?"

My father's eyes scroll over my face like he can't understand the questions coming from my mouth. "I think I read somewhere that lab rats can get addicted to morphine," he says.

"That's not what I mean. I want to know if there are addictive things in an animal's natural environment. Or are humans the only species who sabotage themselves and everyone around them with their addictions?"

My father scratches his forehead. "Is your mother an addict, Beyah?" he asks. "Is that what you're telling me?"

I can't believe I've gone this long and still haven't told him she's dead. I can't believe he hasn't figured it out yet. "She's not an addict anymore."

His eyes are narrowed in concern. "I didn't even know she used to be." He stares at me, unwavering in his worry. "Are you okay?"

I roll my eyes at his question. "We're sitting in a police station in the middle of the night. No, I'm not okay."

He blinks twice. "Yeah, I know. But your questions. They just . . . don't really make sense."

I chuckle. It sounds just like my father's chuckle. It's my new least favorite thing about myself.

I stand up and stretch my legs. I walk to the door and look out of it, hoping to catch a glimpse of Samson somewhere, but he's nowhere.

It's as if there's a gap sitting between the moment I sat down in the police car and the moment I'll get to speak to Samson again. A huge emotional gap where I feel nothing and care about nothing else but that potential conversation.

I refuse to open myself up to whatever is happening, which is probably why my thoughts are all over the place while I wait. If I open myself up to this moment right now, I might convince myself that Samson is a complete stranger to me. But last night, that felt so far from the truth.

For the second time this summer, I find myself amazed at how much life can change from one day to the next.

Officer Ferrell returns, gripping a mug of coffee with both hands. I back out of the doorway and lean against the door. My father stands up.

"We have all your information. The two of you are free to go."

"What about Samson?" I ask.

"He won't be released tonight. Probably won't be released for a while, unless there's someone to make his bail."

Her words kick their way down my chest. *How long is a while?* I press a hand to my stomach. "Can I see him?"

"He's still being processed and will have to see the judge in a few hours. He'll be allowed visitors starting at nine tomorrow."

"We won't be visiting him," my father says.

"Yes, we will," I counter.

"Beyah, you probably don't even know the guy's real name."

"His name is Shawn Samson," I say defensively. But then I wince and look at the officer, wondering if that's something else he wasn't honest about. "Isn't that his name?"

"His full name is Shawn Samson *Bennett*, actually," the officer corrects.

My father waves a hand at the officer while looking at me. "See?" His hands are on his hips when he faces Officer Ferrell. "Do I need to be worried? What exactly is he being charged with and how long will he be in jail?"

"Two counts of breaking and entering. One count of parole violation. One count of arson."

That last one makes me choke on air. "*Arson?*"

"A fire partially destroyed a residence late last year. He was staying in the house without permission when the fire broke out. They have him on security footage and put a warrant out for his arrest. He stopped checking in with his parole officer after that, which leads us to his current outstanding warrants, along with the new charges."

"Why was he on parole in the first place?" my father asks.

"Auto theft. He served six months."

My father begins pacing. "So, this is a pattern with him?"

"Dad, I'm sure he's just a product of a faulty system." My father stops pacing and stares at me like he doesn't understand how such a ridiculous statement can come from my mouth. I look at the officer. "What about his parents?"

"Both deceased. He claims his father went missing after Hurricane Ike and he's been on his own since then."

His *father* went missing?

Rake was his father? That explains so much about his behavior when we found his remains on the beach. I want to go back to that moment when he looked like he was in so much pain. I want to go back and hug him like I should have.

I start to do the math. If Samson has been honest about his age, that means he was only thirteen when Hurricane Ike hit.

He's been alone since he was *thirteen?* No wonder I could tell he was damaged.

"Stop feeling sorry for him, Beyah. I can see it all over your face," my father says.

"He was a kid when his father died. We have no idea what kind of life he lived after that. I'm sure he did the things he did because he had to."

"Is that excuse still valid for a twenty-year-old? He could have gotten a job like the rest of us."

"What was he supposed to do after being released from

jail the first time if he was on his own? He probably never had any kind of identification if he didn't have parents to help him with that. He had no family, no money. People slip through the cracks, Dad. It happens." *It happened to me and you never even noticed.*

My father might think Samson's behavior is a pattern he chose, but it sounds to me like it was a life he might have had no way out of. I know all about making bad choices out of necessity.

"Can we get a restraining order against him? I don't want him anywhere near my property or my daughter."

I can't believe him right now. He hasn't even spoken to Samson or heard his side and he feels threatened by him? "He's harmless, Dad."

My father looks at me like I'm the unreasonable one.

"It's certainly within your rights to protect your property, but your daughter is an adult and would have to file her own restraining order to protect herself," Officer Ferrell says.

"Protect me from what? He's a good person." It's like they aren't hearing me.

"He was *pretending* to be a good person, Beyah. You don't even know him."

"I know him better than I know you," I mutter.

My father presses his lips together but says nothing in response.

Whatever bad things Samson did in his past, he didn't make those choices because he wanted to. I'm convinced of that. Samson was never threatening. He's been the most comforting, nonthreatening part of Texas for me.

My father has already made up his mind about him, though. "I need a bathroom," I say. I need a breather before getting in the car with my father.

The officer points down the hallway. I rush into the bathroom and wait until the door closes before sucking in as much air as I can fit into my lungs. I slowly release it as I walk to the mirror.

I stare at my reflection. Before Samson, when I would look in the mirror, I would see a girl who mattered to no one. But every time I've looked in the mirror since meeting him, I've seen a girl who matters to someone else.

I wonder what Samson sees when he looks in the mirror.

Does he have any idea how much he matters to me?

I wish I would have told him last night when I had the chance.

Twenty-Five

It's seven in the morning when my father and I pull into the driveway. Pepper Jack Cheese is wagging his tail, waiting by the passenger door when I open it.

I just want to be with my dog right now.

I'm tired of answering questions, and P.J. will be the first living thing I've encountered in the last few hours that hasn't thrown questions at me.

My father walks up the stairs and I choose to remain on the stilt level of the house. I sit at the picnic table and scratch P.J.'s head as I stare out at the water. I get maybe three minutes of peace before I hear quick footsteps descending the stairs.

Sara.

"Oh my God, Beyah." She rushes to the picnic table and sits across from me. She reaches across the table and squeezes my hand, forcing a sad smile. "Are you okay?"

I shake my head. "I won't be okay until I speak to Samson."

"I've been so worried. The commotion woke me up last night, and then your father texted my mother and said Samson got arrested. What happened?"

"It's not his house."

"He broke in?"

"Something like that."

Sara runs a hand down her face. "I'm so sorry. I feel terrible. I'm the one who pushed you on him." She leans forward and grips my wrist, looking at me with sincerity. "Not all guys are like him, Beyah. I promise."

She's got that right, but it's a relief that Samson isn't like other guys. He could be like Dakota. Or Gary Shelby. I'd much rather fall for a guy who has a shady past and treats me as well as Samson does than fall for a guy who treats me like shit while looking good to the rest of the world.

"I'm not mad at him, Sara."

She laughs, but it's a nervous laugh. Kind of how she used to do when we first met—when she couldn't tell if I was kidding or not.

"I know it looks like Samson is this terrible person. But you don't know him like I do. He wasn't proud of his past. And he was planning to tell me everything eventually, he just didn't want the truth to ruin the rest of our summer."

Sara folds her arms over the picnic table and leans forward. "Beyah. I know you're upset and you care about him.

But he lied to you. He lied to all of us. Marcos and I have known him since March. Everything he's ever told us is a lie."

"Like what?"

She waves her hand to the house next door. "That he owns that house, for one."

"But what else?"

Her lips fold into a thin line. She shifts in her seat while she thinks. "I don't know. I can't think of anything specific right now."

"Exactly. He lied about where he lived and went along with the rich-boy narrative you guys labeled him with. But he did everything he could not to talk about himself so he *wouldn't* be lying to you guys."

She snaps her fingers. "That guy at dinner! The one who called him Shawn. He lied about going to boarding school in New York with him."

"He lied because we forced an answer out of him."

"I would respect him a lot more than I do now if he would have just told us the truth in that moment."

"That's not true. He'd have been judged back then, just like he's being judged now." Everything is so black and white with people like Sara. The real world doesn't operate under a simple system of right and wrong. People who have never had to trade a piece of their souls just to have food or shelter can't understand the scores of bad decisions desperate people are forced to make. "I don't want to talk about this anymore, Sara."

She sighs like she's not finished trying to convince me to get over him.

It's going to take a lot more than a shady past for me to get over a guy who didn't bat an eye at my own shady past.

Sara is obviously in agreement with my father when it comes to Samson. I'm sure everyone is. "I'd really like to be alone right now."

"Okay," Sara says. "But I'm here if you want to talk."

Sara leaves me to my thoughts and heads back up the stairs. When she's back inside the house, I scratch behind P.J.'s ear. "I guess it's just me and you on Team Samson."

P.J.'s ears perk up as soon as my phone begins to vibrate. I immediately jump up and pull it out of my pocket. My heart is stuck in my throat when it says the caller ID is unavailable. I answer it right away.

"Samson?"

"You're receiving a call from an inmate in Galveston County Jail," the recording says. "Please press one to accept or two to—" I press one and put my phone to my ear.

"Samson?" My voice is full of panic. I squeeze my forehead and sit back down.

"Beyah?"

He sounds so far away, but I can finally feel him again. I sigh with relief. "Are you okay?"

"Yeah." His voice isn't filled with fear like mine is. He actually sounds calm, like he's been expecting this moment. "I can't talk long. I just . . ."

"How long can you talk?"

"Two minutes. But I was just told I can have visitors tomorrow at nine."

"I know. I'll be there. But what can I do today? Is there anyone I can call for you?"

There's a pause on his end. I'm not sure he heard the question, but then he sighs and says, "No. There's no one."

God, I hate that. P.J. and I really are all he has right now. "I don't think my father is going to bail you out. He's pretty upset."

"It's not his responsibility," Samson says. "Please don't ask him to do that."

"I'll figure something out, though."

"I'll be here for a while, Beyah. I really fucked up."

"Which is why I'm going to help find you a lawyer."

"I'll be entitled to a public defender," he says. "I've been through this before."

"Yeah, but they're overworked as it is. It wouldn't hurt to try to find a lawyer who has more time to prepare and fight for your case."

"I can't afford a lawyer. In case you haven't figured it out yet, I'm not actually rich."

"Good. You know your money was my least favorite thing about you."

Samson is quiet, even though it feels like he has so much to say.

"I'm going to spend the rest of today applying for jobs. I'll start saving up to help you hire another lawyer. You aren't alone in this, Samson."

"My mistakes aren't *your* responsibility, either. There's nothing you can do. Besides, the court date won't be for several weeks. You'll be in Pennsylvania by then."

"I'm not going to Pennsylvania." He's insane if he thinks I'm going to abandon him. Does he really think I'm going to leave him to sit in jail while I move across the country as if I didn't grow a heart bone over the summer? "What about Marjorie's son? What kind of lawyer is he?"

He doesn't respond to my question.

"Samson?" I pull my phone back and see that the call has been dropped. "*Shit.*"

I press my phone to my forehead. He probably won't get to call me back. I'll have to wait and talk to him in person tomorrow. I have so many more questions I already need to add to the list.

But I also have work to do, so I walk across the street, straight to Marjorie's house. I beat on her door until she opens it.

I forgot it's still super early. She's in her nightgown, tying her robe together when she opens the door. She looks at me from head to toe. "What in the world has got you so worked up?"

"It's Samson. He's in jail."

A flash of worry floods her eyes, and then she steps aside to let me in. "What for?"

"The house he's been staying in doesn't belong to him. He was arrested this morning because the owners showed up in the middle of the night."

"Samson? Are you sure?"

I nod. "I was there. He's going to need a lawyer, Marjorie. One who can spend more time on his case than a public defender can."

"Yes, that's a good idea."

"Your son. What kind of lawyer is he?"

"He's a defense . . . *No*. No, I can't ask Kevin to do that."

"Why not? I'm getting a job. I can pay him."

Marjorie looks torn. I can't say that I blame her. She admitted to me the first time she met me that she barely knew Samson. I've got more at stake here than she does, but she can't ignore all that he's done for her. One of Marjorie's cats climbs up onto the kitchen counter next to her. She picks it up and brings it to her chest.

"How much did Samson charge you for all the work he's done here?"

It takes her a minute to catch up to my question. Her posture sinks a little. "Nothing. He wouldn't take any money from me."

"Exactly. He's not a bad person and you know it, Marjorie." I hand her my cell phone. "Please. Call your son. You owe Samson this favor."

She sets the cat on the floor and then waves a flippant hand at my phone. "I don't know how to use those things." She walks to the kitchen and picks up her landline telephone, then begins dialing her son's number.

Kevin agreed to get in touch with Samson, but only because he knows how much Samson has helped out Marjorie over the last few months. He didn't agree to take him on pro bono, or take on his case at all, but I'm one step closer than I was before I walked into Marjorie's house.

Now that I'm walking out, she's stuck me with two pounds of pecans. "I'm getting almonds next week," she says.

I smile. "Thank you, Marjorie."

When I'm back inside our house, I drop the nuts on the table and grab both backpacks my father brought over this morning. I'm walking upstairs when he comes out to the hallway. "Beyah?"

I keep walking. "I'll be in my room the rest of the day. I'd rather not be disturbed; I'm going to bed."

"Beyah, wait," I hear him say.

When I make it to the top of the stairs, I hear Alana say, "She asked to be alone, Brian. I think she means it."

Alana is right. I do mean it. I don't feel like lectures from my father about what a terrible human Samson is. I'm too sad for that. And too tired.

I maybe got two hours of sleep last night at the most, and even with the adrenaline that's been pumping through my veins since I woke up, my eyes are beginning to grow heavier by the second.

I drop our backpacks by the bed and fall onto the mattress. I lie on it, staring out the glass balcony doors. It's so bright out there. So warm. So happy.

I stand up and snatch the curtains shut, then crawl back into bed. I just want today to end already and it's not even lunchtime yet.

I toss, turn, and stare at the ceiling for over an hour. I just can't stop thinking about what's going to happen. How long will he be in jail? Or does this mean he'll actually be sentenced to time in prison? If he truly does have that many charges against him, what kind of time is he looking at? Six months? Ten years?

I'm not going to be able to fall asleep without some kind of assistance. My mind is racing too much. I open my door and wait until it sounds like the kitchen is clear. I walk back downstairs and go to the pantry. I know there's a section in here where they keep their medicine. I thumb through the bottles but find nothing that might help me sleep.

Maybe they keep it in their bathroom. My father and Alana should be on their way to work by now, so I go to their bathroom and open their medicine cabinet. There's nothing in here but toothpaste and spare toothbrushes. Some sort of ointment. A container of cotton swabs.

I slam the door to the medicine cabinet shut but startle when I see Alana standing behind me in the mirror's reflection. "Sorry. I thought you were at work."

"I took the day off," she says. "What are you looking for?"

I turn and look at her desperately. "I just need NyQuil or something. I need to sleep. I haven't slept yet and my mind is racing." I wave my hands at my face, trying to push back the tears that have been miraculously kept at bay since last night.

"I can make you some tea."

Tea? She wants to make me tea?

She's a dentist, surely she has a prescription for some horse-strength tranquilizers somewhere in this house.

"I don't want *tea*, Alana. I need something that works. I don't want to be awake right now." I bring my hands up and cover my face. "It hurts so much to think," I whisper. "I don't even want to dream about him. I just want to sleep and not dream or think or feel."

It all starts to hit me in the center of my chest.

Everything Samson said on the phone slams into me so hard, I have to lean against the sink for support. His voice echoes in my head. *I'll be here for a while, Beyah.*

How long do I have to go before I'm happy again?

I don't want to go back to who I was before I met him. I had nothing inside of me then but bitterness and anger. No feeling, no joy, no comfort. "What if he's gone for so long, he doesn't want to be part of my life when he gets out?"

I didn't mean to say that out loud. Or maybe I did.

My tears start falling and Alana immediately responds. She doesn't say anything to make me feel bad for feeling sad. She just wraps her arms around me and tucks my head against her shoulder.

It's a comfort that's completely unfamiliar, but one I desperately need right now. The comfort of a mother. I sob against her for several minutes. It's everything I didn't know I needed in this moment. Just a small morsel of sympathy from *someone*.

"I wish you could have been my mother," I say through my tears.

I feel her sigh. "Oh, sweetie," she whispers sympathetically. She pulls back and looks at me gently. "I'll give you one Ambien, but it's the only one you're ever getting from me."

I nod. "I promise I'll never ask again."

Twenty-Six

I slept way too hard. It feels like my brain is compressed to the right side of my head.

I sit up in bed and look outside. It's almost dark now. I look at the time on my phone and see that it's after seven. My stomach is growling so loud, it may be what woke me up.

I left the ringer on my phone set to high, but it never made a noise and I have no missed calls.

Fourteen more hours until I get to see him.

I reach to the floor and pick up Samson's backpack. I dump the contents of it onto my bed and begin sifting through everything.

Literally everything he owns is on my bed right now.

There are two pairs of shorts and two of Marcos's branded T-shirts. He was wearing the other set when he was arrested, so does that mean he only has three changes of clothes? I noticed he wore the same shirts a lot, but I

290

assumed he was doing it to support Marcos. He probably washed them regularly in hopes no one would notice.

There are toiletries in a bag. Toothpaste, deodorant, a toothbrush, nail clippers. But no wallet.

Did he actually lose his wallet before we went to get tattoos, or did he never even have one? If he's been on his own since his father died, how would he have even gotten a driver's license?

I have so many questions. There's no way our visit tomorrow will be long enough for him to answer them all.

In the bottom of his backpack, I find a plastic Ziploc bag. The bag is filled with what look like folded-up pieces of paper. They're all a little faded with a yellow tint to them, so they're obviously old.

I open the bag and pull out one of the pieces of paper and unfold it.

Little Boy

Bitten by frenzy like me
Exhaustion in his eyes
He's growing angry at the sea
More tired than he should be
So tired of being free

—Rake Bennett
11-13-07

Samson mentioned that Rake used to write poetry. I stare at this poem and try to make sense of it.

Is it about Samson? Are all these notes from his father? It's dated when Samson would have been about twelve years old. A year before the hurricane hit.

So tired of being free.

What does that line mean? Did his father think Samson was tired of living life on the ocean with him?

I pull out the rest of the pieces of paper, needing to read every single one of them. They're all dated from before Hurricane Ike, all written by his father.

She lives

When you were born, so was your mother.
As long as you live,
she too will be alive.

—Rake Bennett
8-30-06

Gone

I met your mother while she was standing on the beach,
her feet buried in the sand.
I regret not falling to my knees to scoop up some of the
granules
into the palms of my hands.
I wonder if any of what we touch has ever been stepped
on by her feet.
Or has every grain of sand she ever came across
already washed back out to sea?

—Rake Bennett
7-16-07

Dear Shawn,

Every child eventually craves a new place to be.
I decided your first home to be a boat, but now I wonder,
Is this boat the home you'll flee?
If so,
that grave mistake is all on me.
Because when a man says *I'm going home*,
he should be heading for the sea.

—Rake Bennett
1-3-08

There are at least twenty poems and letters in the bag. Only a few are written directly for Samson, but based on all the sheets of paper as a whole, I get the impression that what Samson told me about his father was true. Rake lived on the water, but the part Samson left out was that he lived on the water with Rake, too.

Twenty-Seven

"Beyah Grim?"

I practically jump out of my chair. My father stands up, too, but I don't want my father going in with me to see Samson. "You don't have to come."

"I'm not allowing you in there by yourself." His statement is final, like there isn't any room for negotiation.

"Dad, *please*." I don't know that Samson will feel like being honest with me if my father is sitting across from him. "Please."

He nods tightly. "I'll wait in the car."

"Thank you."

I follow the guard as he leads me to a large, open room. There are several tables and almost all of them are full of people visiting with other inmates.

It's depressing. But not as depressing as I thought it

would be. I assumed I'd be on one side of a window made of glass, unable to touch him.

My eyes immediately seek out and find Samson sitting alone at a table on the other side of the room. He's wearing a dark blue jumpsuit. Seeing him in something other than his usual beach shorts makes this all feel more real.

When he finally looks up and sees me, he immediately stands. I don't know why I expected his hands to be cuffed, but I'm relieved to see they aren't. I rush to him and fall right into his arms. He pulls me against him with tightened arms.

"I'm sorry," he says.

"I know."

He holds me for a moment, but I don't want to get him in trouble, so we separate, and I sit across from him. The table is small, so we aren't that far apart, but he feels a world away.

He takes one of my hands and holds it in both of his, resting our hands on the table. "I owe you so many answers. Where do you want me to start?"

"Anywhere."

He takes a moment to figure out where he should begin. I bring my other hand to his until all four of our hands are in a pile on the table. "Everything I told you about my mother was true. Her name was Isabel. I was only five when it happened, but even though I didn't remember much of my life before her death, I knew it changed drastically after she was gone. Rake is my father; I did omit that. After my mother died, he seemed lost when he wasn't on the water. It's like he couldn't imagine being anywhere she wasn't, so he pulled me out of school, and we lived on his boat for several years. And that was my life, until Darya took him from me."

"So that's what you meant when you said Darya broke your heart?"

He nods.

"Where were you when the hurricane hit?"

Samson's jaw hardens, like that's not a memory he wants to relive. He stares at our hands as he speaks. "My father dropped me off at a church. It's where a lot of the residents took shelter, but he refused to stay with me. He wanted to make sure his boat was secured since it was our entire life. He told me he'd be back before dark, but I never saw him again after that night." He brings his eyes back to mine. "I wanted to stay on the peninsula, but there was nothing left after the hurricane. It was hard for a thirteen-year-old to hide there, or even survive at that point, so I had to leave. I knew if I told someone my father was missing, I'd get thrown into a group home, so I just spent the next few years trying to be invisible. I ended up working with a friend in Galveston doing odd jobs like mowing yards. He was the guy you met at the restaurant. We were young and did some stupid shit. It eventually caught up with us."

"What about the arson charge?"

"Technically not my fault. The owner had some shitty

electrical work done, but had I not broken into that house that night and turned on the power, it never would have caught on fire. So, on paper, it *was* my fault." Samson threads his fingers through mine. "Once I knew I had another warrant out for my arrest, I chose to come back here one last time before turning myself in. I don't know if I was looking for closure or hoping to find my father, but I ended up finding both. But I also found you and never wanted to leave." Samson brushes his thumb across the top of my left hand. "I knew I'd be in jail for a while, so I was trying to stretch out my time with you before you left." He sighs. "What else do you want to know?"

"How did you know the alarm code for that house?"

"The owner uses his house number as his code. Easiest digits to guess."

It's hard to judge him when that judgment would be extremely hypocritical of me. If anything, I admire his survival skills.

"What about the Air Force Academy? Was any of that true?"

He looks down, unable to meet my gaze. He shakes his head. "I wanted to go to the air force. That was my plan, until I fucked it all up. But there were things I lied about, like it being a family tradition. I've said a lot of things that weren't true. But I had to back up my reasoning for being in that house with lies I never wanted to tell you. That's why I wouldn't answer your questions. I didn't like being dishonest with you. Or anyone. I just . . ."

"You didn't have a choice," I say, finishing his thought. I get it. I've been there my whole life. "You're the one who said wrong decisions come from either strength or weakness. You weren't lying because you were weak, Samson."

He takes in a slow breath, like he dreads what's coming next. His entire demeanor changes when he looks me in the eyes. The weight of this room begins to close in on me with that look. "Yesterday on the phone you mentioned you weren't going to Pennsylvania."

It's a statement, but he intends for it to be followed by an answer. "I can't leave you."

He shakes his head, pulling his hands from mine. He runs them over his face like he's frustrated with me, then he grabs both my hands even tighter. "You're going to college, Beyah. My mess isn't yours to clean up."

"Your *mess*? Samson, what you did isn't that bad. You were a kid who practically raised himself on the streets. How were you supposed to get back on your feet after you were released from jail the first time? I'm sure if you tell them why the fire started and why you broke parole, they'd understand."

"The court doesn't care why I broke the law; they just care that I broke it."

"Well, they *should* care."

"It doesn't matter how flawed the system is, Beyah. The two of us aren't going to change it overnight. I'm looking at several years, and there's nothing either of us can do about it, so there's no reason for you to stay in Texas."

"You're enough of a reason. How will I visit you if I'm in Pennsylvania?"

"I don't want you to visit me. I want you to go to college."

"I can go to college here."

He laughs, but there's no smile attached to his laugh. It's an exasperated laugh. "Why are you being so stubborn? This was our plan all summer—to go our separate ways when you leave for school."

His words are digging into me, twisting my insides. My voice comes out in a whisper when I say, "I thought things changed. You said we grew heart bones."

Samson's entire body feels that comment. He sinks a little, like I'm hurting him. I don't want to hurt him, but he's worth more than this. He wasn't a throwaway to me.

"I can't be that far away from you," I say quietly. "Phone calls and letters aren't going to be enough."

"I don't want phone calls or letters, either. I want you to go live your life and not be weighed down by mine." He can see the shock on my face, but he doesn't give me time to argue with him. "Beyah. We have been alone on islands our whole lives. It's why we connected, because we recognized that loneliness in each other. But this is your chance to get off your island, and I refuse to hold you back for however many years I'll be gone."

I can feel the tears. I look down just as one falls on the table. "You can't cut me off. I can't do this without you."

"You've already *done* it without me," he says, his voice

determined. He reaches across the table and lifts my face so that I'm forced to look at him. He looks as broken as I feel. "I had nothing to do with your accomplishments. I had nothing to do with who you turned out to be. Please don't make me be the reason you give it all up."

The more committed he is to the idea that he doesn't want me to stay in touch with him, the angrier I get.

"This isn't fair to me. You expect me to just walk away and not have any contact with you at all? Why would you let me fall for you in the first place when you knew this was going to be the end result?"

He exhales sharply. "We agreed this would end in August, Beyah. We agreed to keep it in the shallow end."

I roll my eyes. "You're the one who said people still drown in the shallow end." I lean forward until I have his focus again. "I'm drowning, Samson. And you're the one holding me underwater." I wipe my eyes angrily.

Samson takes my hands again, but this time, it's different. There's an ache in his voice when he says, "I'm so sorry." It's all he says, but I can tell this is his goodbye.

He stands up like this discussion is over, but he's looking at me like he wants me to stand up, too. I fold my arms tightly over my chest. "I'm not hugging you goodbye. You don't deserve to hold me anymore."

Samson nods a little. "I never deserved to hold you in the first place." He turns to leave, and I instantly become terrified it's the last time I'll see him. Samson doesn't say things with that look in his eyes unless he means them. He's not going to allow me to see him again. This is it. This is where we end.

I jump up when he begins to walk away. "Samson, wait!"

He turns around just in time to catch me when I throw my arms around him. I bury my face against his neck. When he folds me into his arms, I start to cry.

So many things are running through me at once. I miss him so much already, but I'm also angrier than I've ever been. I knew this was coming—the goodbye. But I didn't know it would be under these circumstances. I feel powerless. I wanted our goodbye to be a choice I had a part in, but I'm not getting a choice at all.

He kisses the side of my head. "Take the scholarship, Beyah. And have fun. *Please*." His voice cracks on *please*. He releases me and walks to a guard standing next to a door. I feel heavy without him, like I've lost an entire support system and can no longer hold myself up on my own.

Samson is led out of the room, and he never even looks back at me to see the destruction he left behind.

I'm sobbing by the time I make it outside to my father's car. I slam the door, angry and heartbroken. I can't even begin to absorb what just happened in there. I wasn't expecting it. I was expecting the exact opposite of that. I thought we were going to work this out as a team, but instead, he left me completely fucking alone, just like every other person in my life.

"What happened?"

I shake my head. I can't even say it out loud. "Just drive."

My father grips his steering wheel until his knuckles are white. He starts the car and puts it in reverse. "I should have beat the shit out of him the night I pulled him off you in the shower."

I don't even try to explain that he wasn't protecting me from Samson that night. Samson was helping me, but at this point, another explanation would be futile. I just go with a blanket statement: "He's not a bad person, Dad."

My father puts the car back in park. He faces me, his expression unyielding. "I don't know where I went wrong as a father, but I did not raise a daughter who would defend a guy who lied to her the entire summer. You think he cares about you? He doesn't care about anyone but himself."

Is he serious?

Did he actually have the audacity to say he *raised* me?

I glare at him, my hand on the door handle. "You didn't raise a daughter at *all*. If anyone is lying in this scenario, it's *you*." I open my door and get out of his car. There's no way I want to be stuck with him all the way back to Bolivar Peninsula.

"Get back in the car, Beyah."

"No. I'm calling Sara to come pick me up." I sit down on the curb next to the car. My father gets out of the car while I pull out my phone. He kicks at the gravel and motions toward the car.

"Get in. I'll take you home."

I wipe tears from my eyes after I dial Sara's number. "I'm not getting in your car. You can leave now."

My father doesn't leave. Sara agrees to come pick me up, but my father sits patiently in his car until she arrives.

Twenty-Eight

It's been an agonizing week with no news from Samson. Nothing at all. I've tried to visit him twice, but he refuses to see me now.

I have absolutely no way of communicating with him. All I have to cling to are the memories of the time we spent together, and I'm worried those will start to fade if I don't at least get to hear his voice.

Am I really just expected to move on? Forget about him? Go to college like he didn't force me to become a completely different, better version of myself this summer?

I stopped talking about Samson to anyone in the house. I don't even want his name brought up because it just leads to arguments. I've barely left my room all week. I occupy my days with mindless TV shows and visits to Marjorie's house. She's the only one I'll speak to about him. She's the only one on my side.

I've been alternating between the two shirts that were in Samson's backpack all week, but they no longer smell like him. They smell like me now, which is why I'm snuggled up to his backpack, watching a marathon of a British baking show.

I don't know what to do with his things. I doubt he cares to keep toiletries, and there wasn't anything of value in his backpack other than the poems his father wrote to him. But I don't want to give them to Marjorie to get to him because I feel like they're my last connection to him.

They might one day be the only excuse I have to get him to speak to me.

I'm going to have to move on at some point. I know this, but as long as I'm still here and he's still in jail, I can't focus on anything else.

I readjust the backpack in my arms to use it as a partial pillow, but something hard pokes at my temple. I open it up to see if I missed an item, but I see nothing. I move my hand around inside the backpack and find a zipper I didn't catch before.

I immediately sit up and unzip it. I pull out a small, hard-bound notebook. It's only about four inches in length. I flip it open and it's full of names and addresses, and what look like grocery lists.

I flip through several pages, unable to make sense of

any of it. But then I get to a page with Marjorie's name and address on it.

Marjorie Naples

Date of stay: 2-4-15 to 2-8-15.

Ate $15 worth of food.

Repaired roof. Replaced two pieces of siding on north side of house damaged by wind.

There are several more names and addresses that follow Marjorie's, but I need to know the significance of the dates. I pick up my phone and call her.

"Hello?"

"Hey, it's Beyah. Quick question. Are the dates February fourth to February eighth this year of any significance to you?"

Marjorie chews on that thought for a moment. "I'm almost positive those are the days I was in the hospital after my heart attack. Why?"

"Just something I found in Samson's backpack. I'll bring it over later so you can give it to Kevin."

I tell her goodbye and end the call, then I start skimming through all the other things he's written down. The most common address is the one next door for David Silver. There are several dates listed. Most of them between March and last week. Beneath David's name is a list of repairs.

Tightened several loose slats on bedroom balcony railing.
Replaced a broken fuse in the breaker box. Sealed leak in
pipe in outdoor shower.

The lists go on. There are odd jobs he's done for people and how much he got paid for each job, which explains how he sometimes had money for things like dinner and tattoos. There are also lists of people he's done work for that he didn't take pay from.

Every day for the past seven months is accounted for. Every item of food he ate from someone's refrigerator without their permission. Every repair he made to someone's house. He's been keeping track of all of it.

But why? Did he feel like repairing these properties for free was balancing out the fact that he was staying in them without permission?

Could this possibly be the proof the court needs to know he doesn't deserve all the charges being brought against him?

I rush downstairs and find my father and Alana on the living room sofa. Sara and Marcos are together on the love seat. They're all watching *Wheel of Fortune*, but my father mutes it when he sees I've come downstairs for the first time today.

I hand the notebook to my father. "This belongs to Samson." He takes the notebook from me and begins flipping through it. "It's a detailed list of every place he's stayed and how he repaid them."

My father stands up, still flipping through the notebook.

"This could help him." My voice is full of hope for the first time since he was arrested. "If we can prove he was trying to do the right thing, it could help his defense."

My father sighs before he even makes it a few pages into the book. He closes it and hands it back to me. "It's a detailed list of everything he's done wrong. It'll hurt him, not help him."

"You don't know that."

"Beyah, he's only being charged on two counts of breaking and entering. If you take that to the police and show them how many more houses he broke into, they're going to use it to *add* to his charges, not take away from them." He looks frustrated as he takes a step closer to me. "*Please* let this go. You're too young to let a guy you barely know consume your life like this. He messed up and he has to pay the consequences for that."

Alana is standing now. She grips my father's arm in support and says, "Your father is right, Beyah. There's nothing you can do but move forward."

Sara and Marcos are still seated on the love seat, looking at me in a way that makes me feel pathetic.

All of them think I'm pathetic.

None of them cares what happens to Samson. And none of them believes in what we had. For once in my life, I had someone who actually cared about me, and all four of them think I'm incapable of knowing what true love is.

I know what love is, because I spent my whole life knowing what it *isn't*.

"My mother died." It feels like all the air in the room is sucked out after I say that.

Alana's hand goes over her mouth.

My father shakes his head in disbelief. "What? When?"

"The night I called you and asked if I could come here. She overdosed because she'd been an addict for as long as I can remember. I have had no one in my corner. Not you. Not my mother. *No one.* I have been all alone my whole *goddamn* life. Samson is the first person who ever showed up and cheered for me."

My father walks over to me, his face contorted into both confusion and sympathy. "Why would you not tell me something like this?" He runs a hand down his face and mutters, "*Christ*, Beyah."

He tries to pull me in for a hug, but I back away.

I turn around to head toward the stairs, but my father calls after me. "Wait. We need to discuss this."

Now that my rage has surfaced, I feel like I'm drowning in it. I need to get it all out while I have the chance. I spin around and face my father again.

"Discuss what? Everything else I kept from you? Do you want to know about how I lied when I met you at the airport? The airline didn't lose my luggage. I never had anything at all, because every penny you ever sent Janean, she kept for herself. I had to start fucking a guy for money when I was fifteen just so I would have food to eat. So *fuck* you, Brian. You aren't my father. You never have been, and you never will be!"

I don't bother to wait for any of their reactions. I stomp up the stairs and slam my bedroom door.

My father opens it about thirty seconds later.

"Please leave," I say, my voice completely devoid of emotion now.

"We need to talk about this."

"I want to be alone."

"Beyah," he says pleadingly, stepping into the room. I stomp to the bedroom door, refusing to let the look on his face get to me.

"You've spent nineteen years being an uninvolved father. I am not in the mood for you to finally get involved tonight. Please, just leave me alone."

So many things pass through my father's eyes in this moment. Sadness. Regret. Empathy. But I don't allow any of his feelings to affect my own. I stare at him stoically until he finally nods and backs out of my bedroom.

I close the door.

I fall onto the bed and pull Samson's notebook to my chest.

To them, this notebook may be a list of everyone on this peninsula he's wronged, but to me, it's further proof that his intentions were good. He tried to do the right thing with nonexistent means.

I flip through the notebook again, reading every page, touching the words with the tip of my finger, tracing his sloppy handwriting. I read the address of every place he's ever stayed. Half the notebook is filled with pages of his handwriting. It's choppy and hard to read in places, like he'd write these things in a hurry and then close the notebook before he got caught.

I flip toward the end of the notebook and pause on a page that's different from the rest. It's different because my name is at the top of the page.

I pull the notebook flat to my chest and close my eyes. Whatever he wrote was short, but that was my name.

I breathe in and out very slowly several times until my heart rate returns to normal. Then I pull the notebook away from my chest and read his words.

Beyah,

My father once told me love is a lot like water.
   It can be calm. Raging. Threatening. Soothing.
   Water will be many things, but even in all its forms, it will always be water.
   You are my water.
   I think I might be yours, too.
   If you're reading this, it means I've evaporated.
   But it doesn't mean you should evaporate, too.
   Go flood the whole goddamn world, Beyah.

It's the last thing he wrote in the notebook. It's like he was afraid he'd be arrested before he could tell me goodbye.

I read the note several times with tears falling onto the page. *This* is Samson. I don't care what anyone else believes. This is who I'm going to hold on to until the day he's released.

This is also the reason I refuse to leave. He needs my help. I'm all he has. There's no way I can just walk away from him right now. The thought of leaving this town before knowing his fate is a selfish move. He thinks he's doing me a favor, but he has no idea what his decision is doing to me. If he knew, he'd beg me to stay.

There's a light tap on my door. "Beyah, can I come in?" Sara peeks her head in, but I'm not in the mood to argue. I'm not even sure I have the strength to say that out loud. I just clutch the notebook with his words to my chest and I roll over and face the wall.

Sara crawls into the bed with me and wraps her arm around me from behind.

She says nothing. She just quietly slips into her role as a big sister and stays with me until I fall asleep.

Twenty-Nine

The sunrise is the only peaceful thing in my life at this point.

I've been out here waiting on it since five o'clock this morning. I couldn't sleep. How am I expected to sleep after the last week I've had?

Every time I close my eyes, I see Samson walking away from me without looking back. I want to remember all the times he looked at me with hope and enthusiasm and intensity. But all I see is that last moment where he left me crying and alone.

I'm afraid that's how I'm going to remember him, and that's not how I want our goodbye to be. I'm confident I can change his mind. I'm confident I can help him.

I have a job interview at the only donut shop on the peninsula today. I'm going to save up every penny I can to help him. I know he doesn't want that, but it's the least I can do for everything he brought into my life this summer.

It's certainly going to remain a point of contention between my father and me while I stay in this house with him. He thinks I'm being ridiculous for not moving to Pennsylvania. I think he's being ridiculous for expecting me to walk away from someone who has absolutely no one else. Not many people know loneliness like Samson and I do.

I also don't know how my father expects me to just start over again in a new state for the second time this summer. I don't have the energy to start over again. I feel completely drained.

I don't have the energy to move across the country, and I especially don't have the energy to play volleyball in order to qualify for my scholarship.

I'm not even sure I'll have the energy to get up and make donuts every day if I get the job, but knowing every cent will go to helping Samson will likely make it worth it.

My attention is pulled to my bedroom door, just as the sun begins to peek over the horizon. My father pokes his head out of my bedroom and my whole body sighs due to his presence.

It was too late to argue with him last night and it's too early to argue with him this morning.

He looks relieved to see me sitting out here. He probably thought I ran away in the middle of the night when he saw I wasn't in my bed just now.

I've wanted to run away so many times, but where would I go? I feel like I no longer belong anywhere. Samson was the first place I felt I belonged and that was ripped from me.

My father sits down next to me. I don't ease into his comfort like I eased into Samson's. I'm stiff and unyielding.

He watches the sunrise with me, but his presence ruins it. It's hard to find the beauty in it when I have so much anger directed at the man sitting next to me.

"Remember the first time we went to the beach?" he asks.

I shake my head. "I've never been to the beach before this summer."

"Yes, you have. You were young, though. Maybe you don't remember it, but I took you to Santa Monica when you were about four or five."

I finally make eye contact with him. "I've been to California?"

"Yeah. You don't remember?"

"No."

His expression is regretful for a moment, but then he removes his arm from the back of the chair and stands up. "I'll be right back. I have pictures here somewhere. I grabbed the album from our house in Houston when I found out you were coming."

He has pictures of my childhood? Supposedly on a beach?

I'll believe it when I see it.

A few minutes later, my father comes back with a photo

album. He takes his seat in the chair again and opens it up, sliding it over to me.

I flip through the photos and feel like I'm looking at someone else's life. There are so many pictures of me that I don't even remember being taken. Days I have absolutely no recollection of.

I get to a section of pictures of me running in the sand, and I can't connect them to a memory. I probably didn't even realize the meaning behind a road trip at that age.

"When was this?" I ask, pointing to a picture with me sitting at a table in front of a birthday cake, but there's a small Christmas tree in the background. My birthday is months after Christmas, and I normally only visited my father in the summer. "I don't remember having Christmas with you."

"Technically, you didn't. Since you only came in the summer, I'd roll all the holidays into one big celebration."

I vaguely remember that now that he mentions it. I have faded memories of being painfully full while opening presents. But that was so long ago, and those memories didn't carry with me through the years. Neither did the traditions, apparently.

"Why did you stop?" I ask him.

"I don't know, honestly. You started to grow up, and every year when you would come visit, you seemed less interested in the silly things. Or maybe I just assumed you were. You were such a quiet child; it was hard to get anything out of you."

I blame my mother for that.

I flip through the album and pause on a picture of me sitting in my father's lap. We're both smiling at the camera. He has his arm around me, and I'm snuggled against him.

All these years, I didn't think he was ever affectionate with me. There were so many years of him *not* being affectionate with me, *those* are the things I remember the most.

I run my finger over the picture, saddened by whatever happened between us to change our relationship.

"When did you stop treating me like your daughter?"

My father sighs, and his sigh is full of so many things.

"I was twenty-one when you were born. I never knew what I was doing with you. It was easier to fake when you were little, but as you grew up, I just . . . I felt guilty. That guilt started working its way into our time together. I felt like your visits with me were an inconvenience for you."

I shake my head. "They were the only thing I ever looked forward to."

"I wish I'd known that," he says quietly.

I'm starting to wish I'd told him.

If there's one thing I learned from Samson this summer, it's that holding everything in accomplishes nothing. It just causes the truth to hurt even worse in the end.

"I had no idea what kind of mother she was, Beyah. Sara told me some things last night that you told her and I just . . ." His voice sounds shaky, like he's working to hold back tears. "I did so many things wrong. I have no excuse. You have every right to be resentful because you're right. I should have fought harder to get to know you. I should have fought harder to spend more time with you."

My father takes the photo album from me and sets it on the chair next to him. He faces me with an expression full of unease. "I feel like what you're doing—allowing this guy's fate to dictate your own future—it's my fault, because I never set an example for you. But despite that, you turned out to be the amazing person that you are, and that is not because of me. It's because of *you*. You're a fighter, so naturally you want to stay and fight for Samson. Maybe it's because you see so much of yourself in him. But what if he's not who you think he is, and you make the wrong decision?"

"But what if he's exactly who I think he is?"

My father takes my right hand and holds it between both of his. He looks so sincere, staring at me with such raw honesty. "If Samson is the person you think he is, what do you think he would want for you? Do you think he would want you to give up everything you've worked for?" I look away from my father, toward the sunrise. I'm holding all my feelings in my throat.

"I love you, Beyah. Enough to admit that you've been let down by too many people in your life. Me being one of them. The only person who has ever been completely loyal to you is *you*. You're doing yourself a disservice by not putting *yourself* first right now."

I lean forward and hold my head in my hands. I squeeze my eyes shut. I know that's what Samson wants—for me to put myself before him. I just don't *want* him to want that for me.

My father rubs his hand over my back, and the feeling is so soothing, I lean into him, wrapping my arms around him. He hugs me back, running a gentle hand over my head.

"I know it hurts," he whispers. "I wish I could take that pain away from you."

It does hurt. It's fucking brutal. It isn't fair. I finally have something good in my life and now I'm being forced to leave it behind.

They're right, though. Everyone is right but me. I need to put myself first. It's what I've always done and it's worked for me so far.

I think about the letter Samson wrote to me, and that last line that got caught up in my heart. *Go flood the whole goddamn world, Beyah.*

I inhale a gulp of the salty morning air, knowing I won't get very many more of them before I leave for Pennsylvania. "Will you take care of Pepper Jack Cheese while I'm gone?"

My father sighs with relief. "Of course I will." He presses a soft kiss into my hair. "I love you, Beyah."

There's so much truth in his words, and for the first time, I allow myself to believe him.

This is the moment I release it all. Every single thing from my childhood that's made my heart so heavy.

I release my anger toward my father.

I even release my anger toward my mother.

The only thing I'm going to hold on to from this point forward are the good things.

I may not be ending the summer with Samson by my side, but I'm ending it with something I didn't have when I showed up here.

A family.

Thirty

My roommate is a girl from Los Angeles. Her name is Cierra *with a C*.

We get along okay, but I'm trying to stay focused on school and volleyball, so I haven't hung out with her outside of our dorm room. Other than when we're both in here doing homework or sleeping, I don't see her much. It's weird how I lived across the hall from Sara for a summer and saw her more than I see the person living in the same room with me now.

I miss Sara, even though we text every day. So do my father and I.

None of us discusses Samson, though. Not since that morning I decided to come to Pennsylvania. I need everyone to believe that I've moved on, but I'm not sure how to. I think about him all the time. I'll see something or hear something and feel an intense need to tell him about it. But

I can't because he's made sure to cut off any form of communication I could have with him.

I wrote him one letter and it was returned to me. I cried that entire afternoon but decided not to write him after that.

His court hearing was this morning. Based on all the charges, he's looking at several years of potential prison time. I've been waiting by my phone all day for a phone call from Kevin.

That's all I've been doing. Staring at my phone. Waiting. I finally get tired of it and dial Kevin's number. I know he said he'd call me after Samson's sentencing, but maybe he got held up. I look behind me to make sure Cierra is still in the shower and then sit up straight on my bed when Kevin answers.

"I was about to call you."

"What happened?"

Kevin sighs, and I feel all the weight of Samson's sentence in that sigh. "Good news and bad news. We were able to get the breaking and entering charges downgraded to trespassing. But they wouldn't budge on the arson charge because of the security footage."

My arm is wrapped tightly around my stomach. "How long, Kevin?"

"Six years. But he'll likely get out in four."

I press my hand to my forehead and drop my head between my shoulders. "Why so long? That's so long."

"It could have been much worse. He was facing ten years for the arson alone. Had he not already violated parole in the past, he probably would have been slapped on the wrist. But this isn't his first offense, Beyah."

"But did you explain to the judge *why* he violated parole? He had no money. How can they expect people to pay parole fees when they have no money?"

"I know it's not the news you wanted, but it's better than it could have been."

I'm so upset. I honestly didn't think he would be sentenced to that much time. "Rapists get less time than he did. What is wrong with our judicial system?"

"Everything. You're in college. Maybe you should become a lawyer and do something about it."

Maybe I will. I haven't declared a major yet and nothing pisses me off more than thinking of all the people who fell through the cracks. "What prison are they sending him to?"

"Huntsville, Texas."

"Do you have a mailing address for him?"

I can hear Kevin's hesitation over the phone. "He doesn't want visitors. Or mail. My name is the only one on his list besides my mother's."

I figured as much. Samson is going to be stubborn about this until the day he's out. "I'm calling you every month until he's released. But please call me first if there are any changes or if he gets out early on parole. Anything at all. Even if he's moved to a different location."

"Can I give you a piece of advice, Beyah?"

I roll my eyes, waiting for another lecture from someone else who doesn't know Samson at all.

"If you were my daughter, I'd tell you to move on. You're putting too much effort into this guy, and no one knows him well enough to know if he's worth that kind of energy."

"What if Samson was your son?" I ask him. "Would you want everyone to just give up on him?"

Kevin sighs heavily before saying, "Point taken. Guess I'll talk to you next month."

He ends the call. I set my phone down on the dresser, completely disappointed. Helpless.

"You have a boyfriend in jail?"

I spin around at the sound of Cierra's voice. My first instinct is to lie to her because that's what I've always done. Hide my truth from everyone around me. I don't think that's who I want to be anymore, though.

"No, he's not my boyfriend. Just someone I care about."

Cierra faces the mirror and holds a shirt up to her chest. "Good. Because there's a party tonight and I want you to come. There will be so many guys there." She tosses the shirt aside and holds up another one. "And girls, too, if that's what you prefer."

I stare at Cierra as she watches herself in the mirror. There's anticipation in her eyes and very little damage. She's who I wish I could be right now. Someone excited for the fun parts of college life and not at all weighed down by the things she might have had to overcome to get here.

It hasn't felt fair of me to have fun when Samson is stuck behind bars, so all I've done since I arrived on campus is study and play volleyball and research ways to break people out of prison.

No amount of moping is going to change Samson's fate. And even though he's cut off communication with me, I know exactly why he's done it. He knows I'll be too focused and worried about him if I stay in constant contact with him. I can't be angry at him for that.

And when I can't stay angry at him, how am I supposed to forget him?

No one will change Samson's mind, though. I know that for a fact, because if the roles were reversed, I'd want the exact same things he wants for me.

I understand his intentions in every part of me. How would he react if he found out I spent my entire time in college as depressed and alone as I was in high school?

He would be so disappointed if I wasted these years.

I can either choose to stick to a lonely road of hope that may never be met, or I can figure out who I am while I'm in this setting.

What version of myself can I be while I'm here?

I run my index fingers under my eyes. I'm emotional for a lot of reasons, but mostly because I feel like I have to truly release myself of Samson in this moment or he'll weigh me down for the next several years of my life. I don't want that. And neither does he.

"Whoa," Cierra says, spinning around to look at me. "I didn't mean to upset you. You don't have to go."

I smile at her. "No, I want to. I want to go to a party with you. I think I might be a fun person."

Cierra pushes her bottom lip out like my words just made her sad. "Of *course* you're fun, Beyah. Here." She tosses me the shirt she was holding. "This color will look better on you."

I stand up and hold the shirt up to myself. I look at my reflection in the mirror. I can feel the sadness inside me, but I don't see it on my face. I've always been good at hiding what I'm feeling.

"Want me to do your makeup?" she asks.

I nod. "Yeah. I'd like that."

Cierra walks back to the bathroom. I glance next to the bathroom door, at the picture of Mother Teresa I hung on the wall the day I arrived.

I wonder what version of herself my mother could have been if it weren't for her addictions? I wish I could have known that version.

For her sake, that's the version of her I'm going to choose to miss. The person she never had the chance to be. I kiss my fingers and then press them against the picture as I walk past it and into the bathroom.

Cierra is sorting her makeup. I promised myself when I first met her that I wasn't going to prejudge her by labeling her a locker-room girl like I almost did with Sara. No matter who Cierra was in high school, or who I was, we're all made up of more than our past behaviors, good or bad. I no longer want to be the version of myself who judged people before accepting them. I was projecting all the behaviors I resented.

Cierra looks at my reflection in the mirror and smiles like she's just as excited as Sara would be to glam me up.

I smile back at her and pretend to be excited, too.

If I have to pretend my way through this entire year, it's what I'm going to do. I'm going to smile so much that my fake smile eventually becomes real.

Thirty-One

Fall 2019

Today has the makings of being a perfect day. It's October and the sun is out, but it's cool enough that I've been sitting on the hood of my car for the last two hours and haven't even broken a sweat.

But despite the potential for the day, things could still end in severe disappointment. I have no idea.

How will Samson react when he walks through those doors?

Who will he be?

Who has he *become*?

There's a saying from Maya Angelou that reminds me of our situation. *When someone shows you who they are, believe them the first time.*

I've clung to that saying so tightly, it feels carved into

my bones. I always go back to it when I start to have doubts because I want to believe the summer I spent with Samson was the real Samson. I want to believe that he's hoping I'm waiting for him as much as I'm hoping he wants me here.

But even if he isn't, I think enough time has passed that my heart bone has healed. There's still a crack in it. I sometimes feel it aching. Mostly when it's late at night and I'm unable to sleep.

It's been well over four years since the last time I saw him, and my thoughts of him continue to separate further apart by stretches of thoughts that don't involve Samson. But I don't know if that's because I'm trying to protect myself from what could potentially happen today or if it's because Samson really was just one summer fling in a life filled with other seasons.

That's the worst outcome I can imagine—that all the moments we shared that left such a lasting impact on me weren't profound for him at all.

I've thought about saving myself the potential embarrassment. He might see me out here waiting on him and barely remember me. Or worse—he could feel sorry for the girl who hung on after all this time.

Either of those options are worth the risk, because the idea of him walking out those doors to no one sounds like the saddest outcome of all. I'd rather be here and him not want me here than not be here when he hopes I am.

Kevin called last week and said Samson was approved for early release. I knew that's what he was going to tell me before I even answered his phone call because Kevin never calls me. I'm the one who calls him to check if there are updates. I call him so much, I'm probably more annoying to him than a telemarketer.

I'm sitting cross-legged on the hood, eating an apple I just pulled out of my bag. I've been here going on four hours now.

There's a man in the car next to me who is also waiting on someone to be released. He gets out to stretch his legs and then leans against his car. "Who are you here for?" he asks.

I don't know how to answer that, so I shrug. "An old friend who may not even want me here."

He kicks at a rock. "I'm here for my brother. Third time picking him up. Hopefully this will be his last go."

"Hopefully," I say. But I doubt it. I've learned enough about the prison system during my time in college that I have very little faith in the system's ability to properly rehabilitate offenders.

It's why I'm in law school now. I'm convinced Samson wouldn't be in the position he's in if he would have had better access to resources when he was released the first time. Even if I don't end up with Samson by the end of this, I've ended up with a new passion because of it.

"What time do they usually open the doors?" I ask the man.

The guy looks at his watch. "I figured it would be before lunch. They're running behind today."

I reach into my bag, which is sitting on the hood next to me. "You hungry? I have chips."

He holds up his hands, so I toss them at him. "Thanks," he says, opening the bag. He pops one into his mouth. "Good luck with your friend."

I smile. "Good luck to your brother."

I take another bite of my apple and lean back onto my windshield. I lift my arm and run my fingers over my pinwheel tattoo.

I hated this tattoo after Samson was arrested. It was supposed to bring me good luck, but instead it felt like my world became worse than before I moved to Texas. It took at least a year for me to fully appreciate this tattoo.

Aside from everything that happened with Samson being arrested, every other aspect of my life improved after getting this tattoo. I became closer to my father and his new family. Sara is not only my sister now, but my absolute best friend in the world.

I got accepted to law school. I never would have thought when I picked up a volleyball for the first time as a kid that it would lead to me becoming a lawyer. *Me*. The lonely girl who once had to do unthinkable things to feed herself is going to be a damn lawyer.

I think maybe this tattoo really did turn my luck around in the end. Not in the way I expected it to in that moment, but now that I'm at this point in my life, I can see all the good things that came from that summer. Samson being one of those good things, no matter who he is today.

I'm at a point in my life where the outcome of my future won't be determined by the outcome of any potential relationship.

Do I want him to be who I've always believed him to be? Absolutely.

Will I crumble if he isn't? Not at all.

I am still made of steel. *Come at me, world. You can't damage the impenetrable.*

"The door is opening," the man in the car next to me says.

I immediately sit up and drop my apple into my bag next to me.

I press my palm against my chest and exhale as someone begins to exit the building. It isn't Samson.

I would slide off the car and stand up, but I'm scared my legs are too weak to hold me. I'm about twenty feet away from the entrance, but there's a chance he won't see me if he's not expecting someone to be waiting for him.

The man who just walked out looks to be in his fifties. He scans the parking lot until he finds the car next to mine. He nods his head and his brother doesn't even get out of his car. The man walks over and climbs into the passenger seat and they take off like this is an airport and these trips are normal.

I'm still sitting cross-legged on the hood when I finally see him.

Samson emerges from the building and shields his eyes

from the sunlight while he looks down the sidewalk toward the bus.

My heart is beating so fast. Way faster than I thought it would. It's like all the feelings I ever had as a nineteen-year-old girl are waking up all at the same time.

He looks almost the same. More man than boy now, and his hair is a little darker, but other than that, he looks exactly like he looks in my memories. He pushes his hair away from his face and begins walking toward the bus stop without glancing into the parking lot.

I don't know if I should call his name or run up to him. He's walking away from me. I press my palms against the hood, prepared to slide off it, when he stops walking.

He stands still for a moment with his back to me while I hold my breath in anticipation. It's as if he wants to look, but he's scared he won't find anyone.

Eventually, he begins to turn around, as if he can sense my presence. His eyes connect with mine, and he stares at me for so long. He's just as unreadable now as he was back then, but I don't have to know what he's thinking to feel the emotions being released between us.

He brings his hands up to the back of his neck and spins around like he can't look at me for another second. I see the roll of his shoulders as he slowly exhales.

He faces me again, this time with a very touching expression. "Did you go to college, Beyah?" He yells it across the parking lot, like it's the most important question in the world. More important than any other thought that might be going through his head.

As soon as he asks me that, a lone, fat tear rolls down my cheek. I nod.

When I do, it's like all the tension in his soul releases in that moment. I'm still sitting on the hood of my car, but even from here I can see the furrow of his brow. I want to walk over to him and smooth it out and tell him it's finally okay.

He stares at the concrete like he doesn't know what to do. But then he figures it out, because he begins walking toward me with urgency. He runs the last ten feet, and I gasp when he meets the car because he doesn't stop there. He crawls onto the hood and immediately onto me until I'm forced to lean back against my windshield. Then his mouth is on mine and he's apologizing to me with a silent fierceness I feel to my core.

I wrap my arms around his neck, and it's as if a single second never even passed. We kiss on the hood of my car for several seconds, until Samson can't seem to stand it anymore. He pulls away and hops off the car, then grabs my waist and pulls me to the edge, lowering my feet to the pavement. He wraps his arms around me and hugs me tighter than the first hug he ever gave me.

The next few minutes are a combination of tears (mostly mine) and kissing each other and staring at each other in disbelief. I had so many questions coming into this, but now I can't think of a single one.

When we stop kissing long enough for him to speak, he says, "I probably should have asked if you were seeing someone before I did that."

I smile with a strong shake of my head. "I'm very single."

He kisses me again, slowly, and then stares at my mouth like it's the thing he's missed the most. "I'm sorry."

"I forgive you."

And it really is as simple as that.

His eyebrows draw apart with relief. He pulls me tightly against him and releases a heavy sigh into my hair. "I can't believe you're really here." He picks me up and spins me around once before setting me back down on my feet. He rests our foreheads together and smiles. "What now?"

I laugh. "I have no idea. The rest of my day was contingent upon the outcome of this moment."

"So was mine." He grabs my hands and pulls them up to his mouth, kissing my knuckles. Then he tucks my fists against his chest and says, "I need to see Darya."

His words remind me of a line in one of his father's poems. I've read them so many times, I have them memorized, so I say it out loud. "Because when a man says *I'm going home*, he should be heading for the sea."

I start to pull away from him so I can open my car door, but Samson grips my hand and pulls me right back. "My father wrote that. You have my backpack?"

It's not until this moment that I realize Samson probably assumed his backpack was gone forever. "Yeah. I took it the night they arrested you."

"You kept my father's poems for me?"

I nod. "Of course I did."

There's a pained look in his eyes, as if he's trying to hold back tears. Then he closes the distance between us and slides his fingers into my hair, cradling my head in his hands. "Thank you for believing in me, Beyah."

"You believed in me first, Samson. It's the least I could do."

Thirty-Two

When we finally got to the beach, he didn't even pause to appreciate it. He got out of the car, took off his shirt, and walked straight into her. I've been sitting in the sand watching him swim for a while. He's the only one out in the water right now and I'm the only one on the beach. It's empty because it's October and Samson is insane for being in the water when it's this cold.

But I get it. He needs it. Years of therapy, rolled up into a swim.

He eventually comes back to me, dropping to the sand next to me. He's soaking wet and breathing hard, but he looks content. He said very little on the drive here, but I also haven't asked very much. He's been deprived of everything he loved for so long, I want to give him time to soak it all in before bombarding him with questions about the last few years.

He glances behind us. "Does no one live in Marjorie's house?"

"No."

He asks because it's obvious the house hasn't been taken care of since it's been empty. There are shingles missing from the roof. Grass grown up around the foundation.

Marjorie passed away in March, so Kevin will probably put it up for sale soon. I hated that Samson wasn't able to attend her funeral. I know she meant a lot to him. She even visited him a few times before she died.

Samson repositions himself so that he's lying in the sand, his head in my lap. He stares up at me with a look of peaceful content. I drag my fingers through his wet hair and smile down at him.

"Where's Pepper Jack Cheese?" he asks.

I nod my head at our house. "He's an indoor dog now. He and Dad bonded."

"What about you and your dad?"

I smile. "We bonded, too. He's been great."

Samson brings my hand to his mouth and kisses it. Then he grips it with both hands and presses my palm against his chest, holding my hand there.

Everything fell right back into place with him almost as soon as I laid eyes on him today. It's like a single minute never even passed. I have no idea what tomorrow holds, but everything I need is tied up in this moment.

"You look different," he says. "Better. Happier."

"I am." I can feel his heart pounding against my palm. "I'm not gonna lie, I was so mad at you in the beginning, but you were right. It was for the best. I never would have left otherwise."

"It was awful," he says with a contradicting grin. "Complete torture. I can't tell you how many times I almost caved and asked Kevin for your address."

I laugh. "Glad to know you thought of me."

"Every minute," he says confidently. He reaches a hand up and touches my cheek. I lean into his palm. "Can I ask you a personal question?"

I nod.

"Did you date other guys?"

I blink twice. I was expecting him to ask me that, but maybe not this soon.

He lifts up onto his arm until he's face-to-face with me. He reaches around me and presses a comforting hand to the back of my neck. "I'm only asking because I'm hoping your answer is yes."

"You're *hoping* I dated other people?"

He shrugs. "Not saying I wouldn't be jealous. I'm just hoping you actually had fun in college and didn't treat your dorm room like a prison cell."

"I dated," I say. "I even had a boyfriend for a while during junior year."

"Was he nice?"

I nod. "He was. But he wasn't you." I lean forward and

kiss him briefly. "I made friends. I went out. I made good grades. And I even loved my volleyball team. We were pretty damn good."

Samson grins and then resumes his position by laying his head on my thighs. "Good. I don't regret my decision, then."

"Good."

"How's Sara? Are she and Marcos still together?"

"Yeah, they got married last year. She's four months pregnant."

"Good for them. I was hoping that would work out. What about his clothing line? Did it ever take off?"

I point at a house down the beach. Samson lifts up onto his elbows so he can see where I'm pointing. "That's their house. They just finished construction on it six months ago."

"That yellow one?"

"Yep."

"Damn."

"Yeah, the clothing line is doing well. He has a lot of followers on TikTok, so that gave his merch a huge boost."

Samson shakes his head. "TikTok?"

I laugh. "I'll show you later when you get a new phone."

"Oh, how the tables have turned," Samson says. He moves until he's sitting next to me again. He wipes sand from himself. "Can we go see them?"

"Sara and Marcos? Right now?"

"Not this second," he says. "I want more time to catch

up with you. I'd also like to see your father. I owe him an apology or ten."

"Yeah, that's not gonna be easy."

"I know. But I'm persistent." Samson wraps an arm around me and pulls me to him. He kisses the top of my head.

"What am I supposed to call you? Shawn or Samson?"

"Samson," he says immediately. "I've never felt more myself than when I was with you that summer. That's exactly who I want to be. Forever."

I wrap my arms around my knees and bury my mouth into my elbow to hide my smile.

"Where do you live now?" Samson asks me.

I nod my head at my father's beach house. "Staying with my father and Alana this week, but I have an apartment in Houston. I'm in law school."

"No way."

I laugh. "I am. Just started my first semester in August."

Samson shakes his head with a mixture of pride and disbelief on his face. "I didn't know that's what you wanted to do."

"I didn't know either until you were arrested. Kevin has been really helpful. I'm actually about to start an internship at his office."

Samson smiles softly. "I'm proud of you."

"Thank you."

"I took some college classes in prison," he says. "I'm

going to try to get into school somewhere, if anyone will take me."

His eyes drift away after he says that, like he's worried for all the challenges he's about to face.

"What was prison like?"

He sighs. "Real, real shitty. I give it a one out of ten. Do not recommend."

I laugh. "What's the next step? Where are you going to stay?"

Samson shrugs. "Kevin has all that info. Says he set something temporary up for me. I was supposed to call him as soon as I was released, actually."

My mouth drops open. "Samson! It's been four hours. You haven't called him?"

"I don't have a phone. I was going to ask if I could use yours, but I've been a little sidetracked."

I roll my eyes and take out my cell phone. "If you violate parole over something this stupid, I'm driving you to jail myself."

Samson brushes sand from his hands and takes the phone after I dial Kevin's number. Kevin answers after the second ring.

"I haven't heard from him yet," Kevin says, assuming it's me calling. "I promised I would call you as soon as I did."

Samson smiles at me as he speaks into my phone. "It's me, Kevin. I'm out."

There's a pause on Kevin's end before he says, "This is Beyah's number. You're with her?"

"Yep."

"Where are you?"

"We're at the beach."

"Can Beyah hear me?" Kevin asks.

"Yes," I say, leaning toward the phone.

"I guess you were right about him."

"Sure was," I say with a smile.

"I told you you're gonna make one hell of a lawyer with that kind of commitment," Kevin says. "Listen, Samson. You listening?"

"Yep."

"I'm going to email you the information for your parole officer today. You have seven days to check in with him. You'll find your key under the rock to the right of the trash can."

Samson glances at me and raises a brow. "What key?"

"The key to my mother's house."

Samson looks over his shoulder at Marjorie's home. "I don't know what you mean."

"Yeah, I know. My mother made me promise not to tell you until after you were released, which is *why* I instructed you to call me as soon as you got out. You follow instructions terribly. The deed is at my office, I can bring it by sometime this week. I tried to do what I could with the house, but life has been busy. It needs a lot of work."

The look of disbelief on Samson's face is something I wish I could take a picture of. I'm sure the same look is splashed across my own face.

"Is this a joke?" Samson asks.

"No. You made some stupid mistakes, but you also did a lot of good for a lot of people in that community. My mother being one of them. She thought you deserved to be able to call that place your home because she knew how much you loved it."

Samson releases a trembling breath and then drops the phone in the sand. He pushes off the ground and walks away from his conversation with Kevin. He pauses near the water and grips the back of his neck.

I pick up the phone and wipe the sand off it. "Can we call you back later, Kevin?"

"Is everything okay?"

I watch Samson as he struggles to absorb everything Kevin just told him. "Yeah. I think he just needs a while to process this."

After ending the call, I walk over to Samson. I stand in front of him and lift my hands, wiping the tears away from his cheeks like he did for me so many times.

He shakes his head. "I don't deserve that house, Beyah."

I take his face in my hands and tilt it until his focus is on mine. "You've been punished enough. Accept all the good things life is throwing at you today."

He blows out a quick breath and pulls me in tightly. I don't let him hug me for long because I'm too excited to find that key. I grab his hand and pull him away from the beach.

"Come on, I want to see your house."

We find the key exactly where Kevin said it would be.

When Samson goes to insert it into the lock on the door, his hands are shaking. He has to pause for a moment and press his palms into the doorframe. "This can't be real," he whispers.

It's dark when we walk inside, but I can see the layer of dust on the floors before he flips on a light. There's a musty, salty smell to the place. But knowing Samson, those are things he'll have fixed by tomorrow.

He touches everything as we walk through the house. The cabinets, the walls, the doorknobs, all of Marjorie's furniture that's still here. He goes into every room and sighs in all of them like he can't believe this is his life.

I can't believe it, either.

Samson finally opens the door to the stairwell that leads to the roof access. I follow him up the stairs and onto the roof, where he takes a seat. He spreads his legs and pats the area of space between them, wanting me to sit with him.

I lower myself to the roof and then lean back against Samson's chest. He wraps his arms around me, and as beautiful as the view is from here, I squeeze my eyes shut because I've missed the feelings I have for him so much. More than I even knew.

I've gone so long trying not to feel them, I was starting to worry I no longer felt anything. But the feelings were never gone. They never left. I just forced everything to sleep so it wouldn't hurt as much.

Every now and then, Samson shakes his head in total disbelief. I've known him to be a quiet person since I met him, but he's never been this speechless around me. I love his reaction. I love getting to witness his life change for the better right before my eyes.

Look at us. Two lonely kids who slipped through all the cracks but then climbed right back up to the top of the world.

Samson touches my face, urging me to tilt my head back so that I can see him. He's looking at me in the way I saw him look at me so many times that summer—like I'm the most interesting thing on this peninsula.

He kisses me, then lowers his head and presses his lips to my shoulder. He rests his mouth against my skin for a while, as if he's making up for all the years he couldn't kiss me there. "I love you."

Those three words are a simple whisper against my skin, but they provide enough pressure that I feel my heart bone heal completely.

I lean my head back against his shoulder and look out at the water. "I love you, too, Samson."

THE END

Acknowledgments

Thank you to my little sister, Murphy Rae, for designing the original cover to this book years ago. I looked at it all the time, waiting for the opportunity to write the story that would grace the inside of that cover. And now you've gone and made another beautiful version! You are so good at what you do and I love you!

I couldn't be more appreciative of my early readers: Vannoy Fite, Erica Russikoff, Gloria Green, Tasara Vega, Karen Lawson, Maria Blalock, Talon Smith, Ashleigh Taylor, Susan Rossman, Kelly Garcia, Stephanie Cohen, Erica Ramirez, Lauren Levine, Katie Pickett Del Re, Racena McConnell, Gloria Landavazo, Mandee Migliaccio, Jenn Benando, and Alyssa Garcia.

A HUGE thank-you to Anjanette and Emilee Guerrero for your knowledgeable volleyball feedback.

This book went through a series of editors, all at different stages. If you find errors in this book, it is no one's fault but my own. I kept writing, long after they finished editing. A huge thank-you to Murphy Rae, Lindsey Faber, Ellie McLove, and Virginia Tesi Carey for getting this book into shape.

Thank you to Social Butterfly and Jenn Watson for always wanting the best for your authors and the books you represent.

To Ariele Stewart and Kristin Dwyer, you two ladies are amazing and I'm so lucky to have you in my corner, even when you aren't required to be there.

Thank you to everyone at Dystel, Goderich & Bourret for your endless support, encouragement, and overall hard work on every single one of my books.

Thank you to the entire teams at Atria Books, Montlake Publishing, and Grand Central Publishing for supporting me in all my endeavors. There is nothing better than having a team of people surrounding me, encouraging me to write whatever I feel like writing, and working to make it the best version it can be.

A massive thank-you to the readers for supporting my career, my hobby, my dream.

There are numerous people in my life I don't know what I would do without. So many contributors and volunteers to our charities, numerous people who assist with my Face-book groups, all the bloggers who support my books, all the unicorns who show up to help with Book Bonanza, all the CoHorts who make me smile daily. If I named everyone by name, these acknowledgments would be longer than the book, because there are thousands of you impacting my life in such positive ways. I thank you ALL.

I want to thank all the people who contribute so much of their time, not only to CoHorts, but to our charities, Book Bonanza and the Bookworm Box. Susan Rossman, Stephanie Spillane, Sandy Knott, Michele McDaniel, Nadine Vandergriff, Pamela Carrion, Chelle Lagoski Northcutt, Laurie Darter, Kristin Phillips, Stephanie Cohen, Erica Ramirez, Vannoy Fite, Lin Reynolds, and Murphy Rae. What a powerful team of women you all are!

And to the men in my life who are the reason I grew four heart bones: Heath, Levi, Cale, and Beckham. I love you, I love you, I love you, I love you.

About the Author

Colleen Hoover is the author of more than twenty novels and novellas. She lives in Texas with her husband and three boys.

For more about the author, visit her website at **colleenhoover.com** or email her at **colleenhooverbooks@gmail.com**.

Colleen's social media can be found at the following links:
www.instagram.com/colleenhoover
www.facebook.com/authorcolleenhoover
www.twitter.com/colleenhoover
Snapchat: colleenhoover
TikTok: colleenhoover